SPRING IN SIBERIA

SPRING IN SIBERIA

a novel

Artem Mozgovoy

 Red Hen Press | *Pasadena, CA*

Book Design by Mark E. Cull

Library of Congress Cataloging-in-Publication Data

Names: Mozgovoy, Artem, 1985– author.
Title: Spring in Siberia / Artem Mozgovoy.
Description: Pasadena, CA: Red Hen Press, [2022]
Identifiers: LCCN 2022019279 (print) | LCCN 2022019280 (ebook) | ISBN
    9781636280707 (paperback) | ISBN 9781636280714 (ebook)
Subjects: LCGFT: Bildungsromans. | Novels.
Classification: LCC PR9100.9.M69 S67 2022 (print) | LCC PR9100.9.M69
    (ebook) | DDC 823/.92—dc23/eng/20220513
LC record available at https://lccn.loc.gov/2022019279
LC ebook record available at https://lccn.loc.gov/2022019280

The National Endowment for the Arts, the Los Angeles County Arts Commission,
the Ahmanson Foundation, the Dwight Stuart Youth Fund, the Max Factor Family
Foundation, the Pasadena Tournament of Roses Foundation, the Pasadena Arts &
Culture Commission and the City of Pasadena Cultural Affairs Division, the City
of Los Angeles Department of Cultural Affairs, the Audrey & Sydney Irmas Char-
itable Foundation, the Kinder Morgan Foundation, the Meta & George Rosenberg
Foundation, the Albert and Elaine Borchard Foundation, the Adams Family Foundation, the Riordan Foundation, Amazon Literary Partnership, the Sam Francis
Foundation, and the Mara W. Breech Foundation partially support Red Hen Press.

First Edition
Published by Red Hen Press
www.redhen.org

Моей бабушке.

Spring in Siberia

PART ONE

Chapter One

Taiga

All the beauty of it, all the strangeness. Space with no maps, time with no clocks, destinations with no way of reaching them. So many questions with no wise man to look back at you kindly, knowingly, and explain. The feeling of injustice, of being the plaything of someone's cruel decision or stupid mistake. But whose? Who ever had the idea of coming to live here? Who decided to make it home for me or for any human being for that matter? I've never felt at home here. I've always felt alien.

Alien—that was my school nickname. I hated it, both the name and the school. I would wake up at five thirty for classes that started at seven fifteen, feeling that it was not I who should go through this day here but, perhaps, someone else. Perhaps there should be some other little boy who must drag himself through the winter night all the way to the school, four hours before the sun even starts to lighten the sky.

No, it was I.

My mother's hand would reach in through the doorway, turn on the light in my bedroom, and then disappear. I'd pull myself out of bed and walk to the bathroom: the face I found reflected in the mirror was swollen, pale, vacant. Only two thin brush-marks showed on the transparent whiteness of my face. It was almost as if I had melted into the background, as if I didn't yet exist.

Ice-cold water on my face, a hard dry towel. I would have breakfast with my dad. Thin cookies with engraved little houses. I'd put butter on one, stick another cookie to it just as my father did. He'd be reading his detective novel with only the occasional slurp of his tea breaking the silence.

After breakfast, I'd put on all my clothes: a sweater and a school jacket, a pair of trousers and double socks, my *valenki* and mittens, a thin knitted hat, a thick scarf to cover my face and a huge bushy hat on top, then a grey astrakhan fur coat my mom had cut and made for me out of her own. A pair of drawers and, of course, a shirt under all of it. I would be sweating by the time I reached the front door. It'd be hard to bend down, hard to pick up my heavy square backpack and a sack containing a pair of summer shoes to change into at school so that the floors were kept clean—the floors that we, the pupils, had to wash ourselves after class. But the old man at the school entrance wouldn't let anyone in without their dirty winter shoes changed for clean summer ones. '*Smenka!*' he'd yell so loudly for so early in the morning, 'Change shoes!'

The front door of our flat opens, 'Bye,' it closes behind me. Now comes the worst part. I've got to walk down the staircase. It's pitch-dark. I stay immobile for half a minute with my back to the door, giving my eyes a chance to get used to the darkness, but time passes and nothing changes. The world is playing hide and seek with me, and I'm losing the game. Yet I have to move on. I try to feel each step ahead with my right foot, before immersing myself in the darkness. I know by now that the most important thing is not to let fear flood my soul, not to get too scared of that jet-blackness all around. If I let fear in, then I'll run, stumble, fall, lose the sack with my summer shoes—complete failure.

Why is it always so dark on this staircase? Five floors without a single lamp lit. Why, every time some kind neighbour installs a new bulb, does it lie shattered in pieces the next morning? Do other people like things that way? Me—no. I'm scared, I cannot feel the next stair, I hold tight to a railing. One level—I did it. Now another . . .

I remember how one morning I was coming down this devilish staircase, when instead of the soothing firmness of the following stair my right foot met something soft, something squashy and rubbery. My next heartbeat was so intense that it lifted me off the ground and dropped me down a whole level. What *was* that? 'It's only Vasia,' my dad told me later that same evening, with a laugh. 'Vasia, from the second floor. His wife doesn't let him in when he's drunk.' Only Vasia? Why did my dad laugh about it? There was nothing funny about my foot sinking into the swamp of that Vasia.

I keep on going down. Even if I don't see them, the stairs are there this time, firm and empty. I reach the first floor not without relief: there's a patch of light coming through the grimy narrow window above the ceiling from the streetlamp outside. Three walls of the landing are crowded with tin mailboxes, twenty-five of them, five per floor. Most of the boxes are black, hollow, with broken shutters; few are well locked. Ours, in the upper left corner, has its shutter ever-closed and bent slightly—enough for a slim hand to slip inside and check for mail. We've lost the key, or maybe never had one.

There's a more spacious room on the ground floor, a hall of sorts, and I hate crossing it because it always smells so nasty—stale alcohol, bubblegum, and urine—teenagers hang around there each evening and no one kicks them out because they know there are no other places for youngsters to go. Why don't they simply sit at home and read something? I don't understand. I make my way through the hall. It grows even darker than before, but it's level underfoot and quiet. No one is there, nothing but the smell of youth. 'I don't want *ever* to smell like that,' I think to myself.

Finally, with both hands stretched out in front of me, I reach the heavy, freezing door downstairs, the cold of it coming even through my mittens. I push at the door, but nothing happens. I push it harder and harder . . . Only a stream of cold wind comes through the narrow gap, but the door won't open. It's stuck, it's frozen. I push it once again with all the weight of my tiny body . . .

Whoosh!

The door flips open.

The sudden blow to my face!

I can't breathe!

The night winter wind smashes into me so unexpectedly that I am left gasping for air, I am awake instantly. I cannot inhale, because that air is too cold to be inside me. I can only muffle my little face deeper inside my scarf, step forward and give myself up. The wind is more powerful than any turbine, the snow is sharper than any needle. It hurts, but I've got to move on.

After a few minutes of this monotonous effort, of pushing my heavy winter boots through the snow, while leaning into the wind so as not to let it topple me backwards, I begin to get used to it all. My multi-layered outfit indeed keeps me warm. I know the way ahead of me, for there's only one way. It takes about forty minutes before the empty snow-lands reach the ski field of the school and soon after that I can make out a grey cube of cement in the darkness—the Palace of Knowledge, as they call it.

After a while on that path I am fully awake and I even get a little bored. I keep pushing my boots through the snow, I am bored and tired, but I keep on pushing. Keep on pushing through snow. Snow that's whiter than white. Snow that's never grey or yellow for it has never, never touched the soil—and therefore rests pure, always pure—and you too, you also stay that way, by walking above it.

To entertain myself on that path to knowledge, I often play the game I invented one morning. It requires me to shut my eyes completely while walking. I think I invented it only because it was warmer that way, with my head fully hidden in my scarf, with no opening left for the freezing world to prise its way inside. It's impossible to win the game, but perhaps I would find out how far I could go if I were blind. Could I reach the school? The road? The rusty iron fence at the end of the path? To be honest I don't need to look, I know everything that is there: the thin straight line in the snow only as wide as the steps of the early workers whose feet have made it this morning; the big empty field, covered entirely by diamonds and cut diagonally in two by the route. No lights, no people, no sounds, just me.

And yet . . .

Yes, lights! The snow shines brightly, reflecting the moonlight. I don't see it, but I know it's there.

Yes, people! Someone walked here this morning before me, I can feel the deep imprints left in the fresh snow.

Yes, sound! With my eyes closed I can hear the wind, I can hear the snow scrunching comfortingly under my *valenki*. I cannot hear my heart, but I think I do. I know it's there, that tiny oven inside my body warming me up every day, even on a cold sunless day like this one—with all my clothes preventing its hearty warmth from escaping.

My eyes are still shut when I reach the rusty metal fence at the end of the path. I know the fence is there, I stop and open my eyes right in front of it. Through a hole in the fence—big enough for a man folded in half or for a creature my size slightly bowed—I continue on my way to school.

Who made this hole in the fence? Who made this fence on the way to school? Who made this school, anyway? They told me it was a special school (although I don't see anything special about it apart from the fact that it's the only one). 'It's special because it has a sports inclination,' I was told . . .

Inclination? Sports? Me?

Ever since I can remember myself, I recite poems while wheels are turning, and I make dolls out of dandelions; I watch women cooking and murmuring their sad songs, and I draw quietly to them; I laugh when music is playing and I make other people dance to it or I cry if they don't. In the summer I catch white butterflies, because my grandmother tells me to do so. I once asked her why and she said, because they eat cabbage (they are even called cabbage flies), but then, when the three-liter glass jar is full of white misery, I open the lid and let the butterflies rise into the sky . . . To see them fly one last time . . . I still remember how in the air above me this white cloud melts away.

But sports? I couldn't care less about sports. Anyway, today is my lucky day. It's minus thirty. No sport outside.

৵৻৵

My mom hates it when it's cold. She says life in Siberia is like an indefinite exile. A detention that is lifelong, most times much longer. Maybe that's why she's still in bed while I'm walking through the snow. After brushing my teeth this morning, I went into her room to peek at the thermometer outside her window (if it falls below minus twenty-seven, the school excuses us from skiing). I glanced at my mom lying under the blankets and for a brief moment, wanted to ask her if maybe, just maybe, it was too cold to go to school at all, but I knew in advance what her reply would be.

'Don't go if you don't want to,' she'd say as she had already done in the past. And then I'd stand still for a while, thinking . . . *Don't go if you don't want to . . . ?*

'And what will happen to me afterwards . . . later on . . . if I don't go to school today?'

'Then you'll grow up and go work as a yardman,' she'd respond with not much emotion in her voice, without even opening her eyes.

The sharp sounds of ice being broken and of snow being shoveled outside my window were heard every morning—the yardmen seemed to wake up even earlier than the schoolboys. So I didn't say anything and left my mother alone, motionless and quiet, in the dark bedroom.

Maybe, like me, she also feels it's not her who is supposed to go through this day. Maybe she also feels alien and that's the reason why, the last time we were coming back from my grandmother's, she suddenly got out of the car and walked home alone while my father and I remained seated, and he seemed angry at us.

Perhaps it also explains why every now and then her thin black eyebrows gather, forming those dark lines between them, and for no obvious reason she starts moving furniture around within the flat. She even moves the heavy box of the television and our wardrobe (when it won't move, she puts a wet rag under it and then pushes the thing while I pull the rag). I always help her to move furniture around and it can even be fun, but I never understand why we do it so often. Especially when dad comes home and can't recognize the place.

My mom is from the South, maybe that explains everything. It's not much warmer down there, though. It's not really South South. Her place is called Altay, there are lots of mountains and lakes—we go there every summer. She told me she comes from one of those small tribes of people who used to live there long before Russians came and took over Siberia: they are skinny and short, they've got light brown faces, long eyes, and thick, black, straight hair. The hairdresser told me once that I also have that kind of hair even though I'm blond. She said, 'I recognized immediately that you're Lyudmila's son because of your hair.' Maybe she was lying, because my mom was waiting for me outside . . .

Also, in Altay, those people, they are always drunk. When I saw that I asked my parents why.

'Because they are nomads,' my mother replied, 'but they cannot move freely anymore.'

Maybe that's the reason for everything that's wrong with my mom. For her walking alone while we are driving, for her moving furniture all the time, for her staying in bed long after I get up. Maybe she just wants to move freely . . .

It's not easy to move freely here, I agree. Even I, in the mornings, have to follow the path, otherwise God knows what might happen. The moment you turn off the one and only route, you are in the taiga, and you'd better not be there. Our town is even called by that same name, *Taiga*, not a very imaginative name, because, indeed, we are surrounded by this heavy, unwalkable, impassable forest. The jungle of Siberia, they call it.

Even at school, I don't feel like I can move freely. It is also a kind of taiga for me. After walking through the snow in the dark, after noticing the three already-yellowed windows of our classroom on the third floor (What a nasty colour! What an unhappy number!), after crossing the ski fields, then the vegetable patches, after entering the school and switching from *valenki* to summer shoes under the surveillance of the old man, I walk my path one more time. It's rather a ridiculous one— by the wall, hoping not to be noticed.

The hall is long and wide, with windows on the right side. After sports, my biggest problem at school are those windows, more precisely, their sills. The laziest, meanest, strongest boys always sit there before, after, and sometimes during the pealing of the school bell, mocking, giggling, bullying. Here am I. Big white head, thin little body, steps too jumpy, face too shy—a perfect victim.

This is the reason they call me Alien. My big head. They call me Alien not because they think I don't belong here, but because of an American horror film shown on TV that year, when the entire country was scared to death because we hadn't seen any horror films before. Somehow the shape of my head reminds the schoolboys of those alien monsters. What could I do about it?

My grandmother once told me to hit them back if they pick on me. I listened to her, thought of what she suggested.

'Didn't you tell me God always turns the other cheek?' I finally replied.

She went silent.

She's always dreamt of making me a believer—my grandmother—because she was the only one in the family. At first I failed to tell the difference between God and Lenin, but with time I knew who was who: the one hanging above our blackboard at school was Lenin, and the one hanging above the fridge in my grandmother's kitchen was God. I preferred my grandmother's kitchen, and so I liked God more. She always talked about him as if he was the kindest of men. Yet, for some reason she only talked about him with me.

Maybe because the others preferred Lenin?

The summer I was born, Perestroika started. It was a good time, bright and clear, full of hope, accompanied by the sudden gasp of long-awaited change. Or so we later heard on TV. By that year the monster machine which had been spinning its wheels for almost a century finally seemed tired, its route wavering unconfidently for its driver had strayed completely. At the end of May 1985 Mikhail Gorbachev gave a public speech, officially acknowledging the Union's loss of course.

'Dear comrades, we all should restructure ourselves. All of us.'

By the time I was born, two months later, all two hundred million comrades in all fifteen Soviet republics seemed to be, if not already restructuring, then certainly rethinking their lives. By the day I took my first steps, this restructuring, or *Perestroika* as it became known, was in full swing. Some people were scared, some were excited. My grandmother was relieved that she could finally talk about her God and even go to a newly erected church each Sunday.

Perhaps I should blame Perestroika for that feeling of being alien, for having no homeland at my back. They wrote 'USSR' on my birth certificate, but by the time I could read, that united republic had ceased to exist. I kept looking at these four hooked letters, trying to find some meaning for me in them, for them in me. There was no longer any reason for their presence even in my documents.

The leviathan that used to occupy one-sixth of the Earth was shrinking now. One state after another was leaving us, breaking off big chunks of land in all directions as if from a gigantic loaf of bread. Still, it's not as though my family were in danger, for Taiga was in the very center of it all.

Yes, maybe I'd be better off pinning it on geography. When I was barely five I developed a case of asthma, reacting intensely to everything in the world outside the flat in spring, summer, and autumn months. As soon as the snow melted, my skin would get red and itchy, my eyes would become swollen to the point that I couldn't see, and my nose would bung up, preventing me from breathing. My mother would fill a round fishbowl with dried daisies and boiling hot water and let me sit with my face above it, the towel over my head—to let the hot chamomile air help me breathe again.

She did bring me to a hospital too but all the doctors said was to keep me away from fields and gardens (dandelions were said to be especially life-threatening) and to take me to the seaside more often.

The seaside . . . While my mother strove to get sanatorium vouchers to the seaside from her factory, I spent hours alone at home going through my parents' few books, traveling through the pages of a miniature 'Atlas of the World'. The atlas was so small the whole world could fit within my palms. It was the nearest sea that I was looking for. But there lay the trick: very soon I realized that there was no other spot in the entire world as distant from any sea or ocean as our town. When I looked at Eurasia, that ugly crab spread across the blue surface of the globe, I'd find a neat corner where Kazakhstan, Russia, Mongolia, and

China meet, then walk north a few millimeters—and somewhere there would be our town.

Even at that point there would be a few questions as to what precise place we called our home. My parents both came from rural peasant families and both of them—like many of their peers—headed to a big city for work and education as soon as they came of age. They met, got married, and had me while still studying at a polytechnic institute, and the three of us lived in a student dormitory (with one kitchen and one toilet per floor, which meant per hundred students). But they were optimistic because they knew that a young Soviet couple of graduates with a child were entitled to receive a one-bedroom flat, as well as engineering positions in a factory somewhere. Sometimes their salaries would be paid not in cash but in food cards and sometimes there would be no food in the shops to exchange the cards for, but they could expect a degree of certainty about their future. With no right to be picky about it. Even before my parents received their diplomas, they knew that soon our family would be dispatched to a minuscule Siberian town—Taiga.

So what was my hometown, exactly? The one where I was born? The one we moved to? The one where my parents' families come from?

It was the Soviet leaders' conscious intention to move people around the continent, making sure that comrades lost any sense of roots, cultural identity, or tradition. We were all supposed to be equal and feel at home wherever we went. Growing up in Taiga, all I felt was that I was lost and alien.

❧

With the first class starting so early in the morning, the last one would be over by eleven, sometimes even by ten, when the heavy obscure sun would have finally started climbing the sky. The only reason for such a schedule was not having enough teachers and classrooms, so the mass of pupils was split into three shifts with me attending the very first one. Though even that tactic didn't always help and sometimes the lessons

became 'doubled' or 'tripled', with not two pupils but four or six sharing the same desk—unbridled chaos guaranteed.

Usually I'd be back home long before noon and on my own, without
a soul around, starting in on my homework for the want of anything
better to do. I had neither siblings nor friends, and in a small place
like Taiga it proved hard to find anything with which to occupy myself.

In fact, there were only two reasons why the place was called a town
and not a village. First of all, it was located right in the middle of the
Trans-Siberian Railroad. Right in the middle of it, I swear. For when
I looked at the map of the USSR in my atlas, I saw this long skinny
worm crawling all the way from Moscow to Vladivostok (the nearest
seaport—in fact, the Pacific Ocean port!). I would try to distinguish
our bald, grey patch among the greenery (the name of the town itself
was of course not on the map). There it was, right in the middle of the
Trans-Siberian, where my father had marked a little cross with a pencil.

At school I had learnt how to figure out real-life distance from a
map using a ruler, and I did just that, first measuring the distance
from Moscow to our patch (four centimeters) and then from us to
Vladivostok (four centimeters). Then one had to multiply these centimeters according to an index at the margin of the map: four thousand
kilometers to Moscow, four thousand kilometers to the Sea of Japan.

The train would pass twice a day and for some reason stop at our
station only once, but each arrival was announced with a horn so loud
that we could hear it everywhere: in the classroom, at the school's vegetable patch (where we, the pupils, had to cultivate potatoes and then
to harvest them, and then to eat them—the worst part!—as our school
meals), at home, or even in the forest where my father forced me to
practice skiing on the weekends.

At the train station there was a commemorative plaque with two
withered red carnations usually peeking out from beneath. It was the
only such object in our place, so when nearby one would always stop
and read the inscription:

In 1921, Vladimir Ilyich Lenin passed through the station of Taiga while

*leading the Trans-Siberian propagandist expedition from Moscow to
Vladivostok.*

What does 'passed through' mean? Did he actually stop here? What is
a 'propagandist expedition'?

The second reason for our town's existence was an engineering factory. More precisely, the real reason was the Second World War, in
the course of which many factories were evacuated from the European
part of Russia to Siberia (which, so the government was convinced,
the enemy would never reach, and, for a change, it was right). While
the factories were evacuated, most of the workers, apart from the administration, were left behind in the war zone. So, the local Siberians
had to be employed. That was how my parents, on the first day after
their graduation, were sent from the regional center to live and work
in Taiga.

In order to be allocated a flat, the young family would have to meet
all the requirements, then get on the list, and wait in line for a few
years, all the while working at the appointed place.

When we first moved from the big city, we settled in a dugout, an old,
low hut, *izba*, partly hidden in the ground. My parents hoped that it
was temporary—they were already promised a flat in a newly constructed panel block on the edge of the settlement. The only memories
I have of that first home of ours were rather horrendous moments that
seemed to last forever. It was a one-room wooden shack with neither
a heating system nor running water, and with small windows perched
just above the snow. Because the dugout was halfway buried and because the winters were so fierce, a complete army of rats would flood
inside our walls, for they go where it is warmest. My mother and I
would climb onto the bed, while my dad fought the intruders as if leading a war. Later on I fell in love with a Soviet animation based on the
Nutcracker story with beautiful music by Tchaikovsky: the moment
when the prince had to fight the army of rats was my favourite.

While living in the dugout, we had not only rats but human-like
visitors too: in the corner behind the front door, my father kept an

axe to fight off robbers. One night, I remember, we became aware that someone was trying to force his way into our home. My dad no sooner took the axe in hand than we heard a man screaming my mother's name. It was her brother, whom I'd never heard of before. Freshly released from prison, already wasted, he had found our shack from a letter my mother had once made the mistake of sending him.

When we let the unexpected visitor in, he didn't act very differently from any other intruder. Drunk, he demanded that we give him some food, then fell asleep right on the floor, not even caring about the rats. When we got up in the morning, he was gone, together with some of our not-so-valuable possessions. My mother never sent any letters back to her family again.

Right across the street from the engineering factory there was a kindergarten named '*Skazka*'—'a fairytale'—and all the children of the factory workers were brought there for the day. There were not many toys or things to occupy oneself with in that fairytale, and I guess I had issues with making friends as well, because, from what my mother told me, she could see me from the factory windows, standing alone in the middle of the playground for hours without moving.

'Sometimes you'd sit down, grab the ground with your palms, then stand up, clear your hands against one another, and keep standing still, absolutely still like a little tree.'

The scarcities of life were palpable. The only toys I had were the ones my father made for me out of wood. The only clothes our family wore were the ones made by my mother. Most of the food came from my grandmother's garden. But that was more than normal—that was universal in the land of triumphant socialism.

Our common poverty was especially obvious at public events and celebrations when we were supposed to exhibit the best our families had. I remember the New Year's masquerade parties at the kindergarten where every single boy was a bunny and every girl was a snowflake because bunny ears and snow-white fabric were the two costumes available at the factory. However, one year my mother got hold of some aluminum foil. The sparkling material completely mesmerized me. I had never seen anything like that! She made a cape out of the foil for me, and that New Year I was the Star Prince in a world of bunnies and snowflakes.

In a couple of years, we were indeed given a one-bedroom flat in a new social housing block. It felt totally novel—hollow, empty, quiet. In spite of my loneliness and boredom, I rather enjoyed our new home. It was our first real home, and we were its first residents. I remember the freshness in the air captured by the newly constructed walls.

My father immediately started to put together some basic furniture—a table and some stools—as well as decorating the walls of the kitchen with handmade wooden panels, shelves and colourful Russian plates, glued, for a reason unknown to me, to the wall. An extravagantly ornamental, dark-red carpet, which my parents had received on their wedding day, was also hung on the wall, behind my parents' bed, as was done in every good Soviet household.

The two rooms were small, and my parents tried to organize a space so each of us would have a private corner. For a while, mine was behind the wardrobe, placed strategically, in one of my mother's furniture moving sessions, in the middle of the room: on one side of the wardrobe was our living space; on the other, my bedroom.

Happily, I had a long balcony on my side. Back then all our windows—all three of them—faced the limitless taiga, and from my balcony I could breathe it in and observe the forest safely with no need to wander in it. I enjoyed playing on that balcony so much that one summer night I even tried to sleep there, dreaming of watching the stars and listening to the forest all night long. However, my plan was spoiled by midnight rain, which forced me to gather all the blankets and pillows and, quite ridiculously, carry everything back indoors, banging the windows and waking everybody up.

Another happy possession of ours was a bathroom with running water and a tub, which I was supposed to use once a week, on Saturdays—a habit that my parents imported from their own childhood in the villages, where people went to the *banya* only on weekends in order to save water, one after another, while the wood was still burning.

We also had a cuckoo clock, which mystified me for many months until one day I took it down and, using a screwdriver, undid the poor clock, wanting to discover where the cuckoo came from and how it always knew the time right. I put it all back together, as I'd planned, before my parents came back from the factory, but something went wrong, and despite a perfectly untouched look and rhythmic ticking, the cuckoo never came out of its nest again.

That was not such a big drama, for in the Soviet Union it was much easier to get a cuckoo or an Oriental carpet than a real item of furniture. Here again my parents, as a young family of engineers, were given the opportunity to take their place in line for some armchairs and cupboards delivered from another part of Russia. Later we discovered that our neighbours on the third floor, and the ones on the second, and above us, on the fifth, who lived in exactly the same one-bedroom flats, had ordered exactly the same cupboards and armchairs. They, too, had their cuckoo clocks even before they got their furniture (yet they had no glued Russian plates on their walls because that was my father's idea). Those people were exactly the same families of young engineers with one child, who were sent to live in Taiga from a regional center and who were all, needless to say, working at the same factory.

I remember how we once faced a great mystery of our failed sameness: the Azarenkovs, our third-floor neighbours, couldn't manage to install a cupboard properly, even though it was the same one, and the room was of the same size and exactly the same shape as everybody else's, but the cupboard simply wouldn't fit within their walls. All the men of the staircase gathered and scratched their heads, but no one could deal with the problem. In the end, we realized that the builders had made a mistake, making one flat a few centimeters smaller, and we all laughed about it. In moments like this when all the people gathered, didn't look or act very differently from each other and seemed to be ok with that, I had a good, warm feeling of friendly communion.

On every first Saturday of each spring and summer month, the adults would go out to clean the courtyard while their children played together. On those days I remember staying on our long balcony, watching the colourful people down below bowing and picking the bad grass out from the good and planting kiss-me-quicks in flower-beds made of painted tires. A little later, around five in the evening, the cows would appear (our new five-story block was still surrounded by the village *izbas*). The cows were returning from their day in the fields, and they would moo loudly, passing through our courtyard, and eat the freshly planted kiss-me-quicks while people screamed at them and laughed, and I laughed, too, from my balcony.

It was common for adults to take care of each other's children, and so I was left with our neighbours quite often. Once, I recall, a miracle happened: the Borisenkos, our second-floor neighbours, got tickets to the theater over in that big regional center where I was born. They got two places for adults and one for a child (because this is what a young Soviet family was supposed to be), only they didn't have a child yet, the wife was just pregnant. The Borisenkos came to our door and offered to take me to the theater. Everyone seemed excited, and I was as cheerful as ever, for I had never been to a theater before.

The snowy road from Taiga to the city was something akin to my path to the school: pitch-dark from four in the afternoon to ten in the morning, a straight, narrow route in the snow. The drive was not long, only about an hour, but the wind was blowing harshly, the snow falling heavily, and the Borisenkos' old car was crawling along with obvious effort until, at the midpoint, the vehicle gave up.

It seemed funny to me to be in that small metal box of a car in the middle of the snow-land, but the adults didn't look happy. While the man was running around, opening and closing the trunk, trying to fix something, I remember his wife, whispering to herself, '*Pojaluista, pojaluista, pojaluista.*' Please, please, please.

It was rapidly freezing inside the car, and the road was empty of vehicles or people. No lamp posts, no telephones, no lights, no steps in the snow—only blackness and whiteness. Finally, exhausted and scared, the man opened the door and yelled to us, 'Get out! We have to walk!'

We kept walking, on and on, on and on, along the snow road in the middle of nowhere. The man was cursing, and I think I heard his pregnant wife sobbing a little. Strangely, I still didn't feel scared. I'd been told that I was going to see the theater and so I took this walk through the dark snowy land as a part of some amazing performance.

On and on we went. The Borisenkos hoped to see a car coming or a shack on our way, some person somewhere somehow to help us. But the only lights I saw were the stars above, and the moonlight reflected everywhere. It looked magical.

I don't know how long that walk lasted, five minutes or five hours, except that after a while we finally saw a sparkle in the dark. No, there was no village, no cars, no shacks, but there was an electric light somewhere a little aside from the road. We went to it and found a construction site, a factory or a warehouse, big and black, with one small window yellowing in the night. The Borisenkos knocked and the door was opened: there was a night watchman, just an old, bearded man charged with not letting anyone enter the premises, but he did let us in.

The next thing I remember was the feeling of warmth floating up into my body from my feet on the stove. We were saved, and an hour or two later someone drove to pick us up and bring us back to Taiga. The Borisenkos asked me not to tell my parents what had happened. I merely had to say that I liked the theater, and so I told them and didn't feel bad about it because it was true.

Gradually, more and more young families arrived from the regional center to work at the factory, and our place looked more and more like a small town. Another block of flats was built right in front of ours, obscuring any view of the taiga. That building was exactly the same five-story edifice as our own, made of the same panels of cement and, in the same manner, never painted.

Whenever I looked out the window, I would only see that five-story building—absolutely identical to ours standing some hundred meters in front. In between the two blocks a space was formed, people kept calling it a 'yard' but it had nothing of a yard about it. It was just a vacuum: no trees, no bushes, no shops, no other constructions. Only in the summer there were those painted tires with a few feeble flowers growing in them. Once a playground of sorts was installed—nothing more than two poles holding a swing and a ladder—but a couple of weeks later some work had to be done, big cars came, workers threw the swing on the ground, dug there, repaired some pipes here, and left, without putting the swing back in place. I didn't get to swing a single time.

A vacuum, the whole place seemed like an empty bell jar from where everything had been sucked out. Walking home alone through the snow-land, hearing nothing but my own breath, I could feel with my skin how no past had ever happened around me. There was no history and—definitely! I felt it! certainly!—there was no future.

I spent hours on the balcony or the windowsill of my room, behind the wardrobe, looking out, waiting for some life to appear in the vacuum, though, most of the time, all I could see was that other block right in front of ours. And as I kept watching, it gradually started to seem to me that, in fact, I was staring at an immense mirror that reflected our own home—there was the same five-story grey panel block in front of me, with the same four front doors and long balconies. I even imagined that maybe somewhere right in front of me in one of those windows in one of those exact same flats there was exactly the same boy, a boy like me, sitting on the windowsill and looking in my direction.

Soon more people arrived in Taiga, and one, two, ten, twenty housing blocks rose like mushrooms after the rain in between our building and the forest. On the way home from school I had a hard time identifying which one was mine.

It seemed that these towers rising up, these families moving in, these Saturday yard cleanings and kiss-me-quick plantings, and cows mooing in the evenings, might continue forever until there was no taiga left, until the whole country was covered with these identical grey panel blocks, but it was not the case. One day it all stopped.

❧

The first sign of the new time for me was a reindeer. Yes, a reindeer, or, more precisely, a reindeer's head with a massive tree of antlers that carefully made its way through our front door one day. I looked on with round eyes and didn't know whether I should run away and hide or approach and touch it. My father's head appeared behind the rein-deer's as he proudly carried it in. The new member of the family was hung on the wall right above my parents' bed where we used to have the Oriental carpet. Now the carpet was downgraded to the floor, and the central place was taken by the beast.

I had never seen a real reindeer, and so this one seemed perfectly beautiful to me despite its lacking a body. Every other young family from our block came to see it. People were very impressed, only to my mother it didn't seem like a bright idea to sleep under that huge head. One day when my dad was away fishing, she lifted that poor reindeer, dragged it to the balcony and, just when I thought I was going to see a reindeer flying, she hung it on the wall outside, facing the empty yard and that other block in front of ours. Now, on my way from school I had no more problems recognizing our home.

Uncle Kolia, my father's brother, had long been living in Yakutia, in Northern Siberia, where he had met and married a local woman, also black-haired, wide-cheekboned, and with beautiful almond eyes like my mother's. The two women were so strikingly different from the rest of us, all pale and frail, that they were often presumed to be sisters. To me, that idea seemed absurd: their beauty was of different kinds. Whereas my aunt had a softer, kinder appearance—perhaps thanks to the moonlike shape of her face, full lips, and plump body—my moth-er always looked slender and wiry. My aunt seemed much more wel-coming and vivacious. My mother, with sharper features and gestures, made others fear her dark, piercing eyes.

Uncle Kolia, my aunt Lena, her parents and children, spent their lives up above the Polar Circle. I had never met them until I was eight or nine, because the village they lived in was so far north that the only connection they had with the rest of the world was through a helicop-ter which delivered food and mail to them once a month. In exchange, the helicopter would carry away diamonds and furs, for there were plenty of these in my aunt's region.

Uncle Kolia had always been an adventurous, freedom-loving type, not suited to the common standards of Soviet reality. To go on an expedition, to move North, was the typical choice for many poets, musicians, and other freethinkers of his generation. There, up above the Polar Circle or south in the steppes of Kazakhstan, they could live in their own ways, escaping the soul-wrecking banality of communism. He was happily settled in a land where the sun doesn't rise half of the year and would probably have spent all his life there if not for the political turmoil of the nineties.

Perestroika progressed, the old government was disassembled, the dissolution of the Soviet Union had commenced, and as a result, that vitally important helicopter simply stopped coming to the Northern villages. Suddenly, it seemed that no one needed Siberian diamonds or furs, and so there was no means of survival for people like my uncle. They had to leave.

Uncle Kolia, Lena, her parents, their children, with all their belongings, fur coats, and antlers left their homeland for good and descended south into our town on the Trans-Siberian. My parents helped them settle in Taiga, and in return they gave us what they had—furs and antlers. And in my mother's ears, for the first time in her life, there were some snowflakes, little earrings with real diamonds from Yakutia. She slept in them, bathed in them, never ever took them off.

For myself, I have never seen the North of Siberia, except for those late evenings when Uncle Kolia, whom I came to love very quickly, for he was a gentle, playful, sad-eyed, kind man, would present it all in my parents' bedroom. He would lock himself in the room for an hour or so, not letting anyone in, and when he opened the door, when all the kids and adults had gathered, instead of our ordinary window with its ordinary view on another ordinary block . . . there was a deep blue still lake reflecting a dark purple Northern sky, or a hostile snow-land with short frail trees and miniature horses and an almost undetectable white rabbit in the distance, or one of my little cousins with only his dark eyes visible from under the furs, frosted on their edges, or unimaginable, indescribable Polar lights—all of this right there, in our own flat.

At first the marvel was incomprehensible to me—how on earth had our room been transformed into the foreign land?—but the regular click-click of the projector together with an occasional blindingly white screen when a slide got stuck soon revealed to me Uncle Kolia's secret.

After the reindeer's head and the marvelous slideshows, many other signs of change followed. At first, those new flat blocks stopped rising from the ground: their construction was frozen, their frames abandoned. Our 'micro-district'—called that because there were no street names and no streets as such—suddenly stopped expanding into the forest.

When I asked my parents why that was, they told me it was because of Perestroika . . . I kept looking at those fleshless skeletons, those iron railings and blind windows, and thinking, why it was all called *Perestroika*, restructuring, when it should have been called *Nedostroika*, unfinished structuring.

Then, gradually, the wheels of my parents' factory slowed down, too. When I'd asked them some time before what their factory produced, it was difficult for them to explain, for the entire plant had worked on a few individual components, which were then transported, via the Trans-Siberian, west to another factory, where the many separate items were made into a weapon of mass destruction. Even though the Second World War was long over, the Cold one continued on all the way to 1990 when Gorbachev finally stopped the military race. Thereafter our factory's existence came into question, and even the majestic horn of the Trans-Siberian seemed to sound less enthusiastically.

People in our micro-district got very nervous because, without that factory—just like my uncle's family without that helicopter coming—we simply couldn't exist, couldn't plant our flowers in the painted tires or hang up our cuckoo clocks. The management had to do something to restructure the plant from a military-based economy to a market-based one. Soon they had a bright idea: from now on my parents, using the same materials as were used for the weapon of mass destruction, were supposed to produce a three-wheel bicycle, christened the 'Ant', for children under five. However, something went wrong there, and children kept falling off that 'Ant' as a result of its unbalanced construction. The 'Ant' project was over, and the factory itself was soon over as well.

By 1991, the entire Soviet Union was in panic. It so happened that our local factory was just one of hundreds which were rapidly being closed, leaving millions of people, thousands of young families, unemployed—with no social safety net to fall into. People went hungry, people became desperate. Only my grandmother, who always knew to rely on herself, had kept her peasant life intact. With her carrots, cucumbers, potatoes, and the Holy Spirit, she fed our family. For longer and longer periods of time, I was brought to live with her, surrounded by those life-threatening flowers, yet far, far away from all the troubles of the new world.

Chapter Two

Babushka

My grandmother lived in a world of her own, one very different from that of my parents, their friends, and our neighbours. Gradually, I was introduced to her world, and with time it became a part of mine. Yet one of my first memories of that new universe was filled with bitter tears.

After a two-hour ride from Taiga, after my grandmother's boundless joy at our meeting, after spending two happy days with all of us together in her village, I suddenly, in the middle of a bright Sunday, realized to my horror that I had been left behind. That my parents had driven back to town without me. That I was abandoned.

I panicked. I was absolutely convinced that I had been got rid of for good, and for a reason. I spent long hours in front of my grandmother's mirror. The mirror had a front panel and two wings so I could see myself clearly from three separate directions. There, in that mirror-land, I stood fixed, staring at my reflection from the front and then from each side, trying to figure out what was wrong with me, what I had done badly, when it was that I had disobeyed my beloved parents, for it was obvious that I was being rejected and they had decided to lead their life without me. I didn't believe my grandmother when she said that my mom and dad would come back for me one day. There was no telephone on which to call them. I was scared, terribly scared, that I might never see them again.

Days passed, and I held on stubbornly to this fear. I sat by the dirt road that wound up from my grandmother's house and then turned right, parallel to the horizon, before disappearing behind a hill. I kept staring at that point where the road met the hill, waiting for the square blue dot of my father's Moskvitch to reappear. After waiting for hours and hours, I finally decided that enough was enough. Choosing a moment when my grandmother was busy, I simply walked away from the house. Walked until I reached the main road and lay down in the center of it. There I was, no older than eight, small and pale, waiting for some car to come and squash me. Life had become unbearable.

Happily, the village traffic was slow. Within half an hour my grandmother noticed my absence. She ran around the village until she spotted me up there in the middle of the crossroad. Terrified and crying, she lifted me up and hugged me to her breast. I felt her tears on my forehead. I think it was then that I finally understood that I was loved— if not by my parents, then at least by my newly found grandmother.

From that moment on, I paid more attention to my *babushka*. I began to watch her closely, and little by little, I fell in love with her. She was easy to fall in love with—all softness and whiteness. She was all Russian, like my father—and unlike my mom. Her translucent silver hair framed her face, reminding me of the ring of light around the saints' heads on her icons. In the hours of labour, she hid her aureole under a thin white headscarf. She had the most loving eyes and a small, ever-present smile. Her dresses were simply cut and all, all of them, were printed with leaves and petals of various shapes and colours. I remember burying my face in her dress when I hugged her, and in those moments, if I opened my eyes, I found myself in a lush garden. Even in winter, her hands smelled of the sun-hot earth. Every day I spent with her, she worked from dusk to dawn, for her world required a lot of work.

In that world of hers lay a large garden with neat patches of strawberries and raspberries, blackberries and gooseberries, tomatoes and cucumbers, cabbages and pumpkins, cherry trees and apple trees, and potatoes, potatoes, endless rows of potatoes. There was a pigsty with pigs to feed in the morning and to clean in the evening; there was a hen-

house and every time a chicken laid an egg and started screaming fool-
ishly, I had to run and gather the egg, still warm and live in my palms.

The center of my grandmother's world was her house, her pride
and joy. She and her husband had built it out of massive logs some
thirty years before with the help of the entire village, for that was how
houses were built in that world. It was a one-story spacious cottage,
with an asbestos roof and delicately carved window-frames painted a
sky blue. Indoors, one found an airy room, which served at the same
time as a kitchen, a dining room, a work room, and an entrance; then,
two small bedrooms, for her and for him, and a living room in between to seat guests and watch television after dinner. There was also
a *seni*, a sort of inner porch. That light, big room had windows so wide
that it got too cold in wintertime, but it was perfect for an afternoon
nap during summer.

Set in the floor of the *seni*, under a colourful striped carpet, there
was a door that led down to the cellar. Sometimes before or during big
dinners, if I was asked to, I ran to the *seni*, moved the carpet, pulled
up the trapdoor (not without effort), and started carefully descending
the ladder. The air grew chilly and quiet, and gradually I felt as if I
were leaving the real world above me and, akin to Alice in Wonder-
land, found myself surrounded by endless shelves—only in this case
not ones filled with books but with shiny cans and glossy bottles, sparkling with toy-like pickled vegetables and sweetened fruits, compotes
and jams, marinated mushrooms and even salted watermelons. Everything that my grandmother harvested in the autumn she canned and
stored in that cellar during the winter. It was her personal treasury and
no matter how tough the year was, that cellar was never empty and so
there was always the prospect for us, her family, of getting through
the longest winter. Mesmerized by these shining jars, I'd hang on that
ladder for ever and ever, unable to choose between wild strawberry
jam and reinette compote.

In the yard of my grandmother's house, surrounded by its blue
wooden fence, stood a small square pavilion or *besedka*, a place for a
chat. It consisted of nothing but four poles holding up a roof, and beneath that, a table with three benches. Yet that pavilion was the most

popular place of all, one where guests sat out on summer days—eating, laughing, drinking, singing songs. Every spring in the ground around the poles my grandmother planted the type of morning glory that climbs up and blooms in purple flowers, so that by midsummer one couldn't even see the *besedka* itself but only its walls of glory.

Nearby the *besedka* stood another small white edifice with frilly blue window shutters (blue and white, everything in my grandmother's world was painted blue and white, and that marriage of colours was to stay with me forever as the closest to my heart). This small house had two rooms: one a summer kitchen where in the warm months most of the dishes were cooked and served directly through a window; the other was used as the *banya,* the bathhouse.

There was no water supply, no sewage system, no flushing toilets. The basins in the bathhouse, the garden, and the house itself had to be filled by ourselves with water brought from the public pump during the summers and with melted snow in wintertime. To reach the toilet—a shack with a hole in the ground—one had to walk three minutes out the front gate, the journey turning into a grand adventure on ferociously cold or rainy nights. Alternatively, one had to use a chamber pot, a simple metal bucket placed in the corner of the *seni,* behind the main door, which the supplier was obliged not to forget to empty in the morning.

Every evening, before going to bed, I was required to follow one of my grandmother's rituals that I never dared resist: to undress and to step into a shiny tin basin, placed in the middle of the kitchen room. The boiling hot water would numb my feet, the steam would rise up my little body. Her firm gentle hands rubbed my sides, legs, ankles, covering me all in snow-white foam, while I stood still, giggling and glimmering like a little golden cloud, lost at sunset.

When one opened the low wooden gate of the yard and stepped outside, the miniature farmhouse—its pigsty and hen shed, guarded by Alfa, our dog—was on the right. Rows of raspberries and sweet briar, *shipovnik,* stood out front. Encouraged by my grandmother, I'd eat them with great pleasure—both the raspberries and the petals of the flowers.

Another part of this miraculous universe was the so-called *oogliar-ka,* the coal storage. Once a year, by special appointment, a small truck made its way to my grandmother's place, screeched and wiggled to a halt, then suddenly emptied its guts: a hill of black shining stones were piled up in front of the terrified Alfa.

For some six months of the cold season, these stones—this *black gold* as the locals called it—were indispensable for warming the *izbas.* Mesmerizing to look at, once touched, the coal left grimy imprints on your hands, and once rubbed, emitted a grey cloud which hung in the air for a long, long time. Wood was never used to warm the houses, such a crazy idea never even crossed our minds; woods were to stroll through, to look at, to listen to attentively.

A dirt road wound away on the left of the property. From the moment my parents left me, that road became the symbol of my grief and waiting. Again and again I felt attracted to it. Yet the farthest I usually let myself go along it was the hilltop.

When I reached that high spot—labouring to breathe, my eyes swollen and my nose stuffy—and looked back at my grandmother's home, it seemed shockingly small all of a sudden. At first I couldn't understand how something that was so big—this whole new world to me—could look so small from above. It was like a game: down here my grandmother's place is truly enormous, hiding innumerable treasures, while from up there, from up on the hill, it is so insignificant, so tiny.

Then, I understood. My grandmother didn't live in a real village in the full sense of the word: any other houses were scattered across the vast land here and there, seemingly unconnected to each other. There were no roads in between, only narrow paths, no church or shop or city hall or any other major construction to serve as a uniting force. From above, all I could see was my grandmother's white and blue house under the overwhelmingly heavy, immovable sky. In fact, everything, even a palace, and especially that lonely little world of ours, seemed minuscule in relation to that breathtakingly grave Russian sky.

❦

Her world was isolated but not solitary, for within it there was also a man, her husband, my grandfather. While my *babushka* worked every day above ground, he was under it, digging for coal and, later on in his life, serving as a minor clerk in the coal mine office. The man wasn't home most of the time when I was awake, and when he did come back in the evening I was a little scared of him. One source of my fear was the dark lines around his eyes. I was told that all coal miners' eyes are that way because underground they get so blackened by the coal dust that after a few years they cannot wash it out of their eyelids.

Perhaps wishing to make himself more likable, the man sometimes bought me 'caramels', stone-hard candies that one needed to suck on for some minutes before feeling the first sugar hit on the tongue; and one winter he made a sled out of a thin metal board for me to slide down the hill.

Only once did I see that man laugh. It happened when I discovered a curious object in his bedroom. On a desk by his narrow single bed, there stood a large, flat, glittering machine with two 'pancakes' of thin, light-brown film. I couldn't figure out what the thing was for nor how it worked, until my grandfather, noticing my confusion, moved the film, pressed some buttons here and there, and music erupted from nowhere. I shouted with joy! It was a Russian folk dance song, so happy, so gleeful; one couldn't listen to it without a sudden lift in spirits. '*Barynia, barynia, sudarynia-barynia . . .*' the singer commanded in a high-pitched voice and I burst into laughter at the very first sound of it. My grandmother ran from the kitchen to see what had happened.

The song began cheerfully, rhythmically, but with every passing second its harmonicas and balalaikas played faster, ever faster and faster while I bounced with my butt on the bed, clapping my palms to the beat.

'*Barynia, barynia* . . . Dance! Dance, *Babushka!*' I screamed, but my grandmother was already swaying her arms, flexing her knees, and laughing.

'Dance?!' I pleaded, looking uncertainly at my severe grandfather. This most serious, most important of men stood up then, straightened himself, put his fists akimbo and began beating out the rhythm with his feet on wooden floor.

'Dance! Dance!' I beseeched them, and they went on dancing together, without touching, which is the tradition in Russian dances, but smiling, glancing, cheering. I laughed continuously, but then, as soon as the song was over, I paused for a second—one roll of the film was full, another had nothing left on it—and burst into tears at this abrupt end to my happiness. My grandfather pitied me and switched the films, resetting the music to the beginning once again. And then again. And again. They kept on dancing, and I kept on bouncing on the bed, clapping.

'Oh, please, please, Alioshenka,' my grandmother begged me, 'Enough. Enough.'

But I demanded more, more! I felt instantly that there was no such thing as enough of happiness. Grandmother's blushing, blissful face, her luminous eyes, and my grandfather's smile, his forehead covered with drops of sweat were the most evident signs of their shared, simultaneous joy in life.

I once asked my grandmother about her family: whether she had parents, sisters, brothers. She told me that she didn't see them anymore because they all lived too far away. I asked where they'd gone, but she only smiled and replied that it wasn't them but she who had gone away many years ago. She wasn't from Siberia, she said, but from some village far away in Western Russia, where her sister still lived.

'I was just sixteen,' she told me, 'when my parents put me on the train.'

'But why, *Babushka*? Why did they do such a thing to you?'

She shrugged.

'One of my brothers was already living in this land, and so I was sent to join him.'

'But why did *he* come to live so far from home?'

'My brother . . . Well, he settled in Siberia while coming back from the frontline . . .'

'From the frontline? What frontline?'

'Oh, I don't know, really . . . I don't even know . . . Maybe there was just more space in Siberia.'

She grew quiet. But I couldn't stop puzzling over the idea of moving so far away from your native place, from your own home.

'Don't you miss your family, *Babushka*?'

'Oh, yes, of course! I miss my sister very much,' she said, sighing. 'But most of all . . . most of all I miss riding my horse.'

I'd never seen a real horse, only a deer, and so I asked her what it was like to ride one.

'Nothing was ever better than that,' she said. She smiled and drew a picture in my mind that I have never let go of since: a young girl with a long braid of rye hair riding bareback, holding the horse by its mane, along the riverbank. In the moment of telling me about that, her face had an expression that I'd never seen before. Later I learned the word *nostalgia*, and I think what I saw then was just that. Nostalgia.

I also asked her how was it when she came to Siberia and when she met my grandfather.

'Dancing,' she said, her face lighting up again. 'We met at a village dance, and we married soon after.'

'And the house?' I wanted to know. 'Did you build this house also soon after?'

'No, no, we lived in a dugout for a while. We couldn't build our own place until we sold many, many piglets so we could buy the wood for the house.'

'Piglets?' I giggled. 'But where did you get so many piglets from?'

My grandmother laughed too, sparkles in the corners of her eyes.

'Well, the two piglets that we received for our marriage had multiplied,' she responded, stroking my hair gently.

She then told me that for their wedding the entire village had gathered, bringing money as a gift for the newlyweds. The morning after the wedding feast, the young couple counted the money and found it just enough. 'It was just enough, imagine!' They rushed to the market and with all the money they'd received they bought two piglets, a boy and a girl, because they knew this was the way to start their own household.

'This way . . .' she demonstrated, crooking one arm around an invisible bundle, 'We walked back home with the piglets tucked under our elbows. The piglets were screaming and kicking, and we were laughing like two little children ourselves,' my grandmother told me, though herself, she was crying by then.

'But why do you cry, *Babushka*?'

'Out of happiness, my darling. Out of happiness.'

And so I understood that there were also tears of happiness in her world.

Time passed but I kept thinking about my grandmother's family and that land she came from. Even though her sister never visited us, I knew they exchanged letters regularly, because my grandmother used to say:

'Alioshenka, at school you might have a few pages left empty at the end of your notebooks? Don't throw them away. Rip out the last clean pages and bring them to me, please—I will write a letter to Raya, my sister.'

I asked more questions about Raya and her home. I was told that she lived in a much sunnier and prettier village, that they had peaches and apples as big as our pumpkins.

'Don't you want to go back, or at least to visit *baba* Raya?' I asked.

She breathed in deeply.

'Oy, Alioshenka,' she spoke quietly while looking around, 'In these days I have my own house . . . I cannot leave my household and go just like that.'

I looked around then, too. And understood . . . Pigs and chickens had to be fed. Cabbages and tomatoes had to be watered. Bugs and butterflies had to be collected. Branches of lilac had to be picked and brought indoors for the sake of their perfume, and dinners had to be prepared every evening before grandfather came home from work. I knew very well how hard my grandmother had to work, and how early she started.

Each day, when the sun rose and filled our flowery curtains with colours, like the stained glass in churches, I'd get up and look around, sleepily. I was suddenly all alone in our bedroom. I didn't like that feeling. I'd look through the house for my grandmother, but it was empty, with only the bright light from outside falling heavily, silently on the carpets and chairs. I'd run barefoot through the rooms, reach the wooden stoop outside and pause, looking around, still drowsy, in my white underwear and sleeveless T-shirt, with my rye hair all messed, and then, wondering where I should look for her, I would shriek in my little voice as loudly as I could: '*Baaabushkaaa!*'

She was already working somewhere, but I never quite knew what business she had found for herself that day. When later we met people from our village, they would laugh at us, saying that they could hear my rooster's scream every morning. They'd look at me lovingly, but I didn't quite know what was so special about my scream and why it brought this indulgent gaze from others.

Grandmother worked from early morning on through the day, and I helped her as much as I could. I watered things or cut them neatly or—my favourite—went to pick something: raspberries or strawberries, gooseberries or currants. It took me hours to fill a bucket, for I ate far more than I saved.

We had no machines, no electric tools, so my grandmother did everything by hand (I guess that's why her hands always smelled so good). I loved helping her because, I think, it was she who loved working. I never once heard her complain about this daily labour. On the contrary, I remember her always being in a good mood, always singing some song as she worked, which made my life beside her easy and pleasant.

'How can you miss living in a town?!' she would smile playfully at me, 'Living in one of those grey panel blocks as if in a birdhouse!'

Special expeditions were organized occasionally when my grandmother and other villagers ventured into the fields to look for sea-berries (surely, that name must be coming from the sea of snow for there was no other). The gatherers would spread through the fields and hills while singing the same recurring song—and that echoing melody was sweeter than any berry to me. Especially since the tiny bright orange sea-berries covering the thorny bushes were not too much fun to collect—the berries were hard to chew, and the branches prickled the fingers painfully. The sweet syrup that my grandmother produced from these berries lasted the whole winter and, according to her unshakable judgement, was the ultimate panacea.

'I heard you coughing last night, Sashenka,' she would say to her husband. 'Here, take some sea-berry syrup with your tea now. Just vitamins!'

'Your gums are bleeding, Alioshenka,' she continued the very next morning. 'Rub some of the syrup into them, you'll see it works magic.'

So stubborn was her belief in the power of sea-berry syrup that the entire family joked about it, refusing in laughter to submit to this acid orange elixir.

'Just vitamins!' she'd also keep insisting as she offered us her nettle soup, or marinated fern, or 'pineapple' jam made out of dandelions, or numerous herbal infusions—each plant picked by herself, each corresponding to another ailment it was meant to (and often did!) cure. All that—and the perfume of her beloved lilacs, briars, Siberian roses, and the moist, black smell from the cellar, and the metallic, cold aroma of coal, and the clouds of steam rising from the wet wooden planks in the *banya*, and the morning buckwheat *kasha* that had been cooking on the stove through the night 'by itself', and the evening borscht, purple in name, taste, and colour, and all the mushrooms, leaves, and berries drying flat on the trays in the *seni*, and more, more, more!—all of that filled her house with such a unique and complex aroma, into which you entered every time you walked through the door, that you recognized instantly—and even felt the touch of—her own soul.

I observed my grandmother with great attention and care, learning things from her, every now and then being amazed by what was most natural to her. I noticed how she talked to everything around her: the flowers she watered, the vegetables she cultivated, the swampy rivulet, the forest, even the moon and the sun.

'Oh, don't be so harsh on me today,' she would plead on especially hot days, raising her eyes to the sky.

'How beautiful you are this spring!' she'd compliment the lilacs blossoming in her garden.

'Come on, little darling, spring up, spring up, it's about time!' she'd beg some stubborn soldier from the army of carrots she'd planted.

Much longer and more complex were my grandmother's debates with the chickens that always wandered too far from the house, the pigs that were usually making a filthy mess of their sty, and the stray village dogs that appeared every now and then on our walks.

'Well, so why are you barking at us? What has happened?' she would start interrogating a sharp-toothed aggressor in the calmest, friendliest of tones, 'no need to shout so loud. We aren't that easy to frighten. Go away, you silly thing. Find some tree to bark at!'

For all the thousands of words of tenderness and care with which my grandmother used to address plants, animals, and people, there were only one or two harsh ones that she kept exclusively for flies, cabbage butterflies, and other winged creatures that presented some despicable danger.

'Ah, you wait, little scumbag,' she would unexpectedly cry, making me shudder and drop some book or toy I'd been busy with. I'd turn to my grandmother and start smiling instantly: her round flowery body would become tense, while her big kind eyes pierced the wall and her hand reached for the homemade inquisition tool, a fly-killer, nothing but a wooden stick with a flat piece of rubber attached at its tip. 'Dirty, dirty little scum, here's where you get what you asked for!' She'd raise the weapon and suddenly slap it against the wall with a noisy smack—I'd burst into laughter. With time I adopted my grandmother's way of acting and started talking to plants and flowers, pigs and dogs (though I never touched the fly-killer and refused to fight other enemies of the state).

My grandmother's dog Alfa, kept chained outside by the pigsty, was getting sick and growing incapable of protecting our territory, so one day my grandmother took me to our neighbours to choose a new puppy. The neighbour positioned a handful of squeaking dogs in one line by the fence, while my grandmother and I were supposed to call them from some distance to see which one will be the healthiest, the fastest to reach us. I ruined that ceremony, however, after noticing one weak puppy that was dragging behind the rest, lost and confused. The neighbour and my grandmother argued that we needed to take the strongest dog to protect the house, but I showed dogged determination to keep the poor weak one no matter what. Eventually, Dick grew into the fiercest he-dog, so big and powerful that in winter I attached my sleigh to him and rode around the village.

One of my most memorable interactions with the animals was the time when my grandparents brought a few dozen chicks home to live with us. Those days were cold and my *babushka* was afraid that the little ones would freeze in the henhouse. The chicks were dandelion yellow, fluffy, preciously cute, and I couldn't be happier than when standing over them, observing their communal life. From the whole crowd I picked out one which was a bit smaller, slower than the rest.

'Can I have this one?' I asked my grandmother. 'Can I take him out and care for him?'

'No,' she said firmly. 'It's not a good idea.'

'But why?'

'Because the chicks have to stay all together in order to be warm.'

I begged and begged her, promising to take the best possible care of the little one and to warm him day and night. I begged until she gave up. I took the fluffy thing and fed it independently, kept it in my palms in order to keep him warm during the day and let him sleep in my grandfather's fur hat at night. The chick looked so fragile and heartwarming when I let him walk on the carpet. The first thing in the morning I'd check on him, feed him, and watch him grow. One day I found my pet immovable. Heartbroken, I cried, tried to wake him up, but he showed no sign of life. My grandmother did her best to calm me.

'It was because the chick was away from his mates. He couldn't survive all alone,' she said. 'No one can survive all alone.'

❧

After a month or so of living together, *Babushka* and I had already established our favourite things to do. First of all, there was mushrooming in the nearby forest. She would walk slowly through the trees and I'd run in front, jump under each bush, check for a shiny mushroom hat covered by dried grass. I was taught how to tell bad mushrooms from good ones and enjoyed identifying them.

'With your young eyes, Alioshenka, no mushroom can hide from you!'

I was proud counting the trophies multiplying in our basket.

Then there was the birch tree magic . . . One day my grandmother fetched a two-liter jar and walked with me to the hill, my own hill, the observation point. Next to it danced a small group of birch trees, their trunks white and long with black spots as if a painter had dipped his brush into the pot of pitch and dabbed the trees here and there with it.

In spring the birch trees put on earrings, as my grandmother called these elongated fluffy seeds, and in the autumn these trees were the first ones to turn into the clearest shade of yellow, shining like gold all around our village. The birches were both my and my grandmother's favourites. However, on that day she stopped by one of the trees, took a small knife from her pocket and made a cut in the trunk. I looked on, stunned.

'What do you hurt it for, *Babushka*?'

'Don't worry,' she replied, 'The tree is strong and holds some magic inside. Plus, we are going to heal it afterwards.'

Next, she tied the jar to the birch with a rope under the line of the cut she'd made. She took some wax from a pine tree nearby and made a little drain from it, gluing the wax between the cut and the jar.

'That's all for today,' she said, 'let's go back home.'

'But what about the magic?'

'We'll come back for that another day.'

I ran back to the grove the very next morning. As I got closer to our birch, my eyes grew wider. The jar was a quarter full with a transparent silvery liquid!

When grandmother came, she took the jar down from the tree. Then, she gathered more wax from the pine and rubbed it carefully into the cut left on the skin of the tree. Indeed, it looked like our birch was being healed.

'Thank you, my dear, thank you,' she said to the tree, passing me the jar of juice, 'now you try it.'

I took the jar in my palms, brought it suspiciously to my lips and took a small sip. It was sweet, very sweet, and so refreshing. Magic! Pure magic!

'It's very good for you, Alioshenka! It will take all your illnesses away,' my grandmother said lovingly.

Even though I worked and played outside all day long, I was still having difficulties with breathing. The doctors said my condition was similar to asthma; the environment triggered the attacks. The idea of nature being harmful was incomprehensible to us. We couldn't believe the doctors. How could something beautiful be harmful? I came to love it all so much: these flowers and berries, these trees and mushrooms . . . Apart from suggesting a visit to the sea, the doctors didn't help in any way, so my grandmother decided to treat me herself.

Saturday nights we would go to the *banya* together. She'd fill the familiar basin and while I stood watching, she'd immerse her big soft hands in the water, close her eyes and start chanting:

'Moon, young moon, take our pains and take our sorrows, let Aliosha be healed by tomorrow.'

She'd take her hands out of the bowl then, lift it above my head and pour the elixir slowly over me. The flow of fresh water inevitably made me feel renewed, recharged, leaving my head as if cleared from the inside.

I quite liked that homemade magic. It became very natural to me. As natural as her prayers, chants, and conversations with plants and animals, or her other habit of freezing in the middle of whatever she was doing at the first sound of a cuckoo bird.

'Oh, a cuckoo!' she'd rise and stand still, acknowledging the bird's funny call, '*cuckushka-cuckushka*, tell me please, how many years I have left to live?'

Then it was me who stood staring in puzzlement at my grandmother, trying to comprehend this strange inquiry. With each call of the cuckoo, she counted out a further year of her life.

'One.'
'Cuckoo!'
'Two.'
'Cuckoo!'
'Three . . .'
I went on watching her in bewilderment.
'Nine.'
'Cuckoo!'
'Ten.'
'Cuckoo!'
'Eleven . . .'
And all I kept wishing in those moments was that the cuckoo bird would never cease its fatal song.

Not all the birds were given so much trust, however. Among the more adventurous things for us to do was lead a crusade against the magpies. In our yard, there was a handmade sink installed to wash hands after working in the garden. The sink was a primitive thing: a metal reservoir underneath and, on top, something looking like a bucket with a little stick attached to its bottom. When I touched the stick and sort of pressed it into the bucket, the water came out right into my palms.

Grandmother kept a bar of soap next to the sink, but every other week the soap would disappear—that was the great mystery we kept trying to solve for a long time. Until one day, after hearing some noise in the yard, my grandmother ran to check what was happening and found the soap lying on the ground and the bucket upside down next to it. Lifting the bucket, she discovered a wet magpie!

The poor bird was attracted to everything shiny, she explained, and it was this magpie which kept stealing our soap bars over and over. That bird shook its feathers and flew away, but my grandmother was determined to fight the thief. She took my hand and led me over to the tallest tree we had in the area, an old poplar.

'Wait here, Aliosha.'

Babushka advanced on to the tree, lifted her dress a little, touched the trunk here, moved her foot there—and suddenly began climbing the poplar! I couldn't believe my eyes! My dear old grandmother, not that skinny and not that sportive, climbed the tree a million times better than I could ever hope to! After reaching the nest at the top, she yelled back at me:

'Step aside, dear!'

A heap of branches and feathers flew down, together with wires, buttons, forks, and all sorts of other rubbish, including some bars of soap! The magpie never came back to our yard again.

My grandmother seemed to be able to create something incredible out of nothing and to make the most out of whatever little we had. Like those plants, vegetables, and fruits she cultivated from seeds, the seeds that she kept from her last year's plants. The best cucumbers, for instance, were never to be eaten, but to be kept for the sake of their qualities—so that all the cucumbers would be the best next year.

There were no pharmacies in our world, only my grandmother's down-to-earth elixirs. Even such things as eggshells were ground into powder and added to food as a source of calcium. Breadcrumbs were necessarily picked from the table—every single one. The concept of garbage did not exist. We had no trash bin.

Once emptied, glass jars were never thrown away (unthinkable!) and, if broken by accident, provided a reason for a serious family drama. Once used, plastic bags (a very rare commodity!) were washed and line-dried outside for endless reuse. All of that, and much, much more, were signs, no, not of her poverty, but of her deep-rooted careful attitude to everything living and to life itself.

She was not an eccentric, however. There was nothing unusual or even remarkable about her way of living, for such was the way for everyone around us. Such was the simple necessity of life: with no shops to sell things, with no things to be delivered, with no cars to fetch things from afar, with no confidence in anyone set above you, and with no salary ever paid on time at her husband's coal mine, my grandmother knew that her duty was to feed us—in practice that meant that her garden was our best chance of surviving. I couldn't help but feel, see, notice that her life—every one of her daily chores, everything in her behavior, from quiet songs to blistered fingers—partook of the same cast-iron, stone-hard, sun-bright meaning.

One thing she lacked in her life, however, was a cow. At least this was her only complaint, the only desire she expressed regularly. Yet they couldn't afford one, so we had to make a weekly journey deep into the fields, where the cows were grazed under the lazy surveillance of an old woman. My grandmother would talk to the shepherdess while the latter milked the cow. I'd grow bored and tired in the sun, as they went on yakking the hours away. The bucket seemed bottomless and the sun merciless.

When the reservoir was finally full, the two women would let me taste the milk. I remember how they lifted the bucket to my face, how I drew closer, touched the thin slippery edge with my lips, trying to stand still, not to hit the bucket with my teeth. Then, suddenly, the voices and the sounds became echoes, melting somewhere in the distance; there was only the summer heat on my hair and the white infinite surface of the milk all around me—up above . . . below . . . left . . . right . . . all white—with the black dot of a fly drowning somewhere on the edge of the galaxy.

The bucket was tilting more and more, and the milky universe gradually folded in over my head. I closed my eyes an instant before the warmth of the milk reached my lips, wet my tongue, streamed down inside my body—and, for a while, time stood still.

Sometimes in the afternoons, particularly on a bad rainy day or on a special occasion, the villagers paid each other a visit. My grandmother loved such events. Once she took me to a big feast hosted by an old friend of hers whose grandson had been drafted into the army.

The entire village gathered, people laughed and cried and danced and sang until late at night. The newly made soldier looked proud, and all the village girls laughed at his jokes. Then, just before midnight, he finally had to leave. In the dark on the stoop of the house people hugged and cried once more before the boy departed, leaving his old mother with red swimming eyes, exhausted, devastated.

As my grandmother and I walked back home, I remember how my

feet grew weak, how her arms lifted me . . . Next thing—the sun was pouring in through the flowery curtains, and onto the porch, and my own voice was ringing out between the blue and white walls of the yard: '*Baaabushkaaa!*'

On that new day my grandmother, feeling sad for her girlfriend, told me, 'She must be feeling lonely . . . Let's go, Aliosha!' and so we went all the way back to visit the poor woman.

We got to her house, comforted the lonesome friend, and ate some leftovers. The two of them were chatting quietly as they cleaned the house and I played with a local cat, when suddenly the front door was flung open and the newly made soldier, the very same boy to whom we'd all said goodbye only the night before, stepped into the house with a large smile on his face.

'Oh!' the old lady exclaimed, lowering herself slowly, holding onto her heart.

It turned out that the young man had failed his medical test and was sent back home. No army, no reason for sadness and goodbyes. In the turn of an hour, the house was full of villagers once more, laughing and crying all over again, and another party began.

My grandmother's friends and neighbours seemed to like me, the only trouble being that they often mistook me for a girl. I didn't wear girlish clothes, nor was I often seen playing with girls (or boys, for that matter), but something about me confused the village people. As in that occasion when my grandmother and I went shopping . . .

The district had only one store, a couple of hours walk from us, and we hardly ever went there unless we ran out of sugar or salt. Although there was very little on sale, the place was always full of people. People chatting endlessly, discussing the news, standing in line for something, buying nothing.

'Oh, what a pretty little granddaughter you have, Gerasimovna!' some woman exclaimed when we entered the store. *Babushka* then had to explain patiently that I was a boy, and everyone looked puzzled for a moment. 'That's a shame, really . . .' one of them would sigh, before moving on with some local gossip.

I never understood why such confusions occurred. I guess I was too tender with cats, too scared of other boys' fights, too gentle with my grandmother. I didn't like making mess or noise, I always tried to clean up after myself and to make sure everything was pretty in the house. When people gathered, I liked to set the table with plates and cutlery and make soft bouquets of lilacs. I liked to listen attentively to people's loud talk and quiet songs. And when taken to visit others, I was a bit too shy when it came to making new friends.

Only once can I remember making something of a scene when, at a neighbour's house, I was not allowed to play with two big dolls that I found lying on the sofa. The dolls' eyelids, normally opened, closed when you rocked them, and I was happy to do that until the adults saw me and took the dolls away. I began crying, not understanding what I had done wrong.

If left on my own, I would always play quietly. If asked to help, I'd be even happier. I didn't ever want to upset anyone.

Once I overheard the villagers discussing a new problem for the area: more and more often the junkies paid them visits. In the middle of the night, they would break into the village huts, steal whatever of value they found, occasionally get into bloody fights with the elderly dwellers. 'The bastards simply took the ladder and climbed into our *seni!*' I heard them say.

I had no clue who these creatures—'junkies'—were and where they came from, but every night thereafter I was busy imagining someone climbing through my grandmother's window. Since all the *izbas* were the same old one-story huts, it wasn't a hard thing to do. One wouldn't even necessarily need a ladder. There had simply never been any need to protect oneself from each other until then.

During the days I began spending more and more time searching for a secret hiding place—somewhere too high for the junkies ever to reach me. The highest spot I found was the garret above the pigsty. I climbed up, cleaned it a little, dragged an old chair up there and spent hours observing the world from my peephole window, imminently expecting intruders. But during the day there were none. Except occasionally our neighbours, usually old ladies, stopped by our gate wanting to chat, hesitating to enter, and calling for my grandmother.

'Gerasimovnaaa! Zoya Gerasimovna!'

So one day, to ease their troubles, knowing my grandmother's never-failing hospitality, I attached a fishing line to the gate and brought the line all the way up to my garret. From then on, whenever an old lady came for a chat, I would pull on the transparent line and make the gate open as if by magic. Only sometimes it took half a day's waiting for a visitor to come. When a familiar person did finally approach, however, I'd pull and pull on the string, the gate would open, the neighbour would open her mouth in amazement—and my garret was filled with laughter.

❧

When the sun neared the ground and the village dogs—as if suddenly all scared of darkness and eager to reassure each other by joining their voices in choir—filled the air with their hollow barking, my grandmother and I had the last chore of the day: watering the cabbages. For that, we had to go down the path to the swampy area, where the cabbages grew better than anywhere else.

It was the same swamp where in the winter Dick, our new dog, would pull the sledge with me seated gleefully in it, and from where in the summertime I once collected two buckets full of frogs—for my improvised aquarium, a moldy bathtub abandoned in the middle of our garden. After I'd filled this tub with the croaking green misery, however, my *babushka* frightened me by saying that my grandfather wouldn't be happy at all with my new pets, and the two of us had to spoon the frogs out of the basin and to lug the heavy buckets back to the swamp. On our way down the path I stumbled and fell, the buckets 'turned turtle', and their protesting amphibious cargo leapt and jumped all around us—while we could only look on, and laugh, laugh, laugh . . .

So it was down there, near the swamp, where my grandmother and I would venture before sunset to water the cabbages. After that, with all our daytime tasks completed and another happy day over, while I would play at something, or read, or pick the bad buckwheat seeds from the good for my morning *kasha*, my grandmother prepared dinner on her stove. When it was ready she would at last—for the first time in the day—sit quietly by the table, gazing outside.

The table stood right by the window, which faced the raspberry bushes, and beyond that one could see the dirt road stretching all the way up from the house to the hill. Sitting on the floor behind my grandmother, with my buckwheat, books, or toys, I'd look up if she became too quiet, and observe that her eyes were set on the horizon at the precise spot where the road meets the hill. The house would drift in silence . . . Then, all of a sudden, she'd rise from her chair and exclaim with such joy in her voice that I could feel all the strings of her soul tremble:

'Oh, my Sashenka is coming.'

I'd also stand then, and would spot a lone tiny figure appearing from behind the hill, then moving slowly left, turning down onto our road and growing bigger and bigger from that moment on. My grandmother would untie her apron, walk rapidly to the three-paneled mirror, take off her headscarf, fix something, and rush back to start placing dishes on the table for the three of us, singing quietly all the while.

After dinner with my grandfather, during which we kept silent while he talked about his day, the three of us retired to watch television. They had a funny, round TV, not black and white but not exactly coloured either. It had two channels, which was more than sufficient. My grandfather watched his news, got madly worried over some item or other, and then fell peacefully asleep right there on the sofa. My grandmother usually stayed longer, watching soap operas while knitting or sewing. It was ink-dark outside by then and since no more work could be done, my *babushka* could immerse herself in the blood-curdling, spine-tingling, bone-chilling mess happening somewhere in Santa Barbara or Rio de Janeiro.

'Poor people,' she kept saying. 'Poor, poor people!'

I loved watching my grandmother watching television. She grew up without it and so she treated it with great respect and trust. Every newscaster who said, 'Good evening, my name is . . .' would receive a loud, 'Good evening, and I'm Zoya!' from my grandmother. And every

soap opera, even from the most distant social and geographical loca-
tions, would require the maximum attention as if it was our responsi-
bility to solve those troubled people's problems.

'Look at her, just look,' my grandmother would begin, 'she thinks
she knows how to live life! Treacherous, envious woman!'

Sometimes I'd grow scared for my *babushka* because things would
get too dramatic somewhere in Southern California.

'No. No! Don't go there, darling. Please, don't go! Your husband is
a bad man,' she would shout, waking my grandfather, 'Go! Leave him
now!'

After the dramas of the Western Hemisphere had calmed down, we
could go to our bedroom. There were only two narrow beds in their
house so, of course, I preferred to cuddle with my grandmother.

Before going to sleep, to let go of the junkies and other demons, I
begged her to tell me stories. 'But I don't know any!' she would say and
then proceed to recount some funny incidents from the time when my
father and uncle were my age. Those were hilarious anecdotes, like the
one where Uncle Kolia licked the metallic surface of his sleigh while
sliding down the hill on a cold day (it was my dad's idea, no doubt), and
then came back home crying, with the sleigh dangling from his tongue.

I wanted to hear those stories over and over again. But after half
an hour or so, my grandmother, tired after a long day, would start
dozing away right in the middle of some very exciting moment. I was
upset but it was also very funny because she would simply freeze in a
half-sitting position, open her mouth slightly and start to snore quietly.
Then, mischievous me, I'd draw closer, bring my hand near her face,
stretch my pinky finger; thinner than a pencil, and tickle the inside
of my grandmother's nostril. She'd wake suddenly, push herself up on
the bed a little, then look at me, laugh, and continue her story until
I fell asleep. She played no nasty tricks on me, although I certainly
deserved some. Only after a while I'd feel something big and warm
encircling me from behind as that heavy arm of hers was carefully
lowered around me.

'What, again?' she would say the next night, 'But I've already told
you all of my stories!'

I didn't care. I guess it wasn't the stories I was looking for. It was her soothing, tremulous voice which calmed me. Her voice was full of some inexplicable, instinctive trust, some magnanimous care and gratitude which, she believed, this world has to be treated with.

In her world, everything, everything deserved and required her help, her attention, her labour. Everywhere she looked there was something to improve, and that something never seemed to exhaust her, but only made her happier, stronger, calmer . . . I was never that calm and patient.

Take *kissel*, for instance, that viscous, sweet, crimson drink, so popular in rural Russia. My grandmother made a wonderful one from strawberries and big cubes of love. The only difficulty with *kissel* was that after all the mixing, stirring, and boiling, it had to be left for a couple of hours to cool. Because of its thickness, it was impossible to drink even in small sips while it was still hot. Remove the lid from the pot, and *kissel* cools much faster, but a nasty, heavy film forms on top of it. Keep the lid on the pot, and you had to wait for hours before you could even touch it. My grandmother used to place that hot pot of *kissel* covered with its lid outside on the porch. As for me, all I could do was sit nearby and wait for what seemed an eternity for the *kissel* to cool while studying every single flower painted on the dark blue pot. I still remember that pot and the tiny flowers on it, but most of all the taste of *kissel*, which would be even sweeter after such long waiting.

Only much later, much much later, did I understand how treacherous, how recalcitrant time is. Try to speed it up and you get nothing but a heavy nastiness; let it flow slowly, take it as it is, don't rush it, be patient, learn to enjoy every bit of it and you will be rewarded with the most exquisite delight, flowers on top of it.

One morning I woke in my *babushka*'s bedroom and felt something different in the air. The perfume of lilacs, synonymous with her home, had vanished. The light fell less cheerfully on the carpets and chairs. There was something unprepared-for all around. I climbed through the pillows and blankets over to the small window, pushed aside the curtains and saw white crystals over the green grass.

That was my first snow.

The summer was over, and soon after, when I least expected it, a tiny blue car did appear from behind the hill and drive slowly along the dirt road, up there parallel to the horizon. Then the car turned down and rolled in our direction, growing bigger and bigger with every blink of my eyes. Finally, it stopped a few meters from the spot where I stood in disbelief. The door opened and my mother, with tears running down her cheeks to the corners of her smiling lips, stepped out.

They were back! They hadn't abandoned me! They had come to take me away from my *babushka*.

Chapter Three

Eleven

I did go back to my grandmother's place, of course, the summer after that first long stay, and the summer after that. Even my winter holidays I spent with her from that year on. More and more impressions of her world gathered in my head with each visit, good and not-so-good ones too. Including that day in late December when I was sledding down the slope behind our house. On one run my sled stopped moving and I stepped off it into the fluffy snow. All of a sudden the world turned upside down. I cried out, and the next moment there were only cold dark walls around me: I was trapped in a pit, which was covered by snow on the surface, leaving it invisible.

I screamed and screamed until the grown-ups came to my rescue. No one could explain to me what that hole was which I fell into nor why it was there, so close to our house, in the middle of that empty space.

I have another strange, unhappy memory of one evening in the village when a loud conversation occurred at the dinner table, and my father raised his voice to my grandparents. Later on, I realized they were fighting over Perestroika and what it was likely to bring into our lives. Dad was convinced that the changes were for the best, while my grandparents were not so sure. My grandfather was most concerned about what was going to happen to the coal mine where he had worked his entire life.

One thing my *babushka* was certainly grateful to Gorbachev for was the gradual return of her religion. When I think of it, I'm not even sure where she picked up her religion from, because ever since Lenin had taken the place of God, no other variations were allowed. Stalin, rather modestly, volunteered to play Jesus. The Red Terror followed soon after the Revolution when priests were crucified, churches were burnt down, believers were laughed at and gradually chased underground. Still, my grandmother kept praying in secret.

I suppose women like her had learnt their prayers from their mothers. With no churches open, they created their own tiny altars at home with small gilded icons, thin, short, dark-brown candles, and white lace kerchiefs all around. My grandmother had placed her altar above the refrigerator. However, religion in its social forms had died out, and already my parents' generation believed in nothing. Yet for me, born in a free time, *Babushka* cherished a hope that I might pick up her praying. A few times she shared with me her fear that after her death there would be no one to pray for the good of the family, and so there would be no good.

Finally, at the beginning of the nineties, she had reason to rejoice, for the center of the Russian Orthodox religion, the Cathedral of Christ the Saviour in Moscow—which had been converted into a swimming pool by Stalin—was being rebuilt. All around the country people began learning prayers and buying Bibles. After some serious, almost hysterical debates between my parents and my grandmother, the latter had won and took me to a newly built local church to be baptized.

By that time I was nearly nine. I never quite understood what was happening with all that water and chanting in the church, but it reminded me of my *babushka*'s rituals in the *banya*, and so I obeyed her calmly. I was told that I was saved now, and as a material promise of that, I was given a small silver cross to wear on a string around my neck. At home I looked more closely at it, but no matter how hard I tried to like it, I simply didn't. The tortured naked little man somehow didn't seem either kind or loving.

And yet, it was my grandmother, with her chanting and praying, cabbages and potatoes, berries and mushrooms, who shepherded our whole family through the hardest times. My grandfather's coal mine hadn't given out any food cards or money for months. With or without the help of religion, the old country was collapsing, factories were being closed one after another, and people, the people themselves, had no idea what to do with their lives. For nearly a century they were taught to live in one particular way, and now that way had brought them to a dead end.

Lithuania, Estonia, and Latvia were first to express their intention to leave the Union. They didn't want to have anything to do with either our past or our future. Georgia, Moldavia, and Armenia followed them soon after. Finally, in August 1991, something very serious happened. In our isolated town in Siberia, as distant from Moscow as New York is from London, we couldn't really understand what was going on: a few members of the Communist Party appeared on state television announcing that Gorbachev was ill and couldn't keep functioning as head of the Union. They said that they, the true communists, were going to bring the country back onto the right track.

A few hours later, the TV connection died, and when it returned, white swans were dancing. As absurd as that reindeer bursting in through our front door when Perestroika began, those beautiful ballet dancers from Tchaikovsky's 'Swan Lake', broadcast in a loop on all TV stations, served as the sign of something game-changing. Swans danced for hours and hours, people waited.

Later on, we found out that certain politicians, devoted to the ideals of Marxism and Leninism, had locked Gorbachev in a *dacha* in Crimea and attempted a *coup d'état*. Simultaneously a young political leader, Boris Yeltsin (chosen only a month earlier to represent the Russian state at the USSR convention) resisted the hardline communists. Yeltsin managed to get support from the Soviet military and directed tanks to the White House and to Ostankino, the central television station.

Simple citizens like our family were not supposed to know all that at the time. That's why, at Ostankino, they went on broadcasting a recorded version of classical ballet from the Bolshoi Theater instead of presenting a live transmission from the Moscow streets. While my parents, their friends, and the entire town of Taiga lived in fear and agitation, I was quite happy with the 'Swan Lake'. I had never seen ballet before. I couldn't take my eyes off the screen.

Five days later, the *coup d'état* was officially defeated; Boris Yeltsin was triumphantly waving the new old Russian flag, and the Communist Party of the Soviet Union was disbanded. Even though the misery of simple people persisted, my parents and many of their friends were happy about this turn of events.

๖

My dad could never have made a good communist. Ever since he came of age, and his Pioneer service was over, he no longer bothered to attend the Communist Youth Organization meetings. Instead, he was busy listening to illegally smuggled vinyl records of the Beatles, Rolling Stones, Queen, and trying his best to wear John Lennon's hairstyle with Freddie Mercury's mustache. Many years later, I found at home an old Madonna record, brought to Siberia probably via Ukraine or some other Western republic. On the cover, there was a rebellious looking youth and a title translated into Russian: perhaps, with an attempt to censor Madonna's bold ambitions, the title of the album 'Like a Virgin' was turned in Russian into 'As If Still in Virginia'.

In the same way that Soviets were trying to censor Madonna, they were attempting to control young rebels like my father. Even though more and more Western products were leaking into the Union, the KGB presence was ubiquitous. When my dad, a student at the polytechnic institute, began organizing a discotheque (with a disco ball made of a geographic globe and shattered mirrors, and with ABBA-styled outfits made from grandmother's curtains), the KGB took my father directly from his classes and had a discussion behind closed doors.

With Perestroika, people like my dad, who were dancing to Western music and bootlegging chewing gum, were the first to start moving in the direction indicated by Gorbachev. It was clear to my dad that a time of change was here to stay, so instead of joining thousands of strikers, he quit the machine factory even before it was shut down, and my mother soon followed him.

From that summer on, our family was not living in the USSR anymore. We had a new flag, a new anthem, a new leader, and the absolute belief that this was all going to stay with us forever. We believed that there was no way back, and the only way forward was to start building the market-based economy that Gorbachev promoted.

At the beginning of the nineties, when the government finally lifted the Iron Curtain, it seemed that they had opened a dam and we were all going to drown in a rainbow-coloured, cash-smelling, spellbinding tsunami of Coca-Cola.

Western companies, realizing the immense new market opening up, rushed in. The flood of it all was unbelievable. One day we had dandelion jam and bread with butter for dessert, the next day we had Mars, and Snickers, and Mamba, and Skittles. My grandmother's sea-berry syrup completely lost its appeal.

My grandparents were very confused, as were the majority of older people. I remember begging my *babushka* to buy me 'Yuppie', a little plastic bag with an acid-green powder which was supposed to turn into a fun-giving, juice-like drink once mixed with water. And I recall my grandmother's amazed gaze. She couldn't understand me. Did it mean that all that gardening, all that berry collecting and vegetable marinating, all that mushroom picking and cabbage watering were of no use and would soon be over?

According to a 'Yuppie' TV commercial, a child could not be happy without that saccharine powder. I believed commercials the same way as all children of my generation did—wholeheartedly. I had never seen commercials before that year. Nobody had. I spent hours in front of the TV during the commercial breaks, and—oh, God!—they also had rhymes, so I had to memorize them all in the same way as I had memorized children's poems.

In 1994 privatization commenced. That was a simple yet wicked procedure. Because everything, absolutely everything in the Soviet Union was owned by the State, in the brand-new country called the Russian Federation, all property, companies, and institutions were to be sold at auction. Factories and *kolkhozes*, airlines and oil pipes, gas wells and water dams, coal mines, gold mines, and even the Trans-Siberian Railroad itself were now all for sale.

According to legislation, no foreigner was allowed to attend such auctions, and every Russian with money could become a happy owner of one of the world's major corporations. But who had any money in the Soviet Union, where the simple notion of private business was punished by law, and a proud owner of more than one cow risked being sent to a labour camp? Only those in government, of course, had money.

And if you rose to power in Soviet times, it meant that you were a good communist, loyal to the socialist ideals, right? Wrong. Suddenly, in the time of privatization, there appeared to be hundreds of wealthy men who, only recently promoting Lenin's teachings, were now happily buying companies from the State like perfect capitalists.

Further, crime bosses, *avtoriteti* as they were known, individuals often linked to the government itself, were on the rise, acquiring everything that had any value with the help of a gun.

In our small town, a full-scale war broke out between its few criminal groups for control of the engineering factory. There was not much opportunity for people like my parents, and especially like my grandparents, to win in this bloody game. They had neither sufficient capital in their pockets nor cruelty in their veins to climb this deadly mountain. The best thing a young family of engineers could do was to step aside from the big game and attempt to establish a small business of its own.

Together with a couple of his ex-colleagues, my father joined a newly formed small company that was importing goods from the West (meaning Moscow). Goods of all sorts—from juice in carton boxes and children's toys to electrical devices and women's stockings—were arriving in train wagons (via the same Trans-Siberian that some time before had brought Lenin into our premises), then having to be unloaded from the train by my dad and his pals before being put on sale.

This was when my mother became involved in business. Still young and pretty (she had just turned thirty by that time), she cut her long thick dark hair in a shockingly short, boyish style, put on a fashionable, wide-shouldered Tom Claim suit, and turned herself from a young Soviet engineer into an attractive business lady overnight. She was put in charge of selling various items, at first in a tiny shop that was nothing more than a stall and a seat in the side entry of our local hospital. However, things were evolving rapidly, the new economy was gaining momentum, and soon my mother found herself the proud director of an independently standing, first-in-town department store.

A man's soul can be compared to a department store, a wise man once said, and my mother's was a neatly structured one. It was a modest looking place, newly built on the outskirts of Taiga, surrounded by the old wooden *izbas* where people still kept pigs and geese. It was made of grey stone with a small portico and two symmetrical windows on both sides. Indoors, it had an airy entry room with a few doors leading off to separate departments, each no bigger than our bedroom at home. The first was transformed into a clothing and beauty section with one fitting room and a mirror; the second was an electronics stall, the third was a children's department, the fourth was made into my mother's office, where at a stylish black table with a gigantic white computer, she worked in the mornings and evenings when there were not many customers.

From then on, every day after school I rushed to help her. I made my way along the dirt roads trying hard not to mess my shoes with mud and cow droppings—since most of the roads in our town were never cemented, in fact they were, rather, mud roads half of the year and snow roads the other half—and ran under the portico of my mother's neat establishment. I loved seeing my mom that way, all busy and beautiful, with her hair so short, her skin glowing, her suits mostly black, the red lipstick that she was wearing daily now, her fancy, funny, cat-eye shaped glasses, and her perfect long painted nails—which she did herself on the weekends—making fast sounds on the massive keyboard. She looked very unusual to me, I wasn't used to seeing her that way, but she was very happy with her new life and, therefore, more magnetic than ever. Like the sleeping beauty after the magic kiss, my mother seemed suddenly awakened by the new wave of changes rippling through the country.

Very soon her store was attracting crowds, and it became the most popular (or perhaps the only) draw-card in town. No one cared to read that commemorative plaque to Lenin hanging at the station anymore, everyone rushed to the store, if not to buy, then to see things they had never seen before: Maybelline lipsticks and Dior perfumes, Tom Claim suits and Marlboro cigarettes, Barbie dolls and Lego constructors, audiocassettes with British music, videotapes with Hollywood films, watches, electronic items, Asian souvenirs, jeans, jewelry, shoes, and yes, 'Yuppie', 'Yuppie', 'Yuppie'—anything one could dream of. I could not stop wandering through all the treasures in there, hiding under the stalls, exploring each item one after another. Yet there was one place in the store that I loved most.

Every year, on the first of March, even before the snow started to soften, my mother would install dozens of vases right in the spacious entrance by the main door. In those vases, she'd put gerberas and tulips, asters and mimosas, chrysanthemums and roses of all sizes and colours. For most Russian people, who had never seen anything but field flowers and red carnations for Victory Day, this collection of extravagant bouquets looked like an exotic garden. It looked so to me as well. Yet I was much luckier than others.

The reason this flowery happiness took place only in spring was that the eighth of March was Women's Day, which had always been celebrated in the Soviet Union on a grand scale. Ever since the time of Lenin, that date was meant to be a special occasion symbolizing the equality of sexes. Yes, the Soviets were very progressive when it came to women's rights for one simple reason: every woman or man was meant to be a hard worker, a *tovarish*. So, at the beginning of March, every man, so tradition required, had to bring something to his woman, if not flowers or presents then at least a loaf of bread. However, in the new period, even the most exquisite plants could be delivered to Siberia by train. In order to acquire these flowers for sale, every spring my parents drove all the way to Novosibirsk, the biggest city in Siberia, and sometimes I managed to beg my way into the car.

We would drive the devilish, icy, and run-down winter road for about six hours until we reached the industrial city of Novosibirsk, which held as many citizens as Paris. We'd make our way through the center, without stopping, to the city's western outskirts, where all the goods which arrived from Europe via Moscow by train were stored in the massive warehouses. I recall entering one such factory-size warehouse through the floor-to-ceiling doorway and being absolutely overwhelmed by the aroma, the magic combination of all the possible green and blooming plants that were being stored in there and giving out a rich mixture of hundreds of different fragrances. Combined with the cold air from the masses of Siberian snow outside, the effect was breathtaking.

One couldn't see the flowers themselves but only hundreds and hundreds of elongated paper boxes stored everywhere on top of each other. While my mother was dealing with the order and my dad was getting bored in the car, I wandered through the corridors of that warehouse, every now and then sidling up to one of the boxes and quietly opening its cover. Inside, to my surprise, I discovered dozens of white lilies, asleep in their coffins, surrounded by liquid ice in blue containers. Another lid would open up a bit—and I'd find tulips of all colours with their buttons tightly closed, waiting for warmer times to reveal their splendor. Another box, much longer than any other—and I'd admire those deep-red Dutch roses with stems so long that if I took one and put it next to me it would be almost as tall as my body.

After the selection was made and the bills were paid, my dad would help to load the flower boxes into the car, and on the way back I didn't have much space for myself—the flowers were everywhere around me. I didn't even think of complaining. I was happy and smiling quietly all the way back home through the limitless white land, in anticipation of opening the boxes once again and dealing with the flowers.

My mom learned quickly how to make beautiful Western-style bouquets and even ikebana. She had a book, brought by an acquaintance from abroad and in a foreign language, from which, looking at the pictures, she got all the tricks and tips. She taught herself how to make bows and flowers out of ribbons, how to flip a sheet of cellophane into a delicate arrangement, which flowers to combine and which to keep by themselves, how to preserve the bouquets and how to make even the old ones look fresh again. Her hands were quick, and her long, firm nails were of great help. Every March, I couldn't take my eyes off her: she looked wonderful surrounded by all those vases, papers, and petals. Yet, ever since the first such March, she refused to accept flowers as a gift herself.

One spring, after I had already spent a season or two with my mom at work, I noticed many leftovers, short and broken flowers, on the floor. I started picking them up, trying to do what my mother was doing with the good and healthy ones. My bouquets tended to be small and funny, yet my mom was surprised with my initiative and decided to put my little invalids on sale as well.

'If any of them are sold, you'll get the money.'

I was thrilled. I couldn't help but walk impatiently around the shop, looking out of the windows and waiting for some men in search for an eighth of March gift. Whenever a customer stepped inside, I'd hide behind the stall, watching him as he selected a bouquet for his woman. I saw his gaze land on one beautiful composition after another, then stop and ponder over my little monster, then pass on.

The very first client I had was an old man, who found his way into the shop one day. I guess my mother's bouquets were too pricey for him, but when he saw one of mine, he rejoiced. He asked for it. My mother smiled, glanced at me, and sold it to the man. There was no limit to my happiness.

By the evening of that eighth of March, every flower in the store was sold out, including mine. As promised, my mother sat by the stall, counted the profit, and then separated out some sixty rubles for me. How proud I felt of myself! I could go on and immediately buy something from my mom's shop! A new teddy bear! Or a full box of 'Yuppie'!

'Try not to spend all your money,' my mom taught me. 'One has to keep something for the black day.'

I didn't know back then what *the black day* was, but I got her point. I brought the sum into my room and, at night, when everyone was asleep, I took my mother's manicure scissors, said 'I'm sorry' to my old teddy bear, cut his belly open and put the biggest part of my profit inside, before carefully sewing up the wound.

As for the rest of the money, I wandered the streets of our town not knowing what to do with my ten rubles. In fact, before my mother opened her store, there were only two places to buy something in Taiga: a milk factory and a bread factory. Each had a pitiful front stall with nothing on its shelves but the identical bricks of white bread and identical plastic bags (yes, bags) of milk. So now with my own proud sum, I was quite puzzled. I was certainly not going to spend it at either factory, nor at my mom's store, because I had told her I'd keep the rubles for the black day.

Then I reached the post office where I knew there were some postcards, envelopes, and basic stationery on sale. When I entered the place and lifted my eyes to the shelf behind the postman, I knew straightaway how to spend my first salary. Next to the corny postcards with red carnations and point pens in a vase, there were three books of the same size and colour: emblazoned on their dark-crimson leather, golden letters trumpeted the name of the author—Alexander Pushkin.

I passed my rubles to the seller and pointed at the books, but she said they were only sold as a set and cost two times more than what I had. How pretty those books looked! How wonderful was that feeling of having my own library! I couldn't resist such temptation! I ran back home, ripped open the belly of my teddy bear, took out the money saved for the black day and rushed back to the post office to buy my very own three-volume edition of Pushkin. How bad could that black day be, anyway?

❧

The blackest moments I'd known until then were the classes of physical culture (as they used to call sports) that were scheduled at the end of the school day, and so offered endless possibilities for humiliating the weaker beings during and after the session.

Even before the classes themselves began, I had to go through a prelude of bitter confusion. As soon as I stepped into the boys' locker room, seemingly out of nowhere, the strongest feeling of alienation, this powerful sensation of not belonging filled me from top to toe. I had hardly sensed anything more alien, and yet, at the same time, more bizarrely magnetic. Lost and scared, I'd change in a second and rush out of the room, escaping its typical smells of sweat and rubber, its lewd jokes and sharp punches. Unconsciously, without understanding or even trying to understand myself, I'd spend the rest of the time before class standing by the girls' locker room, waiting for one of them to step out and have a chat with me, saving me from my little misery.

Physical culture . . . Why did they call it that? Simply for the want of any alternative? And why was it so vitally important? The school director, himself the sports teacher, insisted that we, the pupils, had to work on the vegetable patches behind the school during the warmer months (to provide for our own meals), had to dig ice and to shovel snow in the colder time (to make our own paths to the Palace of Knowledge), to wash the floors of our own classrooms each day—in order to be well suited to and prepared for a life of labour.

Forced labour?

In the same manner, the objective of our school with its 'sports inclination' was to prepare the boys for the obligatory military service that awaited us. So, from the first grade on, we were required to march while the teacher yelled 'Left, right, left!', to form up in a line according to our height in no less than five seconds and to train ourselves physically.

By that time the country had its first president, Boris Yeltsin, and the school's director—our sports teacher—demanded that we pass the so-called 'Presidential tests' on a regular basis. It was a rather comfortable arrangement for the teacher because all that was required from him was to stand in front of the group with a class book, call one name after another in alphabetical order, and demand that the nominated person publicly demonstrate his or her physical abilities. The whole thing had puzzled me from the beginning because I vividly remembered our president from multiple TV reports as a tipsy, obese, sick man. I could hardly imagine the president himself doing any press-ups or pull-ups, so how could he possibly pass these Presidential tests? With the severest expression on his face, our teacher counted out the series of tasks, compared our results to the test's standards required and distributed our grades accordingly. It was all very simple: if you were strong physically, you got the highest grade, but if you couldn't squeeze those ten pull-ups out of yourself—you got the lowest.

The closer our sports teacher got to *M*, the first letter of my family name, the shakier I became. By the time he called 'Morozov', I was so nervous that all I could think of was a desperate need to pee. As soon as my name was spoken, the class burst out in loud laughter for they knew the show was about to begin. While they were red with excitement, I suffered, hanging on the bar, trying by any means to do a single pull-up. Why couldn't I manage? Oh, why on earth wasn't my body up to the standards for boys of my age? What was wrong with me?

'Well well, Morozov, don't you eat enough *kasha,* or what's your problem? Obviously you have achieved nothing since last week. The lowest grade as usual. If you keep on that way, you will never be able to graduate to the next year!' Ashamed of myself, I had to go back to the line and wait for worse to come.

Fighting and bullying was a regular practice at that school and, for a reason unknown to me, no teacher would intervene in these sometimes absolutely wild rituals. Like the one when the shyest kid, Jenia, got beaten to such an extent that he was absent until the end of the year. Or, another time, when the bully himself, a noisy and mean boy, said something wrong during the physical culture, and the teacher ordered him to hang from the bar. The teacher, a grown-up and a strong man, then punched the boy in his stomach, and the bully fell to the floor.

'This way you will all learn how to respect those older than you,' the teacher finished triumphantly.

My classmates seemed to love fighting more than anything else, and a typical school day would end with a battle in the ski field. Someone would simply yell, 'Today it's Oleg and Igor! Hurry up!' and the entire group ran out to watch the two boys beating each other up until blood flowed. I always tried to avoid it—to go away quickly when something of this sort began. But once or twice I stayed on.

Looking at the boys beating each other with such hatred while the rest of them cheered with joy, I felt as if something inside of me was being tortured, and I would start crying, even if no one had thought of attacking me that day. Some of the boys would stare at me and couldn't understand what my problem was. As for me, I also couldn't and still can't quite understand those tears.

Yet on those occasions when I was the one under attack, my eyes were dry. I would just be there, standing still or lying on the ground if I had already been thrown down, in silent shock. I couldn't fight back, couldn't comprehend, couldn't believe, see, or hear for a while. Why?

Among all our diverse sports classes, my least favourite occurred on the warmer days when the thermometer outside my mom's window showed a temperature higher than minus twenty-seven. That meant that our practice would be outdoor and, therefore, I needed to drag my skis all the way to school. Not plastic skis, but real wooden ones, long and heavy. Not being properly bound to each other, they were constantly falling and sliding in all directions as I made my way through the snowfields.

Once the class began, we had to line up by height outside the school, strap our felt shoes to the wood with some strings and buttons, and begin the marathon around the snow-covered vegetable patches. The teacher stood with a stopwatch. The slowest pupils got the lowest grades. That practice had to be repeated a few times a week until the temperature dropped below twenty-seven or the snow melted.

All our winter clothes, boots, hats, scarves, and mittens were meant to be kept in the wardrobe during indoor classes. But one cold winter day—not cold enough, though, for the skiing to be cancelled—I discovered part of my battle-gear had disappeared from the wardrobe. My coat, boots, and scarf were there all right, but my mittens, and most importantly, my enormous fur hat, three times bigger than my head, had either been stolen or taken by mistake by another pupil.

The winter held me a prisoner—one simply couldn't step out of the building with an uncovered head in such temperatures.

All my classmates got dressed and left the school. I stayed behind by the wardrobe, unable to solve the mystery of my vanished belongings, scared of my mother's reaction, unable to reach home without the hat. I stood there all day, one class after another, counting the bells. The sun rose and lightened the forest outside, the short day passed by and the night descended on the school again as I kept waiting. I simply didn't know what to do, how to reach home, whom to ask for help.

Finally, when the building was about to be closed, the old man, the one in charge of checking that we exchanged our winter boots for summer shoes at the entrance, found me standing by the wardrobe. Quietly, I explained to him what had happened. He spat and grumbled but delved about inside the wardrobe and got a fur hat for me out of some drawer. It wasn't my huge, fluffy, beautiful silver fox fur hat, brought from the North of Siberia by my aunt and uncle, but some miserly thing that looked more like a dead cat (in fact, people always half-joked that the cheapest Siberian fur hats were made out of stray dogs and alley cats). Still, I was saved and could finally face the wintry path home.

There was another problem, however. The skis. Heavy, clumsy, sliding, and falling all the time, the skis had to be carried back home too, and so I got dressed, put the suspect fur on my head, the heavy school bag on my back, the sack with summer shoes on my wrist, got hold of the skis, and left the building. A few minutes later, as I was making my way through the dark snowfields, I started to feel my fingers becoming numb. I still had no mittens or gloves on. On and on I went, my feet in the snow, my skis pointing in all directions, my fingers hardly moving. The dead cat on my head.

The path seemed endless and unwalkable, the skis, which I hated with all my heart anyway, were now forcing my poor fingers to stay exposed to the freezing cold. Just when I was about to drop everything, everything, into the snowdrift—the skis, the hat, the backpack, my own self—a woman appeared out of nowhere. She must have been making her way home from the factory. It was about that time of day. When she approached me, her eyes were not on my face or on my pathetic headpiece, but on my snow-white, naked fingers.

'What on earth are you doing outside without mittens? Your parents must be mad!'

Without another word, she grabbed my wooden skis, ripped them out of my frozen hands, propelled me forward and trudged along silently after me. I thrust my hands into the pockets of my coat, my fingers gradually melting within its warmth.

That gesture of kindness—anonymous, quiet, pure kindness—I have carried through my life, and since then, every time I experienced cruelty, I have tried to restore the memory of that stranger who took my skis and shepherded me home.

❧

Four times a year our grade books were issued with our final marks in them. The Soviet educational system didn't want to make softies out of its students and so gave only five grades: 'five'—outstanding, 'four'—good, 'three'—the lowest possible grade for passing to the next academic term, while 'two' meant failure and the need to repeat the year. Grade 'one', the lowest grade, was only given as a sign of teacher's special disgust towards the pupil. Otherwise, it had no function.

Needless to say, at the end of each term I had the lowest acceptable grade for the physical culture class. No matter how hard I tried to pull myself up or to run or to ski around the school faster, something in my body simply didn't work well enough for the President. Not only was this damaging my academic record and my reputation at school, but also at home nothing seemed to be worse for my dad than having a lousy sportsman for a son. I truly wanted to be good. And I wanted my father to be proud of me. Only I had no clue as to what I was supposed to do to become muscled and mighty all of a sudden.

Coming back home with a newly issued little booklet, containing good and excellent grades for everything, but always having these shaming low marks for sports, the most important of subjects, I knew I deserved punishment. But there was no one to punish me, for my parents were at work till late and I was mostly home on my own. So I would drag myself (and the skis) back home, take off my clothes, and place myself in the corner, facing the wall, while alone in the house. I stood that way for some time (until I thought it was sufficient), wondering over and over again how, in what way, by which method, I might become a good sportsman and a good pupil and, more importantly, a good son.

To be a good father was all my dad wanted to be, no doubt. A true Siberian, a hunter, and a fisherman, he wanted nothing more than to have a son, not a daughter—as my mother once told me—a son who could be a companion in hunting, playing football, and other similar ventures. Seeing that I was not exactly the type who would run around the taiga with a gun, he decided to be on my side, and so every weekend tried to train me to become a stronger man.

In the winter, he took me out to the forest to practice skiing, and in the summer, he attempted to develop my manliness in other ways. He was convinced that every boy had to ride a bicycle, yet I still didn't know how to do that, so one day he borrowed a bike from our neighbour, took me off to the taiga, made me climb a hill, mounted me on the bike and, from up there, pushed me down the hill. I got so scared on that horrendous ride, which naturally resulted in a magnificent fall, that I resolved never to touch that two-wheeled devil again. To this day, I don't know how to ride it.

Unfortunately, that didn't make him abandon his attempts at being a good dad. If I was bad at sports and good with books, he came upon the idea of manning me up using my own tools. Every night, before I went to sleep, he started coming into my room to read me one of his favourite books—*The Wolf-Killer*. The book was about a part-beast part-human who excelled at killing wolves with his bare hands. And every night I stayed in my room, hoping that my dad would forget about his fatherly duties and miss the reading session. Yet he was a responsible father, and so the time of the wolf-killer would inevitably arrive.

Patiently, I kept on listening to his reading, scared and repulsed by the stories. Finally, after a few weeks of these mandatory literary sessions, I told him that I had had enough, that I couldn't listen to it anymore, that I was frightened to death and also that I found that book badly written.

I was only eleven, and naturally my father didn't take my no for an answer. He argued with me, and with all the literary experience an eleven-year-old could possibly summon up, I explained to him why that novel was not a good one, especially for a child of my age. Never the patient kind, he was furious. He refused to read to me again, and after that hardly ever showed up in my room. Before leaving me, though, he asked ironically, 'And what do you consider a good book, then?'

I looked at him from my bed, feeling a little lost and confused in that strange battle and said that I liked my Pushkin, Lermontov, Tolstoy . . .

'What? There's no man in the entire world who has read that monstrous *War and Peace* from cover to cover! It's the stupidest waste of time!'

I had only read some of Tolstoy's shorter stories by then, but I was sure that my father wasn't quite right. Stubbornly, I told him, 'Well, if you think nobody in this world has ever finished reading *War and Peace*, then I'll be the first one!'

He laughed bitterly and left. But I was not joking, and the next morning I took the first tome of the novel from the school library and read it, as well as the other three later on, from cover to cover. While going through the book, I gradually came to forget about our fight. In fact, I even felt grateful to my dad for that scene.

Words, letters, pictures had always had a mesmerizing effect on me, but the most overwhelming thing of all was poetry. I didn't care much if the poems were about frogs and bunnies or heartbreaks and fatherlands. When there were neat lines following one another in a pattern, dedications, elegant titles, or simply three snowflakes on top, and, of course, as soon as there were rhymes, my heartbeat seemed to slow down, my attention was nowhere but on the page. I was enchanted by a poem as if by a magic spell. As soon as I read my first verses, I began learning them by heart. I was not trying to do it on purpose. I was not doing it for the school either. I simply kept reading the poems over and over again until I didn't need to look at the page anymore. At first my family was amazed and, later on, exhausted because I could keep reciting my poems one after another during the entire two-hour ride from Taiga to grandmother's village.

Unfortunately, this little talent of mine was of no help at school, for there was certainly not much poetry in our palace of knowledge with an inclination to physical culture. Even our Russian language teacher saw no point in looking at poetry, focusing instead on despicable Russian grammar rules, which I always struggled to comprehend.

Yet there was one class that I always looked forward to. It was called 'the reading course'. In fact, it was just a literature class, one where we were meant to be simply reading. It had a wonderfully gentle teacher to guide us through the worlds of Pushkin and Lermontov. Not only was this supposed to be a time dedicated entirely to short stories and novels, but also, to my quiet yet intense joy, one day the teacher came up with a new rule for starting every second class with five minutes of poetry. Following her idea, one of the pupils had to stand up, go to the blackboard, face the audience, and recite a poem from memory.

Elena Vasilievna, our teacher, whom we kindly renamed after a Russian fairy-tale heroine, Elena the Beautiful, was simply aiming to develop our memorizing skills. She couldn't, however, have found a better way to make me happy. While the rest of the class was moaning and groaning at this new routine, I did my best to keep silent and motionless, not to express my true feelings, though inside I was dancing. I ran home as soon as the classes were over, opened up one of my volumes of Pushkin, selected a few lines and spent the rest of the afternoon memorizing them while jumping on my parents' bed in excitement (jumping and memorizing at the same time proved to be a very effective technique, I discovered).

Soon enough, Elena the Beautiful noticed my passion for poetry. One day she took my hand in hers and brought me to the school library, tiny, but with an atmosphere of safety. At first, I couldn't understand what it all meant. The teacher introduced me to the librarian as a dedicated poetry lover and asked her to fetch *The Silver Age*. The librarian looked at me warily but, trying not to smile, brought a pile of Yesenin and Gumilyov, Tsvetaeva and Akhmatova, Blok and Mayakovsky. I knew I could only take two. I selected Yesenin immediately because we had already studied him briefly. Among the rest, one edition looked different: all the books seemed very old, their covers were glued over and over again, while their pages were vandalized with scribbles, but one little book looked absolutely new. I asked the librarian if it was a bad book because it seemed like no one had ever taken it.

'Not at all,' she replied. 'It is newly published. We didn't have it until this year.'

'So the writer is still alive?' I asked.

'No, the author is long dead.'

I couldn't understand, but I took that book with me too, hoping to solve this mystery on my own.

I remember walking back home that day in early April, first through the skiing field of the school, still white under the snow, and then down the street in the direction of home. I hadn't put on my gloves that day because I felt it was getting warmer. The spring was gradually winning over the long Siberian winter.

Even some time earlier, in the classroom, I had noticed something strange happening outside when I became bored with the lecture and looked out. Because it was warmer that day, the teacher had opened a *fortochka*, a tiny ventilation window, and through that small opening, I saw an undulating, transparent movement somewhere in between the classroom and the outside world. And when out of school, walking through the snowfield, I felt the same humid air gliding up from the snow, touching my skin gently and making my cheeks blush.

Beyond the field, a path descended, on both sides of which the first springs were already making their way down. I was amazed because they had not been there in the morning. I paused, so that my feet would stop making crunchy noises in the snow. I wanted to listen to the spring water.

Everything seemed to be waking up that day: all the immense power of nature was coming back to life after the endless winter, and everything felt so new to me, so cheerful, so fresh that I wanted to laugh for no reason. I looked all around me—trees, bushes, snowdrifts, and the streams running down . . .

And then I glanced down at that new book I had just taken from the library. It was a small one, thin and pleasant to hold with bare hands. I opened the first page, then the second. The pages were also new and did not part willingly from each other. On the third or fourth page, there was a pile of little black spiders, gathered together in the center. At that I stopped hearing or, it seemed, even breathing. The spiders sped around the page, put themselves in order and, all of a sudden, shaped the first line of a poem. And it felt for that moment as if there was nothing else in the whole world: in essence, a complete vacuum with only me, that first spring and the black Cyrillic letters coming together on the white paper into a verse.

> *Молюсь оконному лучу –*
> *Он бледен, тонок, прям.*
> *Сегодня я с утра молчу,*
> *А сердце—пополам . . .*

I put the book down. With all that fresh air, with that water running on both sides of my path, and that little book, that little poem, I felt my head spinning, as something new and lucid began growing in my chest. Young as I was, it suddenly became clear to me that somehow, inexplicably, something inside of me was also waking up, just like the spring on that first warm day.

This, I understood, was *the only* here and the only *needed* here—art and culture. I felt it as clearly as the sun above me, I heard that voice as distinctly as the joyful springs piercing the snow-land. One little poem bigger than the world around—and I knew it, I felt it, recognized that—this is the soul of one, and the soul of all. Eternal and indestructible.

I saw myself with total clarity standing at the very beginning of that long, complicated thing called life and yet, at the same time, felt a deep sense of connection to the book I was holding, with the name on it that had too many *A*s. I started walking down the street, following the water, and by the time I reached home, both Anna Akhmatova and that poem of hers were deeply rooted in my mind and in my heart.

> *I'm praying to the window ray—*
> *It's pallid, thin, exact.*
> *I have not said a word all day,*
> *Although my heart is cracked . . .*

❧

I knew I would not dare read Akhmatova in front of the class. I sensed that somehow her poems—so delicate and so powerful in their emotions and structure—would not fit those surroundings and could too easily be ridiculed. Also, I wanted to keep her for myself. For the class, I read and memorized some Yesenin and Lermontov instead because I knew their patriotic odes would be accepted more easily.

I had a hard time adjusting to the truly military regime of starting classes at seven in the morning when it only grew light outside around midday. However, this unusual timing—together with the intermittent electricity supply of the town—also made the whole academic process much more exciting. On a few occasions, after classes had already started, all of a sudden the light would go off and the entire building would be plunged into the complete darkness of the taiga. Girls would scream in fright, boys would do everything they could to frighten them more, teachers would beg us not to panic, their voices pitching higher and higher.

One such event took place during our literature class. It happened to be the first class of the day, so when the electricity went off, the full Siberian night fell upon us. Elena the Beautiful asked everyone to stay seated and not be scared while she stepped outside.

To me it was funny to be that way—in the dark yet among others. I stayed immobile and observant at my desk. At first, I was amazed at how bright the forest outside the windows suddenly became. Before it had seemed totally dark out there, but now, with all the indoor lights off, the moonlight was bright enough to capture the contours of the trees and even spread some bluish colours over them. Then I noticed that even the smallest sounds in the room could be distinguished: not only could I hear boys giggling and girls shrieking, but somewhere on the farthest side of the galaxy I could identify a child sobbing quietly. Surprisingly, I was not scared but rather excited about the whole thing.

Soon a soft light came from the doorway. It got brighter and brighter until Elena the Beautiful stepped into the room, holding a short thick candle between her palms.

'Calm down, children. You see, I'm enlightening you!'

She walked in front of us, looked around for a suitable place for the candle.

'I wonder, where should we place our source of wisdom?'

She raised her eyes and installed the candle on the very top of the blackboard. 'See, how suitable it is right under our *dadushka* Lenin.'

Indeed now in the dark of the room—though I couldn't see any of my classmates but only their black silhouettes—the portrait of Lenin was clearly visible. He was always hanging up there, of course, as he did in every classroom in every school in every locality in every republic of the Soviet Union, though somehow, having observed his smooth, dull, emotionless head over and over again during mathematics, physics, chemistry, and other classes, one would totally forget about him and no longer even see his portrait above the blackboard. But now, by the candlelight, we couldn't help but be aware of him. Undoubtedly, it would have made *dadushka* Lenin very happy—he was the best-lit face in the entire room.

'You see, how nice and cozy it is in here now. Well, well, stop crying, Jenia,' the teacher said, noticing the sobbing boy. 'I wonder, what can we do in such unusual circumstances . . . ? We certainly cannot read or write, can we, children?'

Then, the teacher herself suddenly became enlightened.

'How about someone reciting a poem for us? 'Borodino', for instance?'

An unhappy groan went through the class. No one seemed particularly excited about the 'Borodino' option. It was Lermontov's longest poem about war, our great fatherland, and the epic heroism of our soldiers—the most typical of all subjects for primary school pupils.

'Is there anyone who could do us such a favour?' the teacher insisted, but the room was totally quiet all of a sudden. 'Anyone?'

Now, had there been less light on Lenin and a bit more on the class, Elena the Beautiful could have seen from the beginning that there was one hand piercing the gloomy air as soon as she rolled that word 'Lermontov' off her tongue. But the candlelight couldn't reach the one-before-last row where I was seated.

Finally, out of desperation, I called out:

'I can.'

The teacher waved me to the center of the class. I walked quietly to the board and stood right under the candle and our *dadushka* Lenin.

And there I was, a few seconds and even a few minutes later, in the dark of the night, in front of the class, by the blackboard, under the warm fire of the wax candle, reciting with all the emotions and intonations I could bring to it, the long old rhyming story of Napoleon, of the battle of Borodino and Moscow burned to ashes, and the people who went through it all, and their memories. And, to my amazement, finally I could see the faces of my classmates, lit by the candle behind me.

No, it wasn't my moment of victory. It didn't help me win any friends, nor even gain any respect among the pupils. Rather, having exposed my passion for reciting poems, my status as an alien only became cemented and the bullying increased.

'Why are you so weird?'

'Why is your head so big?'

'Why are your eyes so narrow when you smile?'

'Why do you smile all the time? Want us to count your teeth?'

They always had so many questions for me. Questions I could not possibly answer. And if only it had stopped with questions.

On my way to school, right at the point where the broken fence once split the path in two, an unidentified object appeared one day: a rusty metal box with a well-locked door on one side and a barred window on another—a kiosk. This kiosk became the kids' magnet for a while, for behind its barred window innumerable jewels were exhibited: Chupa Chups and canned beer, chewing gum and condoms, chocolate bars and Marlboros (sold one cigarette at a time, a ruble apiece). No child on the way to school could pass by the kiosk without peeking in.

The window of the kiosk was barred for a reason. For the same reason that, if I were lucky that day to receive some pocket money, I'd need to use it quickly and hide that Chupa Chups in my pocket as soon as possible. Though even that wouldn't necessarily help. The teenage gangs lurked never far from the kiosk.

It became the rule of the game: to stop others from bullying me, I had to give away my newly acquired treasures. I had a few, since I was one of the first two kids in our class to have a new box with felt pens, a new backpack with Disney characters on it, and even a small Japanese electrical toy called Tamagotchi that everyone in the school craved.

Tamagotchi had the shape of an egg, with a tiny screen in the middle and three buttons below. On the screen, you saw some sort of creature made out of fat square pixels. By pressing one or other of the buttons you were able to feed, pet and clean the creature. If you did it well, it would grow and send you smiley faces; if you forgot your duties, the creature would die. Yes, die. One day when I hadn't fed my Tamagotchi for a few hours, I looked at the small pixilated screen and saw no pet anymore but a tiny grave with a cross on it. Thanks to the merciful god of capitalism, after an hour or two of bitter tears, I discovered that my Tamagotchi could be resurrected if I pressed a secret button on the back of the toy with a pin.

Another lucky boy in my class, who got treasures like Tamagotchi earlier than others, shocked the school by appearing one day with his own lunchbox. Children of communism, we were all supposed to eat at the same time, in the same place, and indulge in tasting the same menu of self-harvested potatoes and over-boiled cabbage. Teachers looked angry and the kids overexcited when that boy opened his lunchbox and took out . . . a sandwich. A sandwich! What could be fancier than that?! We all gathered around the lucky one, carefully studying the mysterious dark lines on the grilled surface of the bread. Why, where, how had he done it? Those perfectly parallel marks, that crisp sound, that smell!

'It's only a *toosterr*,' announced the classmate, proudly rolling the *r*.

How I begged my parents that evening to buy me a *tooster* too! How bitterly I complained about the over-boiled cabbage in the school's canteen! How eager I was to have a sandwich, with compulsory dark lines over its surface!

Until that year, the only electric tool the majority of Russians enjoyed the luxury of having in their household was a refrigerator. Usually the machine refused to produce anything but noise. Ours was a monster so loud that his energetic drill was heard from every corner of the flat all through the night. My mother kept fighting the beast, unplugging it in the dark hours only to find a pool of water under it in the morning.

Finally, in the midnineties, thanks to the same merciful deities of the new order, my mother was relieved—we got a quieter refrigerator and a washing machine. Until then, like most other women in the USSR, she did the laundry by hand on a wooden washboard with shiny metallic ridges—fingers beaten to blood guaranteed. Our brand new washing machine, however, was so boisterous that during the laundry sessions we both had to sit on top of it to stop the stallion from escaping to the prairies. Nevertheless, it was a big improvement.

I also got my *tooster*.

Soon, however, my tactic to prevent bullying by giving away whatever I owned failed me due to the fact that almost everyone now had the same stuff—while I kept on standing out. They stomped me into snow, they flattened me to the ground, they played football with my backpack, with my hat . . . though at least not with my own head. Not yet.

I knew I couldn't ask my father for any help because if I dared complain he would only remind me of how imperfect, unmanly, improper I was. With every week that passed I could see, I could feel with all my soul how he distanced himself from me. With me growing up and gradually showing more and more of my real self, Father started to learn who I really was. And the more he learnt, the less he wanted to be around. He moved further and further away, and I had no clue how to make him love me, be next to me, protect me. Support me in my own ways.

On my twelfth birthday, he found himself forced to drink the last bitter drop of disappointment. A short time before, I had made friends with our neighbour's daughter. Ksusha was a charming girl, two years younger than me, and because we lived on the same staircase, we started spending some evenings together. Ksusha had a Barbie doll, recently bought from my mother's store. When my birthday came around, I too was taken to the shop and allowed to select any toy I wished from its shelves.

What paradise for a child! You could have anything, anything you wanted! My mother, my dad, and the other people who worked at the store looked at me, running around, searching for something I truly wanted. But of course, I didn't want guns or cars, construction toys or table games. I took out a bright pink box with a Barbie, just like Ksusha's, and cheerfully announced to the entire group that I wanted to have that as a present. That kind of shame was too much for my proud dad to bear.

'I will never in my entire life allow my son . . . !' he yelled passionately in front of everyone.

But what was the point of my choosing freely what I wanted then? Why could other children come here with their parents and get what they liked? Wasn't it supposed to be my birthday gift?

My father was outraged. My mom tried to reason with him. They had a fight in public. Yet I simply couldn't understand what the problem was. Was it too expensive? Too big? Too pink? Surely other kids at school wouldn't like me less than what they already did. Or would they?

My father promptly left the department store. Other people returned to their work. I stayed sobbing there in the middle of the toy department with my mom encouraging me to choose anything else. I refused, of course, and remained with no present.

A couple of weeks later, my mother, pitying me, brought me a gift. A very beautiful miniature theater made of thick cardboard, with little flat dolls, different interchangeable backgrounds and even a real theater curtain. However, soon that theater was also taken away from me. My mom only said that the kids at our local orphanage needed it more than I did, but I already knew what the true reason was.

❦

Ever since that July, my only presents were books. Few of them were of the kind I preferred. The books that others were buying for me were children's stories, fairy tales, and ones with men killing wolves with their bare hands. I stuck to Tolstoy, Akhmatova, and other inhabitants of the school library.

Once, home alone and bored, I wandered through my parents' little collection. I was hoping that maybe something was hidden there, something in between detective novels and dark fantasy fiction. Then I saw a book different from the rest. It had a peach-coloured cover and a butterfly drawn on it. *Lolita*—I read on the cover and turned the first page.

I read the book greedily, in a week. I didn't even realize that it was about an older man lusting for a little girl. Instead, I thought the novel was simply about love and I appreciated its delicate, most elegant, most elaborate language. The main storyline didn't impress me as much as the first thirty pages. In the beginning, there's a story of a teenage boy falling in love with a girl of his age. They are on the beach, surrounded by their families. Not knowing how to express their feelings for each other, how to give way to their emotions, they lie under the sun, build sandcastles and, at some moment, the boy manages to touch the girl's hand by reaching for it under the hot sand. That moment, no, that feeling—of the hot sand keeping one's emotions discreet—stayed forever with me as the tenderest signal of love. Of course, I didn't go around telling my classmates and especially any adult about my discovery, but from that moment on I have always thought that Nabokov was more than brilliant at describing the complexities of the heart.

In spite of the fact that I had failed to share my father's biggest passion in life, it was to his fishing and hunting season that I was grateful for yet another lesson in love. Every September he would disappear, leaving my mother and me to ourselves. It was on that twelfth September of mine, when reading through a newspaper, that I noticed the name of Leonardo DiCaprio on its pages. Even in our movie theater-less town, people talked of the young American celebrity. He must still have been in his teens back then, so when I discovered his photographs in a newspaper I secretly cherished the hope that with my rather long blond hair and fair skin I looked similar to him. That day in September, while searching through the endless minuscule lines of a television program, I saw his name next to a film title that was going to be shown on one of our two TV channels in the middle of the night. I decided to take advantage of my father's absence and my mother's absentmindedness.

Happily, by that year I not only had my own bedroom (my parents sacrificed their space for me, moving to the living room) but I also enjoyed the luxury of having my own mini-TV, the *bull's-eye*. On the appointed night, after I said goodnight to my mother and left for my room, I pretended to be asleep while waiting with excitement for Leo's movie to begin. At the right moment, in the dark of my room, I turned on the bull's-eye, lowered the volume and soon read from the screen the mysterious title of the film—*Total Eclipse*. It was one of the first films I had ever seen, and certainly the first movie which I saw from beginning to end on my own. And that romance, that tormented love story of nineteenth-century French poets Arthur Rimbaud and Paul Verlaine, impressed and bewildered me. Of course, I had no idea who those two men were, and many, many other things remained unclear. I remember asking myself, for instance, if it was the same 'Rimbaud' who was punching and kicking in my dad's action movies. Nevertheless, together with Nabokov, Rimbaud and Verlaine became my own educators on love.

In the morning, when I got up and went to have breakfast, it was my mother who helped me with my tea and cookies. When I took my first sip, she dropped casually, 'So, how did you like the film?'

I blushed to the extent that even my hair, it seemed, turned red. I lied to her that I had just forgotten to turn the TV off last night, but her face said she didn't believe me.

Soon enough I had my first chance to check out my love education in practice. Reading voraciously, I came upon the idea of subscribing to a weekly children's newspaper. For that, I went to the post office already familiar to me and selected the newspaper most to my liking. An interested person, even a child, only had to leave his name and address, and that was enough for a free trial subscription. When the first issue of the children's newspaper *Mourzilka* appeared in our locked-for-good, half-bent mailbox, my parents were puzzled. They'd have done better to prepare themselves for something much bigger to come.

In *Mourzilka*, among all sorts of articles for kids and little stories, there was an entertainment section with crosswords and charades, which I liked the best. On the last page of the newspaper, I noticed an address and decided that if there was an address, they certainly expected some letters. I spent a few hours creating my own crossword, with a neat structure and definitions and, of course, the key. I wrote a letter, attached my crossword and mailed it back. In a couple of weeks, my crossword was there in the newspaper, published! I was so encouraged that I decided to continue the correspondence.

I still had no friends, I was no longer allowed to play with my neighbour, Ksusha, after the scene with the Barbie, and so I decided to ask the newspaper for help. Homeschooled by Akhmatova, Nabokov, Verlaine, and Rimbaud, I wrote a passage of introduction, presenting myself in the most lyrical way possible and stating that I was longing for a friend. When I was satisfied with the content, I mailed my second letter to the paper. A couple of weeks passed and I saw it published, too!

One evening my father got home holding an envelope which had arrived with my name on it. He asked me to explain its appearance in our tin can of a mailbox and I did; yet he only mocked me for the idea of making friends via a newspaper when there were so many kids in my school.

The letter was from a girl living a thousand kilometers away, but she enclosed her photograph and that made it feel like the beginning of a real friendship. But there was a problem to come . . . Just when I began to respond to the first letter, the second arrived with a picture of an enthusiastic redhead from Moscow. So now I had to choose between the two girls. Then, the third letter . . . Then, the fourth, the fifth, the sixth . . . After a couple of weeks, our mailbox was so full that one day when I was coming back home from school, I saw white envelopes that must have jumped out of the broken box, lying all over the floor, all addressed to me from girls and guys from around the country, wanting to make friends. Even though I didn't have a single real friend in my town, now I had a hundred of them living all over Russia!

After discovering that I could very well manage to reach for information and even friendship from another part of the nation via mail, I was soon back at our post office. I learnt that one could also subscribe to an English-language distance learning program and immediately put my name and address on the list. At school we had an English class, but our teacher exhausted her vocabulary with the daily 'How do you do?' and then spoke the rest of the class in Russian (mostly to her colleague next door). Obviously, she had spent her entire life in Siberia, and her own foreign language skills were not much more impressive than her pupils'.

With all the new products and goods coming from the West, we started to be exposed to more and more foreign words: words like 'super', 'expresso', 'ketchup', or 'boomer' and, of course, my favourite, 'yuppie'. I thought that it wouldn't be a bad idea to understand what all those strange words meant.

In a couple of weeks the first few brochure-like English manuals arrived in our mailbox. I was thrilled, and my parents were once again impressed with my ability to get whatever I wanted from God knows where. When the trial period was over, I prepared a big speech for my mother—about the changing times and the need for a modern young man to speak English—and she agreed to pay for a year of the distance learning program. I was a passionate student, and soon, with the help of a dictionary that I borrowed from the library, I went on to translate, rather ambitiously, one of Shakespeare's sonnets (it was short, hence should be easy) and the Beatles' 'Yesterday'. Of course, there was nothing professional about my translations, but I found it incredibly entertaining to try and solve those word puzzles. Latin letters seemed so unusual, so different from Cyrillic ones and, as with everything else different from my own life, my first impulse was to understand it.

No translations, no crosswords, no pen friends or poems were going to impress my dad. I didn't fit his criteria, I didn't satisfy his expectations, I never managed to become good at physical culture or fishing or hunting or even riding a bicycle.

Around that time I started having a nightmare which was to recur over and over for many years. In the dream I am lying asleep in a dog-pulled sleigh, moving rapidly through the snowfields in the middle of the night. Suddenly, I wake up and look back. I see my father running after the sleigh. He's scared of something and screaming for my help, but I'm only a small boy—I stretch my arm to him, but he's too far away to grasp it. The dogs run faster, the sleigh moves on, my father falls further behind. I scream and, finally, wake up.

The nightmare will repeat itself many, many times through the years but I never manage to grasp my father's hand.

Chapter Four

The Black Day

Although I only dimly understood the reasons for it at the time, things in the small universe in which we lived—*Babushka,* my father, my mother, and me—were changing very fast. Caught in a whirlpool of events that was making our former way of living more and more alien, we could never be sure how to react to these changes. Were we supposed to be cautious or excited? Scared or motivated? Thrilled with the new opportunities, or terrified? Perhaps we were all of these at once.

I could sense, even back then, that my father, though he seemed as rock-strong and confident as ever, was bewildered and agitated, excited and confused, but most of all eager to embrace all this new reality. It was only much later, in the cold light of hindsight, that I realized how naive young people like my dad actually were—people who rejoiced in the thought that they were leaving the communist era behind them. Even though many of the political and social structures originally set up by the Bolsheviks in 1917 were reformed by Khrushchev, Gorbachev, and Yeltsin in turn, the very core of the USSR, the iron center of it, always stayed intact.

The KGB, the punitive agency of the Communist Party, born together with the first Revolution and responsible for setting in motion a horror machine that this civilization had not seen before, was equally responsible for the attempted *coups d'état* of 1991 and 1993. When both failed and liberalization seemed inevitable, the KGB decided to act from within, gradually destabilizing the situation inside the country and getting rid of all democratic liberals, including the president himself. They chose a dual strategy, one arm of it bloodier than the other: a military campaign in Chechnya, the southwestern region of Russia, and a program of active collaboration with hundreds of 'organized' criminal groups in every region of the nation. In both cases, the strategy was old and simple: first, attack and assault; second, offer protection; third, take over and possess.

The people of the Caucasus were an easy target because they always stood out in the Union for being proud of their culture and language, protective of their territory, sensitive to any insult from the outside. At the first sight of Russian military action in their region they were ready to strike back. Very soon a full-scale war had begun, and Yeltsin himself was drawn into it. KGB agents must have been celebrating, for it was the Chechen War together with some mysterious personal illness that would cause our first president to resign.

But that was just one region and only the beginning. Soon blood was spilled not just in the Caucasus, but all over Russia. When people started talking of *mafia* (a new word for us), they imagined some rich bastards who had gained their money illegally and now posed a threat to everyone. But who were these dangerous people exactly? Where could they possibly have come from? Were they the same Soviet *tovarischs*, the same comrades as my parents? How did they manage to get into a position of power?

To start with, we had never seen any rich men in our country apart from the Soviet leaders and their cronies. No one had money or weapons in the USSR except those in charge of the USSR, so when the organized criminal groups appeared on our doorsteps, we couldn't help but notice that they had the same guns and the same manners as Russian military campaigners—with the exception of military uniforms. The mafia leaders, *avtoritets*, as they liked to call themselves, wore their infamous 'raspberry jackets'—suit-tops, dyed the colour of rotting blood. We would not have long to wait before this necrotic hue blended, before our very eyes, with the blue of the sky and the white of the snow.

My mother had a prescient feeling about the black day. Despite her business success, she kept repeating her mantra to me every now and then through the years.

'Nothing good will ever happen here, nothing good.'

She knew to expect the worst, and one day did turn black. The vinous-coloured *avtoritets* stepped into my mother's shop: just like that, with their guns hanging from their belts and with their mugs looking like they'd been digging mud with their snouts for a century. They strolled in casually, passed through the flower department, and went on into the room displaying clothes; their leader took the first jacket he saw and put it on, his fellows followed his example. The scene took place in total silence; no one dared ask the men to pay. They went on to the stall with watches and chose the items they fancied. True gentlemen, they grabbed a bunch of bottles of perfume and flowers at the exit.

From there, the leader looked back at the stunned shop assistants.

'Anyone got any problems?'

My mother shook her head silently.

'If you have any,' he added, 'remember, we are here to protect you.'

The rules of the game had changed yet again, and we had better get used to them quickly because it was just the beginning. The so-called organized mafia groups used the same tactics as Russian military groups in Chechnya. They called it *krisha*, 'roofing', meaning that the gang took charge of its chosen territory under the guise of providing security for its residents. In fact, the greatest danger posed to my mother's store was from this 'security' itself.

My father was furious, my mom nervous yet self-controlled. She played nice and tried to smile next time the heavily armed men showed up. She knew very well what happens to those who disobey, those who refuse to accept kindly the protection on offer. What might they do to us? What could happen to me, for instance? There were a few possibilities.

First, there was the cement—the most widespread punishment. A disobedient citizen would be kidnapped, tied up, and brought to a construction site. He or she would be thrown to the ground, then the liquid cement would be poured on top of the body. No noise, no fuss, no need to deal with any aftermath. No one would ever find the victim.

God knows how many roads and office buildings, blocks of flats and children's playgrounds constructed in those years across Russia contain corpses of innocent civilians.

One cement plant in a nearby town had increased its output tenfold. This way of 'solving the problem', by the way, is firmly set in the traditions of the Bolsheviks. In fact, the last tzar's family, Nicholas, Alexandra, and their five children, were disposed of in a similar way: it took seven decades to find their bodies, covered with sulfuric acid and pressed under railroad sleepers.

Speaking of acid . . . In the second form of punishment, widespread in nineties Russia, a victim would be notified that she or he was not acting in accordance with an unspoken agreement. If the victim continued to disobey, their child might be kidnapped. And if the victim still didn't satisfy the requirements within a given time, the child would be dropped into a container filled with acid. When the body had dissolved, the liquid would be delivered to the victim. They called it *rassolchik*, a 'little brine'.

Of course, there were also banal shootings and stabbings. The most common spot for this to take place was a victim's staircase, always pitch-dark in any block of flats. In such cases of 'ordinary' crime, the family would never be able to prove whether they were victims of KGB agents, local mafia, or ordinary street lowlifes. And prove it to whom? To the police? Another state agency? Ever since the early nineties, calling the police in Russia was taboo. Every time you saw a police car nearby, you knew you were better off disappearing from the spot. Police were never there to protect you from assault, but to protect the interests of your assaulters.

In such conditions, the worst thing a businessman, or any person, for that matter, could do was to aim for success and fortune. 'Don't show off, don't stick out,' my mother kept repeating to my dad, who was all too often agitated. She also asked me to stop coming to her store after school, and to always, always lock our apartment door.

The bigger and more important your enterprise grew, the more initiative you had, the more dignity and disobedience you showed, the more men with loaded guns and ugly mugs would circle around you, until one of them decided to stop providing 'security' and to pocket your business whole.

❦

Our store was open every single day and my mother usually had to be there from the moment doors opened till the late evening. Dad most often went to pick her up and sometimes I joined him. One evening the two of us were walking through the town, passing by the old *izbas* still standing outside our micro-district, when I saw a surprisingly neat, pretty house with a richly decorated porch. Among all the surrounding misery, this house was old-fashioned but retained its cared-for look.

'Whose house is it?' I asked my dad.

'Nobody's,' he said gloomily.

'*Nobody's?*'

He paused by its gate, peering into its black windows.

'It used to be Yeniseyenko's.'

I sensed he knew the story behind this, and I pressed him with more questions. Yeniseyenko, he told me, was one of those trustworthy men, those still loyal to Socialist ideas, who were not so rare in the Soviet era. My dad had never been fond of the regime, but I felt that he respected and liked this man. Yeniseyenko was the director of the factory where my dad was employed. Sometimes they would meet in the early morning on their way to work and discuss the country's problems.

I took another look at the house, and I could see exactly what kind of man might have built it. Walls not very tall but sturdy, material of white brick, not wood, windows decorated with grilled shutters, the fence sagging a little but still looking trim—the whole property gave off the image of a good master.

When the Soviet Union collapsed and the engineering factory was suddenly nobody's, Yeniseyenko's position became a slippery one. In fact, those old-timers, faithful to communist principles in their most ideal form, would be the biggest obstacle in the way of those who didn't care either about the old ideals or about the new ones. Yeniseyenko couldn't be bribed, couldn't be taken down legally, so one day he was found stabbed in the staircase of our block where his children were living, and where not a single bulb was left unbroken from the ground to the top floor.

Oh, those Soviet social housing staircases, that clearest symbol of communism! How frightening, how mortifying they had always seemed to me, whether our own, or the staircase of the block where my aunt and uncle lived, or that in any other typical five- or nine-story housing project in Russia. Those staircases had always served as a perfect example of the fatal flaw at the heart of the communist system: if everything belongs to everyone, then no one is responsible for anything. We might have taken care of our own minuscule flats because those were our own to a certain extent, but staircases were communal, and so completely neglected. On entering one of them, a foreigner visiting our small town was heard to ask, 'Was the war damage so bad?' The irony was there never had been any war in our region. Only the victory of socialism. One was always repelled when using the staircase in the morning and always terrified coming back home at night because everyone knew that, in the communal zone, horror was always looming on the next landing.

Indeed, horrendous stories became part of our everyday life. At first, I suppose, my parents tried to protect me from it, but it proved too difficult for them to be a shield between me and the world. One night someone came knocking and ringing the bell at our door. Like everyone else who could afford it in those days, my parents had installed two heavy safe-like steel doors that looked as if they were sheltering some immense fortune while in fact leading only into our one-bedroom flat. I was absolutely forbidden to unlock the door when alone at home, no matter who was knocking. 'We have our sets of keys, so don't even come to the door', my mother had taught me. But that night there was no gangster at the entrance, but a victim.

When my dad finally unlocked the door, he found my mother's best friend, Marina, covered in blood and tears. The woman, who was with my parents at the polytechnic institute and later at the same factory, was terrified and begged for help. For some time she'd been living alone with her daughter in the same apartment block as we did, just one staircase over from ours. She was a single parent since her husband had got mixed up with local mafia and soon after was stabbed on his return home one evening. But on this occasion, in the middle of the night, her husband's ex-associates had come banging at her flat. She said she didn't know what they wanted, but they wanted it badly.

I woke up in the midst of all this noise in our corridor and went to see what was happening. I don't know if the adults saw me because I was standing around the corner, watching our beloved friend with my eyes wide-open in horror. Marina was telling my parents how scared she had got, how loud her little daughter—the same age as me—was crying when the men started breaking through the doors to her flat. The little girl and her mother had moved all the furniture they had—wardrobes, bookshelves, a washing machine—to block the entrance, to stop the men. To no avail. What could they be after? What could she and her little girl be hiding in their one-bedroom flat? What treasures? I still don't know their reasoning, but ever since that night I had even bigger problems sleeping than before.

At bedtime each night it became my habit to gather my stuffed animals and place them all around my body in such a manner that, covered with a blanket, it wouldn't be possible to see where exactly I was positioned. That way, I believed, if some men came to stab me in the middle of the night, their knives would hit my toys or pillows, sparing my life.

Around three in the morning I would usually wake from a nightmare, and, scared to walk through the corridor to my parents' room, scared to lie alone in my bedroom, scared of the world outside my window, I'd start crying for help. I'd begin doing it quietly, ashamed of my own misery, then as my panic grew I'd yell more and more loudly, until my mom woke, hearing me from the other room, and came to calm me down.

Seeing the state I was in, she'd set me on my feet and tell me to go wash my face with cold water. When I came back, I'd see her throwing all my toys, blankets, and pillows on the floor, and smoothing the bed linen with her palms: she'd try to wipe away all the dust and wrinkles as if those were my pains and fears. She'd shake the pillows in the air and put them back in place. Then she'd ask me, in a serious, sober tone, to jump in. After I did so, she would raise the blanket and wave it in the air above me. One. Two. Three . . . The blanket descended slowly upon me, it felt fresh and new—and I slept quietly till morning.

It was also around that time that I started following a ritual of my own, a habit that sometimes helped me to fall asleep and not think about all the atrocities. Yes, I felt that I feared the world more and more. And the more I feared, the more I looked for something of the opposite. Something calm, quiet, predictable. Something beautiful, yes, beautiful because I knew, I felt, that in beauty lay safety.

Before going to sleep in the evening or even in the middle of the night, while lying in my bed, I started to repeat in my head my poems, or, not mine, but Akhmatova's, Pushkin's, Lermontov's. I spun out those lines over and over, over and over in my mind—lines that never change, that always keep harmony with the next one to come. Their expected rhyming, their predictable flow, their melodic beauty left me at peace with all the troubles of the universe.

Many, many years passed before I realized that those poems, recited from my heart before going to sleep, were to me the same as Christian prayers and pagan chants were to my grandmother—the simple reminder of a superior force, soothing all worries, bringing strength and hope and relief.

❦

Changes were happening at school as well as in the world outside, though my social position in class remained the same. I was in the seventh grade by then, and so mathematics changed to algebra while geometry, physics, and chemistry were added to our schedule, and the classes of physical culture were brought to a whole new level.

It was 1997, and yet we were still being prepared for war with the West. From first grade on we were made to march like soldiers, taught how to follow an order, and even how to produce and use our own gas masks (in case the Americans started a gas attack).

Now, when we were practically adult, we were also taken to a military base to learn how to use an AK-47. I remember the rifle being heavy and cold, and even though it was fun at first to dismantle the gun and then put it together all over again (just like Lego, I thought), when I realized we were also expected to shoot, I panicked. Of course, I got the lowest grade for my AK-47 session.

Once or twice a semester an alarm would go off at the school and all of us were evacuated. Pupils screamed and ran, and teachers had to guide them. But we were not supposed to hide in some safe cave—oh, no! Boys and girls, little kids and teenagers, we all had to put on our gas masks (that nasty feeling of bad-smelling rubber over my head is hard to forget) and then run, run, run around the school, suffocating in that wretched mask while the teacher in charge rated our performance. If you dared take the rubber mask off, not only would the entire school mock you but, of course, you would also get the lowest grade.

One positive thing about the state of being 'adult' was that we had a new teacher in charge of our class. Vera Zurabovna was not from Siberia and looked different from most of us. Very tall, with impressive posture, she had a notable aquiline nose that I couldn't stop admiring—'Just like Akhmatova's!'—while she silently stared out the window as we wrote some essay. We almost never saw her smile, and when she did, her eyes were somehow still distant, serious. Nevertheless I liked her because she knew how to put some order into our chaotic group. By now most of the boys were drinking beer in the breaks and smoking heavily (another reason to ridicule me, because both the alcohol and the smoke had always disgusted me), and the fights became even bloodier. But Vera Zurabovna had some experience in handling all that.

I asked my mother at home if she knew anything about my new teacher. In a small town everyone knows the entire family history of a newcomer. I was told that Vera Zurabovna and her two adult daughters came from Chechnya: they were war refugees. I liked our teacher even more from then on. Though young, I'd heard a lot about Chechn-ya. I couldn't understand why the war was happening (no one could explain it to me clearly back then) and I didn't even know where the place was. Yet I knew about the war: those families in our block who had sons in their late teens or twenties had no sons anymore. Boys were drafted mandatorily. We never saw some of them again, and their mothers turned green-faced and mean.

Vera Zurabovna never talked about her homeland, never tried to be friendly with her pupils, but she once asked me if my mom could stop by her office. It didn't bother me because while my grades were never excellent, they weren't bad, so I passed the message calmly and was very curious about the subject of their discussion. The teacher knew about our shop. It was one of the few places in town that was neither run by the mafia nor by the state. Vera Zurabovna wanted to ask if her daughters might, perhaps, be needed in the shop as assis-tants. The salaries and the hours were not important so long as they weren't working for the government. I think my mother—family-less, motherless—felt pity for this small group of refugees. In spite of her tough and businesslike attitude, I always knew that there was a very soft heart inside her iron chest. Soon both girls were working at our shop, and I silently rejoiced, imagining how very scary it must be to live as a refugee in Siberia.

On my way from school to the shop, one rather peculiar building al-ways attracted my attention. Surrounded as it was by *izbas*, the build-ing had a massive entrance with four fat columns holding up a cracked portico; its doors were impressively tall, but one had fallen off its hing-es, and the other seemed permanently locked. Besieged by a circle of empty black tires—the days of forget-me-nots were long gone—an ugly dirty-grey statue of Lenin (one of our small town's four) pointed off into nowhere. This queer, pseudo-classical ensemble looked as if a UFO had been dropped into our snows so many years earlier that by now everybody had forgotten it was there. In passing one day, I approached its entrance and read the dusty plaque hung to the left of the doors.

Pioneers' House of Culture.

Hundreds of these strange monsters had been built around the Union some fifty years before with the ambition of turning nine-year-olds into loyal Communist Party members. The whole thing now looked very tired and ridiculous, but one word from its official title clung to my mind. It was soon to be linked, just as permanently, with the name of a person also totally unknown to me until that year.

She had appeared out of the blue, knocking one day at our class-room door.

'Come in!' commanded Vera Zurabovna.

A small, pale woman entered hesitantly. Her face instantly appealed to me. She looked somehow different from other people: more gentle, more innocent, more . . . otherworldly. She was probably in her fifties. Her hair was cut short like my mom's, except that this woman was so blonde that, with her pale features and bashfulness, she must have seemed like a white moth to my classmates.

'Stand up, children! This is Olga Sergeyevna,' the teacher intro-duced our guest. 'She is from the Pioneers' House of Culture.'

We stood, noisily shuffling our chairs and tables about in the pro-cess (this had to be done every time an adult entered the room).

'Good day, Olga Sergeyevna,' we said in chorus.

She smiled shyly at us.

'Sit down, children. Sit down, please.'

Olga Sergeyevna then proceeded to tell us about her job and why she had come: she was looking for kids who would be interested in attending an audition for her theater. If by chance any of us were, she asked us to stop by that peculiar building in the afternoon.

I felt as if there were no icy roads, no snowdrifts, no freezing winds as I ran my legs off to the Pioneers' House of Culture that afternoon. I didn't need to prepare anything for the audition, I only had to choose a poem out of the diverse selection stored on the shelves of my mind. Olga Sergeyevna greeted me enthusiastically: there was no one else in her theater troupe. I performed one of my poems for her, and just a few weeks later I found myself standing on the House of Culture's minia-ture stage, reciting Pushkin to a group from the Old People's Home across the street. I was very, very proud and happy, though I didn't tell a soul about it. Not my parents, and especially not anyone at school. I was afraid of their showing up to see me performing, and ridiculing my recitation, full as it was of pathos and awe.

I think that Olga Sergeyevna was the first adult from the world outside my family who really liked me, and I liked her in return. As she watched me recite my verses, the expression on her face was one of admiration, or perhaps, simply one of being glad that her own self, her little job and her little theater had found a purpose in me.

She dragged me from the Old People's Home to the local hospital, and from there to the House of War Veterans and then to the orphanage, and so on. She taught me how to declaim Shakespeare and Lope de Vega. She was amazed that I could learn by heart full passages not only of poetry but prose. She did her best to improve my enunciation and to make me feel like a real theater actor. Every word, she said, or even every single emotion behind every word, should be expressed by my intonation, my gesture, my expressions. She kept training me, and I performed regularly. She made a costume for me out of the puppet theater curtains: the theater itself was long-abandoned, but the gorgeous red velvet stage curtain was left behind, so Olga Sergeyevna created a cape out of it. In that massive scarlet cape I performed the most dramatic passages from *Hamlet* and *The Dog in the Manger*. She gave me nothing from those propaganda stories about Lenin that every Soviet instructor had been required to pass on to a Pioneer. She was my hero, and each day I couldn't wait for school to be over so I could run through the snow into her shabby world of culture.

After a few months of our work together, Olga Sergeyevna began to prepare me for the regional poetry-reciting contest devoted to the national celebration of Victory Day. It was the only talent contest in the region, so neither of us cared as much about its theme as about the opportunity to perform. We selected a Pushkin poem called 'Flower' with a very simple but delicate storyline: nothing to do with victory, war, or patriotism. The poem is about a young man who discovers a dry flower pressed between the pages of a book, and while he is contemplating the flower, he starts to wonder: to whom could the flower have belonged to in the past? why was it picked? for whom? for what occasion? The poem ended with a question: 'Or have they already withered like this unbeknown *tsvetok*?'

Every day Olga Sergeyevna coached me in when to raise my voice and when to move my hand, when I should speed up and when I should slow down, when my eyes should gaze at the audience and when I should look with a meditative stare into space. I loved my little poem, and I practiced it all day long till I fell asleep with the verses still on my lips.

Finally, the ninth of May had come, the day of red carnations, red flags, red balloons—the day of the Red Army's triumphant victory over Hitler. Olga Sergeyevna and I reached the House of Culture of Construction Workers where all the demonstrations took place in our town, and the contest began. One after another children came up on stage, introduced themselves, and recited in front of the jury—some old members of the long-withered Communist Party and a few teachers from the regional schools.

I don't remember very well performing my part, but I didn't stumble, and I think I really felt every single emotion beneath each of Pushkin's words. People applauded, and the jury looked satisfied, especially the women. Yet I didn't win that contest. I was given the second prize. The first was taken by Misha Osadchiy, a pale, lanky, dark-haired boy, who recited a long poem about our *dadushka,* dear grandfather Lenin and the Red Army's heroism.

I wasn't upset about losing the competition, but it certainly didn't make me love patriotic poems. The only important thing for me was the opportunity to continue meeting with Olga Sergeyevna. She didn't stop being proud of me and soon managed to transform my second prize diploma into something far more precious.

A couple of weeks after the poetry-reciting contest, when I came to the Pioneers' House, Olga Sergeyevna, blushing with excitement, told me she had some big news. She sat me next to her and said in a whisper, as if it was something nobody had to know:

'Alexey, tell me, have you ever been away alone? Have you ever seen the ocean? I've got a place for you in a summer camp for especially gifted children!'

I was overwhelmed. Not only was it a special camp, but it was located on the other side of the planet, not just by the sea but on the Pacific Ocean!

'The camp is in Vladivostok. Do you know where that is?'

The thrill in her voice as she asked this made it seem as if she was the one who was going on vacation.

'Four centimeters to the right of Taiga,' I remembered my calculations from my dad's atlas, 'four thousand kilometers to the east.'

I ran back home. I was ecstatic and no longer scared of confessing my poetic sins and where they had led me. My mother was very proud. She said that when she was small she was also sent to a camp for talented kids, one called 'Artek', on the other side of Russia by the Black Sea.

That was the typical Soviet method of encouraging loyal, trustworthy Pioneers. The best of them, the ones who had good grades, were great at arts or sports, would be granted this special time at a summer camp free of charge. And even though it was almost the year 2000, still I was given a chance to become a Pioneer. No, of course, I wasn't excited about carrying the Lenin sign on my collar. But the idea of the sea, the thought of laying eyes on the ocean . . .

One early summer morning, two months later, my parents took me to the train station, kissed me five million times, made sure I had enough provisions for a three-day journey, and with the first horn blasting through Taiga—the very same sound that I had heard so many times while in the classroom, at home, in my mother's shop—I was there, I was on the train, I was on my way to the sea!

☙

'To the sea!' That's what Siberians would say when they were asked about their dream destination. 'To the sea!' would be exclaimed triumphantly if they had managed to obtain a voucher to a sanatorium. No other questions followed as to what sea, what city, where, when. 'To the sea' would mean the three-day train ride to the West from Taiga to the coast of the Black Sea.

My mother had managed to take me to the sea for the first time when I was about seven, after the doctors became quite desperate about me. It was another season of swollen eyes and difficult breathing when one of them explained in the most mystical manner that Nature was provoking some sort of liquids to rise inside my head, and once the waters grew too high this risked inundating my brain. But even without him saying that, I already felt how, on especially hard summer days, the seas inside of me kept rising, rising, rising—and with it the pressure mounting in my head.

After another windy, hot, sun-bleached afternoon in the fields with my grandmother, I remember sitting quietly on a sofa in her house, unable to breathe, as my *babushka* ran and ran around me, crying, trembling, praying, mumbling her chants. I couldn't understand why she was so worried. All I felt was that her dear voice, her flowery body, and everything, everything else around me grew more and more blurry, distant, irrelevant . . . And the next thing—I'm at the hospital, wearing a white shirt with extremely long sleeves, and a group of adults tying those sleeves around my body, then a long thick hollow metallic needle being forced into my nostril, and then—stamp!

It was my birthday, I later realized.

In a communist country with a free medical system, there isn't much choice of treatment. The one which followed the metallic needle was called a 'cuckushka'. Tubes were installed through my nostrils, cavities, head and as the waters kept floating through me, I was instructed—for whatever reason—to keep repeating, 'Cuckoo, cuckoo, cuckoo.' I did what I was asked, thinking all the while of my grandmother's end-knowing bird, and our home cuckoo clock, and how I opened it one day, and how it never sang again.

After that month in the hospital, the tides inside of me were low for a season and when the autumn came, I walked to school with a precious, flimsy piece of paper, announcing that I was temporarily freed from the classes of physical culture. It was also the year when my mother finally received a sanatorium voucher for a sick child with a chaperone.

Whether due to my sudden ability to breathe freely or for some other reason, that first ride on the Trans-Siberian remains in my mind as an overwhelming concentration of smells. The sharp, omnipresent stench of somebody's unwashed socks. The hit of the aroma of salami that, like an alarm, would go off at nine o'clock, noon, six o'clock. The delightfully intoxicating smell of the huge basket of rotting pears that my mother attempted to bring home on the return journey. (One of my few other experiences with fruit at that age was a sack of green bananas that my father once very proudly brought from a trip to Moscow. I wasn't allowed to touch the bananas, only to look, waiting until they turned yellow. Of course, I don't remember if they ever did turn yellow; all I can recall is sneaking under the kitchen table every morning to check their state of never-ending greenness.)

Yet, now I think of it, even that trip with my mom wasn't actually my first ride on a train. My grandmother missed me dearly and would sometimes make a trip from her village to Taiga to pick me up. I remember being with her on the train, sitting on the light brown slippery seats, counting crows' nests in the trees outside the window, and watching the incredulous faces of other passengers amazed at my endless recitations. But that was not the real Trans-Siberian, but a local, so-called electric train, *elektrichka*.

When my mom and I did at last get on the train and after three long days saw the Black Sea, I was confused because it wasn't black at all. It was perfectly blue, with palm trees all around and an enormous sun above, with late evening music and plenty of ripened fruit. I remember my first boat ride, which seemed to me a cross-Atlantic voyage, while in fact, of course, it must have been some half-an-hour trip to a dolphinarium. Yes, the dolphinarium! It was located on an island, and on the way there from the mainland a storm began, the crew ran back and forth, and all the passengers, seasick, leaned over the side of the boat while I couldn't understand what the agitation was about. Sitting calmly with my mom on the deck, I got very sleepy from all the rocking and swaying, and the next thing I remember was the voice of a man in a beautiful blue and white uniform who'd stopped in the middle of the chaos and, staring at me with a handsome smile, said: 'That's gonna be one good sailor!'

I think it was also that sailor who brought a watermelon to us one warm evening, and I was asked to sit still on a bench and eat that enormous fruit, while he and my mother went away—for an hour or so—laughingly.

I recall that night alone in the park, more amazingly warm than any I'd ever experienced before. And the perfume of exotic flowers in the dark. And the never-ending watermelon on my lap. And once she returned, alone, I remember how on our way home through some shadowy alley, I stopped and stared at what lay in front of me: the world seemed to turn itself upside down, and the stars went on moving, dancing, swaying all around—I felt as I were flying, leaving the ground. 'Fireflies!' my mom's voice resounded as we stepped into the cloud of glittering stars.

One other memory from that trip recurs . . . We are walking in a park full of dark green and fuchsia colours. Mother wears a matching pink dress. Then I look up and see a big group of men coming towards us. Seven or eight of them walking in such a way along the alley that we are unable to pass. Suddenly, I lose my mom's hand, I see those men surrounding my mother in her pretty pink dress. The men laugh. I cry. She clutches our brand-new camera stubbornly in her hands while one of the men is pulling at the strap. Terrified, I feel like all my body is pierced with metallic needles at the sight of my own beloved mother being pushed and tousled like a rag doll—she screams for the last time and falls to the ground. The men get the camera and run away in all directions like cockroaches. Mother is already hugging me, calming me. 'It's all right, it's all right'. But holding her, I feel my hands wet. I look at her dress and see a darker shade of pink on it. 'Oh, Alioshenka, dear, we have to go back home,' she whispers to me, 'I think I wet myself.' I clutch her hand tightly all the way home.

❦

This time, however, I was on my own. This time I was aboard neither

Babushka's local *elektrichka* nor the train which took my mother and me to the sanatorium by the Black Sea. This time the train was crawling through Russia in the opposite direction—from Moscow to Vladivostok, to the East. Just three and half days on the Trans-Siberian—and you are by the ocean!

As it slowly made its way through the country, the train stopped every now and then to pick up a specially gifted child or two as if they were some rare berries. It was so exciting to look at them from my compartment, watch their parents cry and wave, guess with what particular talent this new lonely kid was crowned. Some may have won a biology Olympiad, others mathematics; some were good at singing, others at painting. The children were of various ethnicities: Buryats, Nenets, Tatars, and once, far, far away east, when we were already approaching our destination, the train stopped for three minutes in a town with the bewildering name Birobidzhan, and a couple of very shy, skinny boys stepped into the wagon.

'The Jews! The Jews!' exclaimed a girl who had won a national history Olympiad. 'This is where Stalin sent the Jews to live!'

We made friends with the two boys as quickly as with the other fellow travelers. With each new stop our train was getting louder and louder, more and more joyful. There were two chaperones in charge of five railway carriages loaded with talented children. What paradise it was! What bliss! I still cannot think of a better definition of happiness than being on an endless train ride, surrounded by like-minded friends and favourite books, watching the world passing by from the window. No worries. No places to go. No decisions to make. Nothing depending on you: the rails are set in steel. There is absolutely nothing you can do about the direction your life is going to take. You are in the hands of your destiny, on the way to your destination.

As the train kept chugging on through the forests and swamps, fields and hills, we talked and laughed, played games and sang songs. Yet I would leave the happy company early in the evening and go to my own berth. There were four kids per *kupe*, or sleeping compartment. My berth was an upper one, on the right. Those evenings, while the others were still singing and laughing somewhere in the train (they would all gather in the same compartment, sitting on each others' heads), I enjoyed lying on my upper berth, peacefully watching the world pass by. Gradually the sun set. I covered myself and placed a pillow in such a way that I could follow the landscape from the window: by then everything outside was in the night—the dark, dark blue night. Every now and then a constellation of lights appeared on the left—a village or a town—the lights slowly crawled like a group of travelers to the right before disappearing somewhere in the softness of my pillow. Then again dark, dark blueness. And again a constellation of lights. On and on in that way until I fell asleep.

On its route to Vladivostok our train passed through hundreds of settlements, lakes (including Baykal, of which I have no distinct memories), and rivers (including Amour, so wide that when we were crossing it, I saw from my window the entire length of the train suspended on the bridge above the water).

Most of all I was impressed by a place called Chita in Eastern Siberia. The train didn't stop there at all, but while it was making its way through the city, dozens of children, dirty and miserable, ran after our carriage screaming for food. We threw bread out the window to them and, for the first time in my life, I felt very privileged and ashamed of my capricious self.

In sight of those hungry children I overheard one of the Jewish boys asking our chaperone a question, quietly and humbly:

'And us . . . How often are we going to be fed at the camp?'

And the adult replying laconically:

'Five times.'

'Not bad,' the child said to himself, 'five times a week, that's not bad.'

The chaperone raised her eyes to the child and added:

'Five times a day, dear. Five times a day.'

Finally, on the fourth night we reached Vladivostok and were driven to the camp in a magnificent cortege of four buses and two police motorbikes. The camp was set right next to the ocean, in an impressive building shaped like a cruise liner. Each dorm had access to a common balcony (like those on real liners, I suppose) and from our rooms we could not just admire but *inhale* the ocean.

Later, thinking back about that time in the summer camp, I came to realize how incredibly fortunate I was. Not only because I was considered to be talented enough to be fed five times a day for three weeks, but also because in any other year, at any other time before that particular summer, I would inevitably have been immersed in a typical communist setup with songs about Lenin, red and white outfits, and heavy brainwashing. However, that year, on the cusp of the millennium, there were no red flags waving, no patriotic songs. All that Pioneer craziness was gone, and the new ideology was not yet formed. As a result, in those three weeks by the ocean we enjoyed the best of what there was in socialist Russia: sitting all together by the fire at night, singing songs about a bright future while holding hands with mates, playing games on the beach, preparing and performing our final concert. Surrounded by these friendly, creative people, for the first time in my life I didn't feel scared, I didn't feel alien, I felt like a perfectly happy, normal kid.

And I'm certain, that is what one wants deep inside: to be completely normal.

As if overnight, it was all over and once again I was put on the train. Only this time the entire wagon, crawling west, was soaked in tears. All of us seemed to have grown up so quickly in those three weeks; now we knew for ourselves what the word *nostalgia* meant.

When my parents met the train in Taiga, they couldn't understand why I looked so devastatingly sad. I remember how they brought me home, how my mother had changed the wallpaper in my room in the meantime, and how excited she was to open the door for me. But the moment she left me alone, I fell on my bed, sinking into tears. I guess it was the first time I had the feeling of losing something vital, something that I had just found and had been forced to let go of too soon, too soon. What I didn't know back then was that that feeling would never pass, but only increase with years.

Not knowing other ways of dealing with the bitter sadness that had overwhelmed me after my return from the camp, I began writing everything down. I wrote one diary after another, filling the pages with summer memories. Before leaving the camp and getting off the train, I had collected the addresses of all the new marvelous friends I had made, and now, back in Taiga, I began writing and sending endless letters. For a while it helped, but with time the responses whitened our mailbox less and less often when I checked the post on the way from school, until there was nothing in the box but an empty darkness.

Then I found a new way to keep my spirits up. I took my father's Walkman and a few music tapes, and began recording my stories about that summer over the pop songs. I liked that practice. I kept whispering my joys and sorrows, my memories and secrets into the recorder, and then, late at night, I played my own words back. It felt like a conversation.

There was a boy in my class, Dima Yevdokimov, whom my mother liked. Dima could be quite funny, although it didn't seem funny to me at all when, together with his pals, he buried me in the snow one afternoon. Nevertheless, when by himself Dima would ask sometimes to come and play at my home. Knowing that my mom approved of his company, I allowed him and one of his friends to come over.

The boys would kick my stuffed animals around, make sordid sketches in my books, and laugh at my inability to fight back. Unable to cope with their cruel games, I still found it hard to refuse them when they'd ask to come back.

One day that autumn, after I had returned from the camp, Dima and his friend were over at my place when they saw the tape recorder lying on my desk. They grabbed it and—before I could protest—pressed 'Play'.

That feeling is hard to forget.

I chased after them. Tried to silence their laughter. I begged them, crying by the bathroom door, when the two of them locked themselves inside while listening to my recorded confessions about the camp, and laughing, laughing, laughing.

Finally, I caught up with Dima on the balcony, to which he'd escaped, still clutching my audio tape. I begged him to give it back to me, but he only stared into my eyes, held the cassette over the balcony railing, and then, with the thin film between his fingers, released the cassette . . . The plastic case fell to the ground from the fourth floor where we were standing. The shining film unrolled on and on, on and on, casting my memories, my stories, my joys and sorrows to the wind—while I kept crying, with my heart violated, and he kept watching my face with great curiosity.

One Sunday at the end of summer 1998 we were in the car driving back home from my grandmother's. It was stiflingly hot, as is usual in August in Siberia, and the ride seemed endless. My dad kept switching from one radio station to another. 'A driver is a DJ,' he used to say. Then he found a news program. The reporter's voice seemed nervous and we all paid attention to it.

'The government of the Russian Federation has decided to devalue the ruble.'

My parents gave each other a silent look.

'What does it mean?' I kept asking them. 'What does it mean?'

Neither of them replied.

'Mom?' I pleaded. 'Dad?'

'It means we're fucked,' was his answer.

What my father meant was that the train from Moscow, bringing all those Western goods, would not stop at our station anymore. Those rice boxes and pasta packages, the toys and clothes, the washing machines and microwaves, the stationery and all other items our life totally depended on by then would now be out of reach.

Inflation would soon be eighty-four percent. All local banks, so recently opened, would close down one after another. Communists would start yet another nationwide strike, and our region's coal miners would block the Trans-Siberian railroad with their own bodies, demanding the last year's delayed salaries. Russia could not afford a Western style of life any longer. Our family's newly born business would sink like a holed fishing boat in a storm.

People blamed the war in Chechnya, which by that time had cost some six billion dollars. People blamed the poor harvest and, by October, Russia was appealing for international humanitarian aid. But most of all, people blamed President Yeltsin, who was getting increasingly sick (though no one could explain what he was suffering from). His face and body appeared to be getting wider and wider on our TV screen, he couldn't speak in a natural rhythm, he was losing his thoughts, seemed not himself anymore.

All of a sudden there were no more people to buy things, and there were no more things to sell to people. No flowers, no clothes, no perfume. With the weeks passing and the news getting worse, our fridge grew emptier by the day until we had nothing left but frozen dumplings, made by my grandmother long in advance for just such a black day as this. Her own world began to crumble that same year.

※

When he died, I remember standing by his coffin with a frozen face. I didn't quite understand what had happened. I only saw and heard my grandmother's unstoppable flow of laments.

'Why did you leave me, Sashenka? Why did you leave me so early? Oh, dear God, why so early? Why did you take him so early? Who will be here with me now, Sashenka? Oh, for whom did you leave me here?'

Those tears were more horrifying to me than the fact that my grandfather wasn't moving any longer. I was staring at my beloved *babushka*, taking inside me every single word of hers as if it were to me they referred.

A few days earlier I was told that my grandfather had died unexpectedly, but I didn't comprehend what that meant exactly. The last time we saw him, he looked somewhat strange, perhaps because he wasn't working anymore. He was forced to retire. It was a shock to him; he felt insulted because he'd spent all his life in that coal mine.

He did everything he could to be a good coal miner, a good comrade, a good communist. He was frightened when the Soviet Union collapsed. People like him, village people, knew nothing about the dark side of paradise. It was all one great promised heaven to them, one where if you worked hard and were loyal to your leader, you would be guided to a bright future.

Then, all of a sudden, there was no Soviet Union anymore and no promised land. Heavily armed men had appeared at the coal mine one day the same way they had entered my mother's store. They looked at my grandfather, sitting pitifully at his desk with those dark circles around his eyes, and they mocked him: 'What did you put the eyeliner on for, old man?'

A few more weeks and members of the coal mine administration started to disappear one by one. The new, rude, angry young men with guns ran the place now. My parents begged my grandfather to resign, but he clung stubbornly to his position. After a few minor arguments with his new bosses, they simply changed the locks on his office door—a sign that they pitied him. Less than a month later, he had a fatal heart attack. He was sixty-five.

At my grandmother's house, in her lovely sitting room decorated with flowery curtains and colourful carpets on the walls, the table was moved into the middle, and the coffin placed on top. The three-paneled mirror in which I used to stare so often was covered with black cloth now.

'Why did you leave me, Sashenka? Oh, why did you leave me so early?' she couldn't stop crying for hours now.

My eyes were glued to my grandmother from the moment we'd entered, I didn't know what to do. She didn't seem to notice me. I knew there were many people around, they were talking, eating, drinking, but for a long time I could see nothing and no one but her and her excruciating grief.

After some time, I noticed a woman by my grandmother's side. I'd never seen that old lady, but now she was standing the closest, hugging, caressing, rocking grandma like a child. I was told that this was Raya, my grandmother's sister, who'd travelled from very far away, from those sunny places where my *babushka* used to live, where she used to ride her horse bareback by the bank of the river.

Looking at that unfamiliar face I recalled how my grandmother used to ask me to keep unused pages from my school notebooks for the letters to Raya. I also remembered why she could never go to visit her sister in that sunny far-away land . . . Her household, her pigs and chickens, her garden, and making dinner in the evening—what will now happen to all of that, I wondered.

Then, finally, I also thought of the evenings when, after a day full of work, songs and berries, my *babushka* and I would retire to the kitchen, where I'd pick the bad buckwheat seeds out from the good ones and she'd sit quietly by the window, staring out at the road. I remembered how she'd rise up suddenly and say, 'Oh, my Sashenka's coming!'—I have never heard greater love in any voice than in hers in those moments.

'Why, why did you leave me so early? Why? Oh, dear God, was there a need to take him so early, so early?'

I heard my grandmother crying all morning, all day, all evening long. She would calm down for a little because so many people surrounded her now and then, as if trying to stifle her grief, to distract her, to do something to relieve her pain. But I don't think her grief was ever over. I think her own life was over that day.

Some time later in the same room I caught sight of my kind Uncle Kolia from the North of Siberia. I loved him, and every time I saw him I couldn't help but think of that story of when he licked the sled on his way down the snow-hill. And when now, on this strange, very strange day, I looked at Uncle Kolia's face, I felt a little better, I almost felt like smiling.

After so many hours by the coffin, when the sun began to set and the room fell into twilight, my uncle stepped aside. My eyes followed him: I saw how he drew his palms over his face as he made to leave the room and paused like that for a couple of seconds in the doorway. When he let his hands fall, he looked back at the crowd around the coffin and noticed my gaze.

'Enough,' he said abruptly. 'Children, follow me!'

It was only then that I realized how many children were actually there: not only my two cousins but also some village boys and girls with haggard faces, trying to comprehend what had happened in the room that day.

Uncle Kolia made us dress warmly. We all put on our *valenki*, tied our fur hats tight under our chins, belted our coats firmly and went out. It was dark, crispy cold, and quiet outside. It seemed as though the entire village was inside our house.

It had snowed so much that day that one of my cousins climbed the car repair ramp standing a meter high above the ground and jumped from it into the snowdrift. Some boy laughed, and it was a strange sound to hear that day, but I looked back at my uncle (to check if we were allowed to laugh), and he didn't seem to mind.

'Wait a second,' he said. 'How about building an igloo, a real Yakut house?'

Everyone was excited by the idea.

'How do we make one?' a village boy asked.

'Just look around you. Isn't there enough snow right here?'

'Yes, but how do we start?'

'Simple,' my uncle said. 'First, we press the snow in from all sides to the ramp.'

'And then?'

'When we have enough . . . ' he paused and let his eyes pass over our rapt faces. 'Then we can start digging a den!'

On our knees, with snow on our clothes and a blush on our faces, we forgot about everything except the igloo. We pressed and dug and pressed some more. In a while—it might just as well have been five hours as one—I found myself looking into the snow tunnel: its walls and the ceiling seemed firm, and there was enough space to crawl through. My uncle went in first, saying he would call for us. When we'd already begun wondering if he was all right in there, we heard him yelling:

'Come on in, boys! Come on in!'

Someone brave crawled in, then another, and another. Finally, I, too, followed, kneeling down and moving on all fours through the blue corridor. Then it disappeared. Everything disappeared—the walls, the boys, the uncle. It was just me and the cold air in total darkness.

Shhp!

Someone had lit a match.

All the faces were illuminated then and so were the walls, the ceiling, the floor. The faces were glowing like pearls surrounded by thousands of crystals. My uncle took a small candle from his pocket and lit it . . . We were inside some magic little home. It was small, and one couldn't possibly stand up, but we could sit comfortably, giggling at each other. After a minute everyone became silent for no reason. No one made any noise. We were all quietly amazed with the entire world shrinking to this tiny snow house.

I don't know how much time we spent inside there because, I guess, time, too, disappeared. It froze like the whole universe around us. I don't recall being cold in there, nor scared. I remember glancing at my uncle's face. He seemed as excited as everyone else around. Then, watching him more closely, it all came back to me—my grandmother's tears, her sister Raya who had come from so far away, my grandfather's unmoving body on the dining table . . . My uncle kept sitting still, holding the candle silently, his eyes fixed on one point. At that moment I felt with all my heart that he was no more than another boy among us. A boy who had just lost his father.

That was the last time I went to my grandmother's home. From that day on, there was no need for anyone to take care of pigs and chickens, raspberries and tomatoes, dinners and breakfasts. Very soon my *babushka* was taken away from her house that had grown so hollow all of a sudden. Her sons sold everything she owned in the village, and all they could buy with that money was a tiny gloomy room in one of Taiga's apartment blocks, in one of the 'birdhouses', as she called them with scorn.

It took me some time to get my mind around it all. I was told that my grandmother would be living near us from now on, and I was glad. But I couldn't understand . . . I couldn't comprehend the insane scenario by which a whole reality, the whole world of my grandmother, which had become such a big part of my own soul, could cease to exist.

The next summer, and the summer after that, and the summer after that one, too, I kept expecting that I would be taken back to that place. And every summer I was told over and over again that we couldn't go back there. That it didn't exist anymore, that it was all gone, vanished, left in the past—I couldn't understand.

It was all so very much alive inside of me. There I still held onto the same white house made of thick logs, and the summer kitchen with its frilly blue shutters, and the *besedka* covered with millions of morning glory blossoms, and our songs, stories, prayers, chants, and the living room filled with the scent of lilacs, and the endless rows of shiny jars and pots in the cellar, and our mushroom picking, our birch tree juice magic and the birch tree itself standing nearby, marked with some pine wax over the cut, and our neighbours with their grandsons who couldn't manage to leave for the army, our cabbage field that we had to water in the evenings, and even those cabbage butterflies, rising up into the sky above me. All of that and many other things from my grandmother's world were still breathing inside me, with all their colours and smells as vivid as ever . . . so how, how, how could they possibly tell me that it was all gone?

When I shared my feelings with my mother, she said some strange things to me. She told me that *Babushka's* world wasn't as wonderful as I imagined it. She said that the house was old and its wood was rotten, that there was no running water, no toilet, no stable electricity supply; that the water in the pump was not good for drinking, not even for washing, that the living conditions were very bad there. I couldn't believe my ears. I thought that she was just being mean and jealous of my love for *Babushka.*

'No,' my mother said. 'This is the truth. Your grandfather's coal mine was one of the biggest in the country. They've been digging so wide and deep,' she went on, 'that there's a hollow space, a huge hole under their own house . . .'

'A *hole?*'

'Don't you understand, Aliosha, people aren't even supposed to live there.'

'But why not? If they've always lived there?'

'They didn't have any documents. They couldn't prove that this land belongs to them,' she said. 'Why, there aren't even any streets, any house numbers. They never even had an address!'

'And worse, in fact worst of all,' she continued mercilessly. 'The whole place—your grandparents' house, the vegetable garden, the pigsty, the henhouse—they are all sinking into the ground, falling into that wretched coal mine!'

It sounded surreal to me. As if taken from some horror storybook of my father's.

How could the house stand over the coal mine? How could it not have an address? How could it not exist?

'Do you remember that day when you fell into the pit after sledding down the hill? Do you, or do you not? What do you think that pit was?'

I looked at my mother sheepishly.

'A cellar?'

She continued as if I hadn't spoken.

'And do you remember how you used to suffocate every summer? Do you remember how you couldn't see or breathe? Do you? So what do you think that was all about?'

I began to tremble.

'Flowers, I guess, plants, maybe . . . pollen?'

'Oh, no, darling,' my mother kept on. 'It was all because of the coal mine. The coal mines and the coal dust are all around us here, but in that region the conditions are inhuman. There's a gigantic open coal basin close by,' she was desperate to make me understand, 'and every second person in the area has asthma, and every tenth one dies of lung cancer! *That* was the only reason for your condition! That's why you had to be hospitalized! That's why the only reasonable thing the doctors could suggest was to take you to the sea—as far away from here as possible—understand now?'

I listened, and yet I didn't.

I was truly stunned.

I refused to believe what my mother was telling me. I refused to admit that we, all of us—my parents, my uncle, my grandmother, her neighbours, the people in our village and in our town—all of us were capable of living in this way, moving on with our lives, doing our chores, exploring the new, creating something, and yet letting the most precious things, the most cherished, the most wonderful things simply disappear, sink into the ground, and be turned into some black dust.

How? How could I believe that?

❧

Perhaps my mom was indeed jealous of the love I had cherished for my paternal grandmother and her world, which I had accepted as my own home. Or maybe she was losing a part of her own soul in those days, and that's why she was so bitter. In any case, I wasn't angry with her because—especially at that time—she truly deserved my gratitude and love.

Only a few weeks after my grandfather's death I remember being alone at home late at night. My parents were still at work and I was scared, as usual: every time they were late I began to worry that something might have happened to them. I heard so many odious stories about the mafia and what they did to people that as soon as the sun had set, I began imagining the most extreme scenarios. I couldn't stop being anxious. I couldn't phone them. The only thing I could do was to repeat over and over again my poems.

The Oriental carpet we had placed on the floor of my parents' bedroom had a complicated geometric pattern with a few lines drawn parallel to the edges. So, on nights like that one, when my parents were away, I would pick one colour line in the carpet's pattern and walk it in circles. With every round I started a new poem and kept walking for hours, spinning out the verses inside my head. I normally continued that way deep into the night until the key finally turned in the lock and my parents appeared, cheerful after some party.

However, on that particular night at the end of 1998, I knew there could be no parties due to the recent death of my grandfather. When my parents had still not returned home by three in the morning, I was sure something had happened. Eventually, when I was on the point of collapse from circling the carpet, I heard a key in the lock and ran to the door.

'Who is it?' I asked in a loud low voice, imitating an adult, as instructed.

'It's us, sonny,' came my mother's reply.

I opened the inner bolt. They stepped in.

They were all right, but I smelt a very strange odor accompanying them into the room.

'What is it, Aliosha? Why aren't you sleeping?'

'I can smell something,' I said.

'Nothing, it's nothing. Go to bed.'

In the morning when I woke, the smell was still there. In the early dark hours I could identify its components: there was the stench of burnt plastic, an odor of hot dust and the distinctive presence of some other alien substance. Without any additional questions, with my mom still in bed, I got dressed quickly, ate my breakfast in silence and went to school.

As soon as I entered the classroom, I realized all the kids were staring at me, whispering something to one another. I became even more confused. Then, finally, one boy from my class, the leader of the team, four years older than most of us since he didn't pass his final exams three years in a row, poked me with his pen and said, 'So what, sissy boy, now it's all over for you?! Say goodbye to your mommy's shop!'

The others laughed coarsely, and only then, only then did it become clear. I understood where that strange smell had appeared from and why my parents were so late last night. Our shop had been burnt down.

I still don't know who did it. And I don't know why. In that period, in that particular year, anything could happen in that miserable land. No, not *anything*. Anything *bad*. All I knew for sure was that another part of my world had turned to dust and that there was no way back.

With no job, no way of making money, not even a factory to go back to, my parents struggled to find a way to exist. While my father sold his car and kept running around the town in search of any opportunity, my mom was away most of the time. She would leave before I woke, before six in the morning, and come back alone late at night. I kept waiting for her, scared, nervous that something else might happen. When she did finally get home, I'd run out of my room and bury my face in her old, grey astrakhan coat. I'd be so happy that she was back that this feeling, this touch of cold astrakhan fur, is still one of my most treasured memories.

What she was doing was simple: my mom would take the first interurban bus to the big city—a long, tiring road in an old Soviet vehicle so badly made that in winter its walls and windows froze, becoming white and reminding its passengers of a refrigerator on wheels. The city she'd go to was that very same regional center where she had studied, where I had been born, and which she had been forced to leave ten years earlier. Perhaps, due to my mother's nomad blood or maybe just because of her business initiative and the simple need to feed her family, she knew very well that, if she weren't moving, she wouldn't get anywhere. And the further she moved, the better. Of course, if there were a chance to go to Moscow, she would do just that, for even in the worst times all the money from around the country was dragged into that black hole. But Moscow was as far as Tokyo and the flights there were so inexplicably expensive, that the best thing my mother could do was to search for a job in the regional center.

After getting off that crowded refrigerator on wheels still so early in the morning, she would search for a place where she could work, if not permanently then at least until the end of the day. If she was lucky, she'd find some bizarre way to make her daily cash.

I remember how once . . . it was seven, eight, nine—ten!—eleven at night, and she was still not home. I began panicking. Finally, my father left me alone in the middle of the night and went to the bus station to check whether perhaps something was wrong with the buses. I still remember how I sat on a little red plastic stool by the front door, not even crying but simply horrified by the thought of what might have happened to her—waiting for the sound of the key moving in the lock.

An hour or two later, my father came back carrying my mom unconscious in his arms: the bus had broken down halfway, and people were forced to sit in it, gradually freezing until the next one came and picked them up. By the time they made it back to town, my mother had no more strength, she collapsed into my father's arms the moment he fetched her off the bus.

In September 1999, in four cities across the country, blocks of flats were bombed one after another with over three hundred innocent people killed and thousands injured. Those were exactly the same social housing projects as everyone else was living in, so now the entire country fell into a panic.

On September 22, something strange happened in Ryazan, an ordinary town in European Russia. A resident of a block of flats had seen a group of people bringing into the cellar sacks filled with something. Aware of other bombings in the country, he gathered the residents of the building and together they called the police. But when the police arrived, they merely took the sacks away, explaining that it was a military training exercise and those sacks were just filled with sugar. Simultaneously, however, a KGB representative went on state television to inform the country that the incident with the sacks in Ryazan was indeed another planned terrorist attack but that, thanks to the vigilant residents, it was prevented.

It seemed to many that those officials, the policemen and KGB agents, were lost in their own arrangements. The residents of the Ryazan block of flats, who had discovered the bomb and who felt that something deeply wrong was happening, went so far as to reach out to the media, making the case public, blaming no one but the KGB itself for arranging the bombings across the country.

But it was too late to react. A new face had already appeared on the screens.

While Yeltsin's mysterious illness was getting worse and worse, with a shaking index finger he pointed at someone called Vladimir Putin, a KGB agent. Appointed as Prime Minister precisely one month before the bombings, this man took on the role of hero from the start, promising to save the nation.

While the majority cheerfully greeted their savior, I remember seeing his jaundiced face for the first time on the television, watching his close-set porcine eyes, his sardonic smirk, and thinking to myself, in my childishly exaggerated manner, that if the devil were to come to Earth, he would look exactly like that.

On September 23, only one day after that unsuccessful bombing in Ryazan, Vladimir Putin announced that investigators had already reached the conclusion that those were indeed terrorist attacks on Russian civilians and they were organized from Chechnya. At 7:00 p.m. on the very same day, Putin called for the air bombing of the Chechen capital Grozny. The Second Chechen War had begun.

In his message that day Putin added, 'I'd like to thank the public. No panic, no sympathy for the bandits.'

The true hero, the real man.

Even though the world around us was shaking, behind the thick walls of the Pioneers' House of Culture music was playing, plays were being performed, poems were being recited, and I was hiding a secret. Ever since that *coup d'état,* when 'Swan Lake' was broadcast on TV in one continuous loop for hours, I dreamt of being a ballet dancer. Every now and then, when at the Pioneers' House, I passed by the dance group's door. Hearing the music coming from within, I'd peek through the keyhole and watch others twirl and sway with my heart trembling. I simply couldn't be indifferent. Something inside me was jumping and swinging to the sounds and rhythms as well.

Following the empowering summer at the camp, I felt much more confident, and one day I asked the choreographer whether I could join the group. 'You're too old,' I was told, 'It's too late for it.' The only ones who were allowed to receive professional dance training were those who had been practicing full-time since the age of five or six. Nevertheless, they let me assist other dancers, water the floors, run all sorts of errands. Even if they had enslaved me and demanded that I wash their pointe shoes after practice, I think I still wouldn't have minded.

Nothing stays secret forever. Ours was a small town, and one day my father found out about my involvement with the dance class. He could barely tolerate my poetry, but dance! He made another scene: once again I was not strong enough, not brave enough, not manly enough. I wasn't good at sports, I wasn't fishing and hunting and so on and so forth. And as he indulged himself in expressing his utter disappointment at home that evening, my eye was drawn to my mother's face: she looked so gaunt, so miserable, so fed up.

By then I had for some time been aware of how my parents were growing distant from each other. I had already noticed how their wedding rings first migrated to their neck-chains, and then disappeared altogether. I felt that our family was falling apart, and this feeling was a horror to me because in my childhood world everything centered and turned upon me, and so I was sure it was entirely my fault. It was my inability to fight, to ride a bicycle, to hunt, or to simply protect myself; it was my love for poetry, for books, for flowers, for butterflies; it was my clinging to my grandmother, to my mom, to Olga Sergeyevna; finally, it was my dancing that made me a failure in my father's eyes. And as my mother was protecting me again and again from my dad's criticism, I started to realize that *I* was the barrier between them, that *I* was the rock on which the boat of their union had crashed.

Traditionally New Year is the most important, most joyful celebration in Russia. All around the country, people gather for that day. They set the table, decorate a fir tree, give one another presents. However, that particular year there was not much festive spirit in the air. People still gathered, but they were more scared and less excited than usual. With the financial crisis, mafia attacks, Chechen wars, apartment block bombings, nobody knew what to expect next. A good many, on the other hand, were expecting the end of the world: it was December 31, 1999, and not only the century but the entire millennium was going to be left behind that night.

Another tradition in Russia is to turn on the television at about ten minutes before twelve to hear the Kremlin clock chiming in the New Year. On that night, one hundred million Russians gathered around their TVs. As usual the leader was speaking. This time his speech was very unclear, slow, it was the speech of a very sick man. All we could understand from Boris Yeltsin's monologue were his last words.

'As I go into retirement,' a long, heavy pause, 'I have signed a decree,' a few troublesome intakes of air, 'entrusting the duties of the president of Russia,' the entire country went silent, 'to Vladimir Putin.'

That simple.

Some people were surprised, others expected it. Some people were angry, but the majority seemed happy to have a young, healthy man in power. Some people were already dead drunk and didn't really care. But it seems that very few realized that it wasn't just another man coming to power.

For the first time in history, total control of the biggest country on Earth was being taken over by one organization—an organization that was already responsible for taking the lives of some twenty million of its own citizens, for erecting Gulag camps all across the continent, for poisoning the souls of each and every one who happened to live in its territory, the organization that in the course of one century had managed to bring to their knees a dozen other nations and fear to the rest of the world, the organization that was constantly changing its name—Cheka, NKVD, MGB, KGB, FSB—but always retaining its essence. Despite all its might, this organization had never held unlimited power, for there was always someone standing above it—Lenin, Stalin, Khrushchev, or Yeltsin—but now, by the third millennium, the KGB had finally managed to put its own agent in charge. With the New Year, a new, very frightening era seemed to have begun.

From the very first days of January 2000, my mother must have heard an eerie call of freedom. Her marriage was collapsing, her business had been reduced to ashes, the country where she was born had disappeared and the new one didn't seem to be any better. There was no strength to move furniture anymore, no time to fight the winter with blankets, no need to walk all the way home while my father and I drove in the car, for there was no car and no driver.

On the first Monday of the new millennium, my mother grabbed a bag in her left hand, took my hand in her right, pushed the door open, and left for the big city. For the first time, she could move freely, as she'd always wanted.

Spring in Siberia

PART TWO

Chapter Five

In the Big City

The sun hadn't risen yet. The bus slid on and on through a corridor of snowdrift, with no left or right, traveling from nowhere to nowhere. The silhouettes of passengers, drowsing in the early hours, were black in contrast to the glitter all around. All the windows of the old Soviet vehicle, from top to bottom, and even the edges of the windscreen, were glazed with a layer of silver-white frost. It was as if we were locked in a jewelry box richly inlaid with mother-of-pearl inside and out: one could see nothing but that ambient luster.

I pressed my bare palm to the iced glass. I kept holding it there. Five seconds. Cold biting my skin. Ten seconds. It felt like tickling. Fifteen seconds. Drops begin sliding down inside my sleeve. Twenty seconds . . . The ice had melted, I removed my numb hand and looked out through the imprint of my own palm into the passing world.

The bus moved slowly, hesitantly.

'The diesel must have frozen,' my mother whispered.

Someone snored behind us. Outside my five-fingered window, there was only a dark blue nothingness, interrupted every now and then by yellow patches of light coming from scattered lampposts. Every time the light flashed, I saw the snowdrift. Wavelike, it stretched as far as the road itself, piled high enough to be at my eye level.

As we trundled on and on, the snowdrift seemed to be moving too, seemed to be flowing like a river, indeed, like water. Frozen water. Iced water. Solid water. Sparkling, flying, crystallized water. Heaps of snow, hills of water. All kinds of water, except liquid water. And we, we were only its passengers, rocking in our tippy vessel through the open sea—the sea of snow.

Mother seemed to be dozing or was perhaps just keeping her eyes shut. There was nothing for her to see, nothing but sparkling silver. I went on peering out, hoping for the sunrise to come before the imprint of my palm iced over again.

With every second, every minute, every yellow patch of light, we were moving farther and farther away from Taiga. I tried to think about what we had left behind. I knew I was supposed to think of my school, of my father, of my *babushka* . . . But somehow those images seemed blurry, refused to stick to my sleepy mind. What seemed clear and vivid then was the pretty face of Tania Ospelnikova, a girl from my class whom I'd always liked, secretly. I had hoped to make friends with her, tried to summon the courage to go and talk with her one day, but never did. Now in that frozen bus, I kept thinking of her disappearing somewhere outside the imprint of my palm.

The sun wasn't rising, no. But the dark blue gradually grew a shade lighter, a shade lighter. I took off my glove again and placed my hand over the outline of my palm. I waited for the glass to become transparent once more. Then I looked out and finally saw something other than the endless wavy line of the snowdrift: in the distance, deep in the white fields, groups of ghosts swayed in circles—naked trees.

Finally, the silhouette of a shack appeared. Another. And another. And then, piercing the horizon, long black lines—the sharp teeth of the factories. The opening which my palm had made in the ice now seemed too small to accommodate the world outside.

Approaching the big city, on that first Monday of 2000, my mother and I received a cold welcome. As if feeling the need to explain its own existence, the city bluntly presented its major source of pride right at its entrance: a colossal industrial zone with a bunch of factories trumpeting their names on the billboards—ZOAT, HIMSHAH, KOX, ZGORM. All of them were coal-processing plants, producing a vast range of chemical substances. The industrial zone was right next to the city center and at night when people reached home, locked their doors tight, and turned on their television sets, the factory pipes gave off a final elephantine belch, spouting thick smoke into the air. If there was any wind, then by morning when people went out to work, the smoke would have virtually vanished; if not, a grey, malodorous cloud would cover everything and everyone as if under a bell jar for days.

Taiga was the epitome of innocence by comparison with this so-called regional center. I'd heard of that city before, of course. I'd even dreamt of living there one day (the status of the center had held out the promise of some wondrous things). Once I'd even set out for the city to experience its theater, but our car had got stuck in the snow and we'd never reached our destination. In fact, I was born and spent my first two years in that regional center while my parents were still students at the polytechnic institute, but I had no memory of it, and the early winter morning when my mother and I took the icebox of a bus from Taiga and got off at the boisterous main station, I was surprised by the unfamiliar stench in the air.

The center of the city was made up of three avenues, running parallel to each other—Soviet Prospekt, Red Army Prospekt, and the longest, the widest of all, Lenin Prospekt—and a few streets which ran perpendicular to those three: Red Street, Kirov Street, Street of Fifty Years of the October Revolution, and Spring Street. Not surprisingly, the last of these was the only one with a touch of aesthetic intent: Spring Street had rowan trees planted along its sides (twenty-two on the right, twenty-two on the left), a few benches set at exactly the same distance from one another, flat housing blocks constructed before Khrushchev and so preserving a pretension of dignity.

The massive cube of the theater was thrown down at the junction where Spring met Soviet. It was the same pseudoclassical box of cement as The Pioneers' House of Culture in Taiga, only much bigger. Those who expected to find culture in that theater would be disappointed, for it was intended to be a source of communist propaganda, had a triumphant scene featuring Lenin on its ceiling, another portrait of the Greatest with the hammer and sickle above the stage and, in spite of all those charming effects, was empty most evenings.

At the head of Red Army Prospekt, the colossal Lenin Library had planted its fat columns with caryatids posing as milkmaids and construction workers. I expressed my excitement to my mother as we were passing; finally, I would get to visit a real library! 'Don't even think about it,' she responded, 'only legal residents are allowed in. We aren't legal here.'

Stepping off the interurban bus, at the central station we boarded a tram, and I prepared myself to see the rest of the city center, but within a minute or two the decorative part of the tour was done with. The residential area, 'the sleeping zone' as it is called in Russian, began to unroll itself: a humongous beast the size of Amsterdam. The place I was now meant to call home was nothing more than a limitless concentration of five-story social housing blocks, grimy, never painted, crumbling: the plaster flaked constantly from its ceilings and walls. The buildings, the look of which made my heart shrink at first sight, lined the prospekts in a sickly, hypnotic sequence: block, block, block, school, block, block, block, hospital, block, block, block, police station, block, block, and so on. Needless to say, the blocks were all identical, as were the public buildings, the only difference being that the first had five stories, and the latter only two.

Three sites of ultimate wonderment, three sixteen-story apartment towers, graced the major intersections along Lenin Prospekt which stretched for several kilometers from the central station to the outskirts of the city. On the journey from the station into the depths of the metropolis, one's eye would inevitably dwell on those towers, exactly the same as any other block but three times higher, three times scarier.

As if the surrealism of it all had no limits, each public place, whether it be a bus stop or a square, was pierced with multiple poles holding massive banners, screaming at the viewer: 'We love our city!'; 'We are proud of our Homeland!'; 'We thank the Governor for our happy childhood!' The letters were painted in brick-orange or red and, below them, the images of some awkwardly smiling children with dark circles under their eyes.

Who are 'we'? Why do 'we' love our city? Who has put these words into our mouths? As my mother and I rode along that never-ending

Lenin Prospekt, staring at those billboards, flat towers, and other ur-
ban gems, a fear was churning in my chest that this big city, this new
home of ours, was going to swallow me whole one day and there would
be nothing left in the place where I had stood.

Half a million citizens inhabited these countless blocks under their
cupola of coal dust. So, in spite of its dispiriting conditions, there was
life here. Life attracted my mother. She was hoping that, perhaps, when
everything lay in ruins behind her, the best thing was to go to a place
where you had never built anything at all.

✤

The only person we knew in the big city was Marina, my mother's
friend, the woman who had once appeared crying for help in our doorway in the middle of the night. Soon after that dramatic incident, Marina had taken her seven-year-old daughter and run away from Taiga,
wanting to escape the mafia friends of her late husband. She'd sold her
two-room flat (the one given to her by the factory in the same fashion
as we were granted ours) and managed to buy a place in the big city.

Her new home was literally one room which had to be used as a
combined living space, bedroom, dining room, study, and playroom
for her daughter. Altogether it was no more than twelve square meters. Even as a child, I was always puzzled by this typical Soviet habit
of economizing on space: when your country occupies one-sixth of
the Earth's land with only three persons per square kilometer, why do
you press people together in these minuscule cement cages? How come
you always have the resources for gigantic Soviet Prospekts or Lenin
Squares, for immense administration buildings, and even absurd and
always empty theaters or libraries accessible to the few, yet ensure that
your citizens don't use up too much space for their living quarters?

Marina welcomed us in. There was no discussion of how long we
could stay, or what we would owe her. She just smiled knowingly and
made us feel at home. While the women were preparing dinner, I remember sitting in their tiny room, playing with Marina's red-haired
girl, and finally feeling safe.

Yes, after the road to and through the big city, Marina's new home, no matter how small, felt comfortable and secure. The two of them were living modestly but everything was so clean and neat: the girl's books were carefully arranged on a desk in the corner; the walls were decorated with drawings and paintings (the girl was attending art school after classes); the old, flimsy pull-out sofa had snow-white pillows and blankets piled up.

Then Marina called us for dinner and we all sat at their table. The table was also miniature, with not enough space for four people, but we moved it a little, sat with our shoulders touching and with plates and glasses clinking, laughed and ate the most delicious homemade dumplings.

With children around the two women didn't want to talk about problems, but instead they talked about us, the kids. Marina said that she had found a really good school since they'd moved, and her daughter was very happy there. That was important—finding a good school—for most of the schools in the new Russia were equally squalid.

It didn't matter whether it was Moscow, the Far East, the Caucasus, or Siberia, most of the schools were set in exactly the same shabby buildings, pupils wore the same uniform and studied the same ancient textbooks with pages disintegrating under the fingers. Lenin's portrait hung above each blackboard, of course. There were no private schools, not even schools for kids of different ages: all the children from seven to eighteen studied together.

However, Marina had found a slightly different establishment. After all, it was the year 2000 and there should have been some changes. Her daughter was attending classes at the *Humanities Gymnasium*. I didn't quite know what 'humanities' or 'gymnasium' meant, but I liked the idea of going to the same school as that girl. Marina explained that what turned an ordinary school into a gymnasium was the arrangement with the local university: professors came to give lectures to the gymnasium pupils, so that, by the end of the study program, a few of the most talented kids were chosen to enroll in the university without entry exams.

The Soviet education system had involved a rich assortment of regular oral and written tests. There was one exam for each subject at the end of each of the four semesters, another at the end of each year, and a final one before graduating from school, and yet one more on entering university. If you failed even one of them (meaning, you got less than three on a scale of five for one of your courses), you were not allowed to proceed to the next level but had to repeat the year (if granted permission). Perhaps, it was all so strict because the entire education system, including the kindergarten, the school, and the university, had remained free since Soviet times. Free, that is, except for the heavy bribes required.

Before dinner was over we had all agreed that I should find a way to join the Humanities Gymnasium. The women mentioned that I was always good with poetry, theater, and other 'humanities' (again, they used that word which I thought meant being kind to other people). But, before dealing with my studies, my mother first had to find a job.

When our department store in Taiga was burnt down, one of the only things that she managed to rescue was a curious little white-stone figurine that someone must have brought her from Novosibirsk or even from nearby China. It depicted a scene from a monastery: two boys with shaven heads performing their duties, one drawing water from a well and the other lifting the filled bucket. When she brought the little monks home that night of the arson, the white-stone of the statuette had turned dark beige and smelled of smoke. The shape itself was not damaged except that, as a result of the heat, a few small bubbles had formed on the forehead of the boy who was lifting the bucket: it looked as if he was sweating from his hard work.

After sweating her own way through the shops and department stores in the big city, my mother found that there was not a single one which sold Asian talismans, souvenirs, incense sticks, and other Oriental bric-a-brac. Maybe it was her sentimental attachment to those two little monks, or some superstition that she—an Altay woman with slanted eyes and yellow skin—possessed, or maybe it was simply a practical calculation that made her decide to open an Asian kiosk. It was hard to imagine that such a minor, highly specialized business would ever come to the attention of gunmen running after the big money.

Obviously, she couldn't afford to rent a place in one of the big stores, let alone a shop with a separate entrance. The best thing she could hope for was to rent a space in a basement. There was nothing strange about running a business from under the ground in a country which lacked any market-oriented strategy. Virtually none of the Soviet flat blocks had a place for shops or offices. In post-Soviet Russia, if one wanted to open a store, one had to acquire a ground-floor flat (usually by kicking some old lady out onto the street) and build an entrance via the window. Alternatively, one could convert a smelly windowless cesspit into a trading space.

Mother couldn't afford to rent an entire basement either, so the solution she found was rather special. If you turned off Spring Street and walked into one of its spooky inner yards, you saw an iron door at one corner of the block, with stairs leading down. After descending into the sewage system and making your way through its grim tunnel, you suddenly found yourself in a sort of waiting room: no reception desk, no signboards, no windows, just a few chairs, a humid air, and a heavy silence. From that space, another door took you into a very particular 'cabinet', which housed an integrated medical center, private detective agency, and psychotherapy practice. The person in charge of that peculiar establishment was a stout, incredibly tall, deafeningly loud gypsy woman.

Isabella Davidovna was there to improve your family life, to set your career straight, to save you from some incurable disease, to find your kidnapped child, to bring new lovers together or to get rid of old enemies. She was there to help you.

In a country where juridical, political, and medical systems were dysfunctional, where people were scared to call the police in cases of emergency, where a hospital was synonymous with a graveyard, and where financial crises, wars, and *coups d'état* happened with the regularity of a repeating nightmare—in that sort of environment, thousands of psychics, healers, and even TV hypnotists had flourished since Perestroika, providing people with the aid and comfort they lacked in their everyday lives.

In spite of running her business successfully, Isabella Davidovna—that underground Siberian psychic, that gypsy queen almighty—had problems with the local police. The woman was in need of cover and was looking for someone who could take over that dull windowless waiting room adjoining her cabinet, and turn it into a shop where clients could pass the time while waiting for their sessions. According to her perfect gypsy logic, if the police appeared, they would see nothing but an ordinary small business with all its licenses approved and taxes paid, and hopefully not open that extra door which led to the gypsy's headquarters. For Isabella Davidovna, my mother and her project of selling little buddhas and incense sticks was the perfect match.

In the mid-1990s, when the mafia were already running riot and the ruble had not yet been devalued, various tricks were practiced which allowed people to secure their future. One such was to buy gold in any shape or form. In those years, when a business could be commandeered by police and 'sold' to another person, when cars could be burnt or blown up as a form of revenge or warning (with no insurance ever available), and when money could lose all value and you could find yourself tossed out on the street in the blink of an eye, your last chance of survival might yet be hanging around your neck. It was around that time that my mother bought me, my dad, and herself simple golden chains (mine was the heaviest one, for there were fewer chances that some bandit would rob a child). Also, my uncle and aunt had known very well what they were doing when they brought my mother a pair of diamond earrings from Northern Siberia—they were not just giving a present but securing the future of our family.

Now that the black day had arrived, as predicted, my mother could use our necklaces and her earrings to start a new life. We were not the only ones: in those years, when the banks still didn't trust people enough to give them loans, pawnbroking shops had sprung up all around the country. My mother pawned our few precious treasures and had one month to try to make enough profit to redeem them before they were sold on to someone else.

She pulled together the money, rented the gypsy's waiting room and, in order to purchase goods for sale, took the bus to Novosibirsk the very next morning. I went with her, clutching her hand tightly on that first mercantile journey as well as on many others to come.

Our Marcopolian crusade usually began long before sunrise. We would take the earliest bus to the capital of Siberia, spending six hours in that wobbling wheeled refrigerator before reaching the city. Having made our way through its densely inhabited center to the wholesale markets on the outskirts, we selected and paid for the items we wanted, dragged the boxes back through the city to the bus station, loaded the cargo, and rode back to our underground cabinet where we attempted to sell, at a small profit, what we'd bought. One such trip usually took us about fifteen hours: three hours for the purchase, twelve hours for the road. This had to be repeated once or twice a month.

I remember how once, by the time we reached our basement, I felt so exhausted (it was almost the morning of the next day) that I collapsed on the gypsy's daybed. A sudden thunderous laughter woke me in what it seemed like a moment.

'What a client I have today!' Isabella Davidovna's low, loud voice rumbled.

I was quite afraid of her. She was one of those people with a larger-than-life personality and absolute indifference to the opinion of others. She would constantly make you feel like you were keeping some repugnant secret in the depths of your soul. I was never courageous enough to raise my eyes when I sensed hers watching me, yet I couldn't stop myself from peeking when she was busy with someone else. With her long heavily muscled arms and thick masculine legs, her impressive chevelure of crow-black hair, her small piercing eyes, and that thin but conspicuous mustache above her narrow lips . . . every part of Isabella Davidovna's being made me shiver. I felt that no one could ever hide anything from her, even though I had absolutely nothing to hide but my own fear, which I knew she sensed just as cats sense the mice behind the wall.

On returning from Novosibirsk, my mother and I would unpack the boxes we'd brought back, she'd set up a stall in the waiting room, lay out all her stock of shivas and buddhas, put on her old red lipstick and one of her so very nineties Tom Claim suits, and there she was— the smiling Siberian geisha, selling talismans to strangers waiting for the help of the big gypsy woman.

The first spring of the new millennium came, and then the summer followed, but we still had found neither a place of our own nor a school for me. But, as my mother said, get a job, and the rest will follow along.

❧

Whether it be a Humanities Gymnasium or a school with a sports inclination, any palace of knowledge in our ex-Soviet land had the same four floors, the same walls painted in sickly green, though only up to the windowsills, the same vast corridor where the cool kids gathered to mock the lousy ones, the same squat toilets with no cubicle doors and the *fortochka,* the small corner window, slightly open because someone had just disobediently smoked in there. Even the old man at the school entrance, who checked whether you had changed your street shoes for clean ones, seemed familiar when my mother and I stepped into the gymnasium for the first time.

The fact that this particular school had the inside track running to university entry meant that many parents from around the city craved a place there for their child. All that had led, naturally enough, to the gymnasium administrators' expectation of bribes. The classrooms were quickly filled with rich kids (no one really cared whether they had any inclination towards any humanities), the walls seemed recently repainted, and the school principal's jewelry dazzled our eyes when we entered her spacious office.

My mother seemed not to notice the fresh wallpaper in the room, the lush Oriental carpets on the floors, the gigantic white computer on the secretary's desk, and other posh items that the gymnasium flaunted. Either that, or she wanted everyone to think she didn't notice. She knew very well that this gymnasium was owned by the state and was therefore, like any other school in Russia, not only meant to be free but compelled to accept any pupil who lived in its vicinity. The five-story Khrushchev block, where my mom had just rented a one-bedroom place (fat cockroaches and junkie neighbours included) was right across the street and so she was confident that the school, whether it called itself a gymnasium or not, was obliged to take me in.

'Hmm,' murmured the gymnasium principal, her lips pursed in a sceptical grimace, when we showed up in her doorway. Her black hair was mounted in an impressive beehive and her eyebrows lifted high above her horn-rimmed glasses. She went on sighing wearily while my mother introduced herself and explained our situation. 'Hmm,' the woman continued while glancing at my grades from the previous school, demonstrating with every gesture the hardship of her position.

'Aha!'

That didn't sound good to me.

'So the boy, I see, has not only missed one semester but has some average marks on his grade list! You must know very well that this is not an ordinary school! We cannot accept pupils with average . . .'

'Yes, Dear Respected Galina Georgievna,' my mom replied promptly, 'we have just moved to the city and have had some difficulties in settling in, but we are here now. And Alexey has got only one average grade, which was for the sports class. You're not focusing on sports here, I'm sure. His grades for the humanities are all excellent.'

My mother smiled politely; her voice kept a calm, reverent intonation. I listened to the conversation and couldn't believe she would manage to pull this trick off here. From the moment we'd stepped into the building all I'd thought of was running away back to Taiga.

'Well, well . . .' the principal proceeded unenthusiastically, 'you must already be aware that our Humanities Gymnasium is exceptional. Ex-cep-tional, you understand?' The principal shook her head decisively, her heavy earrings lending a ringing affirmation to her words. 'Here we don't accept just anyone who wanders in off the streets. Or in your case, from . . . Taiga.'

I raised my eyes, noticing the scornful smirk in the right corner of her lips.

'Yes, yes . . .' my mother acted as if not noticing the intended insult.

'No, no, we don't, *damochka*,' the principal interrupted, raising her voice and looking strictly at my mother. Then she sighed and looked away from us, fixing her eyes on the window or, perhaps, on the freshly painted window frame as if investigating whether the job had been properly done. After a few seconds, without looking back at us, she continued.

'We give young people a chance to enter the highest, most cultivated, most exclusive academic world,' her hand spiraled upward in three movements, then lowered itself gently. 'And in return their parents have to make sure that they satisfy the gymnasium's demands.'

With a crooked smile, the principal looked directly at my mom now.

'The demands are high, you know. I hope you understand me correctly . . . Do you understand me correctly?'

'Yes, of course, I understand you.' Mother was invincible. 'My son has always been an excellent pupil when it comes to humanities. Take a look at his grades for literature, languages, history. He won the regional poetry recital competition last year. I'm sure he will satisfy your demands just fine!'

The principal wasn't happy at all. Glancing at my mother with obvious anger in her eyes, she nonetheless kept her guard up, gradually raising her voice.

'You understand that many, many parents are willing to give everything, everything they have in order to secure their offspring's future?! Families from all the neighbourhoods of our city are literally fighting for a place here!'

'Of course, we are very conscious of it, Respected Galina Georgievna,' my mother parried. 'You have created a very special environment in this school. That's why we are particularly lucky to live right across the street.'

Flap!

The principal dropped her palms to the desk with considerable force. That was all. Her patience was exhausted.

'Ni-notch-ka,' she called in a slow, very articulated way . . .

Then pursed her lips tighter, looking hatefully at the door.

'Nina!' she yelled like a fool.

An ageless blonde appeared.

'See these two out,' the principal commanded without a proper farewell.

I knew we failed but had no bad feelings about leaving the office and then the school itself.

'Take the boy to your classroom, Nina.' Suddenly, I heard the woman's voice bellow from behind me. 'Let him try to pass your test.'

What made the gymnasium principal let me have that chance, I still don't know. Certainly there was nothing she could hope to get from my mother, and yet she didn't kick us out. Maybe she wasn't so corrupt after all or was indeed forced to accept all pupils who lived nearby. Maybe she simply realized that one quiet boy from Taiga who'd been obsessed with poetry ever since he could read would not bring any dramatic discord into the Humanities Gymnasium.

Her colleague Nina, or Nina Olegovna as I was required to call her, had a similar style to her superior's: the same beehive hair, though rye-coloured, the same golden earrings, though more modest, the eyebrows a little lower. Beneath her left eyebrow, on the lid of her eye, there was a pea-shaped mole, which I kept staring at no matter how hard I tried not to. The woman seemed to be very self-conscious and kept talking, gesticulating rapidly as if trying to take one's attention from her pretty young face spoiled by the dark-brown mole. She was one of the vice-principals of the school and for about an hour or so Nina Olegovna set about testing my knowledge of various subjects, from the Periodic Table of Mendeleyev to Russian classics.

'Now please tell me . . .' I still remember her final question after I'd replied to many other easier demands. 'Tell me now . . . Of all the characters from *Dead Souls* which one has a chance for spiritual resurrection?'

It was the end.

A failure.

I didn't know the correct answer. Yet one was always expected to have a grasp of that single possible truth in the Soviet schools. I had read Gogol's *Dead Souls*, I loved it, yet I was puzzled by her inquiry: Gogol had many memorable characters, but none of them, not a single one of them, had any chance to improve, or so it seemed to me. No hope for spiritual resurrection. All of them were unforgivably egoistic, corrupt, pathetic.

'Well, you don't know, I see,' Nina Olegovna concluded in a soft manner, observing my hesitating gaze. 'Then you'd better learn and remember that the correct answer is Plyushkin,' she said with a friendly smile while smoothing her left eyebrow with the tips of the index and middle fingers of her left hand, hiding for one moment the ugly mole.

'Plyushkin?' I exclaimed, 'But he is the very worst of them! That pitiful scrooge who leaves his own daughter with no help, only to sink into misery himself?'

'You are absolutely right, young man. He is just what you've described,' the teacher said, puzzling me even more. 'But that's exactly the reason why Gogol is giving him a chance for spiritual resurrection! Look here.'

Nina Olegovna took a sheet of paper and started to draw something reminiscent of a pit, positioning the little figures of the characters on the different levels.

'You see, it is only when one falls to the lowest level, only when one loses all moral and spiritual values, when one reaches the dead end,' the teacher pointed with the pencil to the lowest point, 'that *there*, at the bottom of the pit, one finally has no other choice but to start climbing. Plyushkin is not complacent, but miserable. He is a tragic hero. He knows he has done wrong.'

She drew an arrow pointing upwards out of the pit.

Even though I was embarrassed at the time about not knowing the correct answer, I did remember it forever: only when one reaches the dead end has one no other choice but to start climbing . . .

'So, tell me,' continued Nina Olegovna in the same amicable way, crossing her thin hands over the drawing, 'Which of the gymnasium's specializations do you prefer? You have to make a decision in order to secure your future.'

Once again, it seemed like I didn't know the correct answer.

Never in my life had anyone asked me such a question. I hadn't heard of any specializations. Willing to help, Nina Olegovna explained that at the gymnasium each pupil had to choose whether to focus on history, philology, foreign languages, or journalism.

History reminded me of Lenin's portrait. The meaning of the word 'philology' was unknown to me. So I had to pick either of the last two.

'Maybe, journalism?' I replied hesitatingly.

'Journalism?' Nina Olegovna was surprised. 'Aren't you scared of becoming a journalist in *this* country?'

I felt completely lost.

Was it a wrong answer again? What was so dangerous about that job? Why 'in *this* country'?

'Well,' she added, 'The journalism class is the least popular. We might need another pupil there, indeed.'

❧

No one in Taiga believed my mother when she told people that I'd been accepted into the Humanities Gymnasium without paying any bribes. Even if she'd wanted to offer a gift or some money to the principal, I knew she couldn't afford to do it, because the flat she'd rented for us was so poky and smelly, because the business she ran with the gypsy woman wasn't bringing in much profit, because our golden necklaces and her earrings were still at the pawnshop.

I saw how much effort my mother was making to start everything from scratch in the big city. Silently, I watched her as she stood by her underground stall, I followed her on the journeys to Novosibirsk, I saw her fighting off the drug addicts in our staircase. I admired my mother for her seemingly endless patience and strength.

Our new home was on Lenin Prospekt, a parkway ten kilometers long, eight lanes wide, flanked by a monotonous procession of red-bricked five-story blocks. At first, I had the same old trouble of identifying which home was ours. But then I noticed a group of old ladies—*babushkas*, just like my own—selling sunflower seeds near our building. The old women, kerchiefed and ragged, in a final effort to add a few rubles to their miserable pensions, would always be there, sitting on the turned-over boxes or, more often, right on the pavement and offering, all as one, their humble produce to passersby: fried sunflower seeds or, for a few kopecks extra, shelled and fried sunflower seeds. On returning home, I once asked my mother to buy me a cornet of the shelled ones.

'Sure, but do you understand by what means those seeds are shelled already?' she replied.

I only needed to use my imagination to know that I didn't want any.

And yet, each time, the sight of those *babushkas* served me a good sign of our home nearby, and a warm memory of my own grandmother.

In our new one-bedroom space my mother and I had ripped down the old, blood-stained wallpapers and glued on new ones, covered the nasty rotten floors with fresh linoleum, declared war on the troops of cockroaches and ants that felt much more comfortable in our flat than we did (we used a special tool called 'Mashenka', a white chalk of poison with which you marked out the zone that the insects wouldn't dare cross). Finally, when our business grew steadier, we managed to buy a rug to keep the house warmer during the winter. I remember how we carried the long heavy tube of carpet on our shoulders from the shop, and laughing at ourselves, both short and frail, all the way back home. Soon the two of us achieved a relative coziness in our place, and only the never-ending noise of speeding vehicles and bestial fistfights outside my window—barred with a metal net—kept me awake at night.

In contrast, everything at the Humanities Gymnasium was intimidating: my classmates with their loud stories about vacations abroad (I recall someone's photos from Turkey that amazed me with their vividness, which I naively attributed to the quality of the film, not to the fact that the world outside our coal-dust bell jar was, in fact, brighter); the classrooms with real computers (the only one I'd ever touched was burnt along with our shop); and last but not least, those headmistresses of the gymnasium with their high expectations (I recall our principal's outrage when my mother, responsible for doing the flower arrangements for a school event, put nine roses in the teachers' bouquets and only seven in the administrators'—an error for which she had to make public apologies).

Some of my classmates were brought to school by cars (a rare luxury), others were already taking drugs. Those kids were also smarter than me, more experienced, more sophisticated. I remember the very first day at the gymnasium when I was seated in the very back row with Volodia Skorniakov. When the teacher mentioned the Epicurean current, I whispered to Volodia, 'Could you tell me how to spell that?'

'Hm?' Volodia gave me an arrogant glance, 'Where did you say you are from?'

'From Taiga,' I replied sheepishly.

'I see.'

Doing my best not to participate in conversations, I kept observing the new people around me. I listened very attentively to what they were saying, studied carefully the details of their appearance, noticed the little gestures, glances, hints. It was exciting to be immersed in this whole new world and at the same time to be left totally alone, as if invisible, on the margin of this colourful society.

During the nights at home, I kept writing my observations and guesses down in my diary about each of my classmates. Every colleague of mine was like a fictional character for me. I noted down the colour of their eyes and hair, the details of the clothes they wore, the patterns of their speech and behavior.

There was Yana, for example, the girl who always sat with her back to me, so I spent hours admiring how the sunshine changed the shade of her hair over the course of the day. And in between classes I continued to sit, pretending to read or do my homework, while listening to the stories Yana told her girlfriend. At that tender age, the girls already had plenty of drama going on: boyfriends finding out that they were not the only ones, parents providing soft drugs, plans to travel abroad. At home, I put all my impressions of Yana in a poem about a blue-eyed angel who, of course, had fallen.

There was a clique at school, of which Yana was a member. The group consisted of very diverse boys and girls and I kept asking myself what united them, until it became clear that they were all the daughters and sons of local government officials. I observed many times the way Yana, always vivacious, full of funny ideas and jokes, mingled with those kids: they all seemed so comfortable with each other, joyful, easygoing. I kept trying to imagine how good it must feel to live that kind of life, social and carefree. The families of those working for the government were known as the only caste that enjoyed a relatively stable, secure living.

The name I kept hearing most often in the conversations of others was Xenia Chernova. Indeed, it was impossible not to notice that girl: very tall, slender Xenia with her chestnut-coloured hair and the whitest skin was not only the most popular, the prettiest girl in school, but she also possessed a very special, overwhelmingly confident way of acting. So many times I observed how others would not be able to take their eyes off Xenia when she was cat-walking through the corridors and not dare strike up a conversation with her either. But what impressed me most about her was not her looks or her superior behavior, but the fact that sixteen- or seventeen-year-old Xenia Chernova was, according to the gossips, already running her own modeling agency, with herself as the face of the company. I overheard Yana, my fallen angel classmate, discussing the chances of her being cast as one of Xenia's models.

'Modeling,' I kept thinking to myself at home in the evening, 'What a strange, mysterious thing . . . What is that for? What on earth do they do there? How could one run any sort of agency while being practically a child?'

Another character, who would very much appreciate a poem written about her, was a girl with the rare name of Vilena. A rebellious outsider, she enjoyed shocking people with her looks and would not be stopped from speaking her mind aloud, often insulting both students and teachers. Nevertheless, I liked her, perhaps because she was leaving a wonderful imprint in my diary.

'This city is like a toothless beast that keeps chewing you but cannot swallow!' she used to say, and I couldn't agree more even though I had only felt its first dull bites.

Vilena wore a safety pin in her left ear, seemed never to wash her long, ash-blonde hair with its tips dyed raven-black, and preferred wearing beat-up, long-to-the-ground overcoats in all seasons. I guessed she was linked to some goth or emo subculture, present in every school in those years, but there were no such individuals in Taiga and so to me she seemed perfectly extraordinary.

There were not many boys in the gymnasium, probably because the humanities were more popular among female students. One boy, however, was to take a very special place in my pages. Andrey seemed to be the leader of our journalism class, even though he always acted low-key. His personality puzzled me the most. It was as if there was some code to his character that I couldn't crack. I saw that everyone respected him, even though he treated the rest of them with obvious disregard. I felt that even teachers were especially careful with Andrey, always listening attentively to his infrequent comments. During the breaks he never fought, gossiped, or bragged but instead sat silently, letting some girl prattle on nonstop while he doodled in his notebook.

To amuse myself I also tried to pair people up, guessing which boy and girl might end up married, who had a crush on whom, which couple might make a happy family and which would not last long. Only with Andrey did I have difficulty matching him with anyone else. No matter how hard I tried to imagine him walking hand in hand with Yana or Xenia or some other girl, it seemed unlikely. There was something frighteningly lonesome about him as if all his existence was throwing out a silent 'no' to the world around him.

Of all the new teachers my favourite by far was the literature professor Tamara Alexeyevna. With her silver-grey hair, always pulled up in a bun, and somber outfits, she looked much sterner, much more old-fashioned than other staff members, and seemed to hold herself aside from the general issues and events of the gymnasium. She had a great calmness and seriousness about her, but with us, her students, Tamara Alexeyevna could be enthusiastic and lenient, listening to our big debates calmly with an ever-present, all-understanding smile. Asking us to discuss some philosophical concept of Dostoyevsky, every now and then she would interrupt our talk, look at us with a loving gaze, and all of a sudden exclaim with huge emotion in her voice:

'Oh, how silly you all are, my darlings!'

Such an attitude was insulting to some of my all-too-cool class-mates, but it made me laugh. Of course, we were silly and kept shock-ing her with our twenty-first-century morals.

'Oh, this new, bright Generation Next!' she mocked us, quoting some stupid Pepsi commercial.

Nevertheless, patiently listening to our analyses of literary works, she directed our way of thinking, asking questions in such a manner that we felt that she really cared to hear our opinions. Considering lit-erature the most important subject for gymnasium students, Tamara Alexeyevna also protected us from other teachers when something went wrong in our algebra or chemistry departments.

In spite of her being my favourite, I don't think Tamara Alexeyevna liked me very much. I remember only one time when she turned her mind to me. During a class on Akhmatova, she once asked if anyone knew any of the poet's works by heart. I raised my hand and so was asked to recite, standing in front of the class.

'It seems to me, that you sense the meaning of every word of the poet with your heart, Alexey,' she commented on my recital, which made me very happy.

But that was all. The rest of the time she seemed not to notice me, instead paying a lot of attention to Andrey, who was obviously her most loved student. Him she asked many questions, him she praised more than anyone else, and once during the break, I saw Andrey giv-ing Tamara Alexeyevna a few sheets with handwritten poems, which seemed to please her very much.

Something similar was also evident in the geography classroom. Andrey was the one whom the teacher, Leonid Josephovich, adored with a special zeal. This was obvious because, although every other student dreaded 'the geographer', Andrey stood out as the single ex-ception. When Leonid Josephovich entered the room—hunchbacked, sallow, with crooked teeth and wrinkled smelly clothes—everyone tried to keep low and silent as if desperate to become invisible. Invisi-ble, because the geographer usually found his first victim straightaway and started mocking him or her in the nastiest, most caustic manner.

'Ivanova,' Leonid Josephovich would call his students only by their family names, 'Everyone! Come on, look at Ivanova. Just look at her,' the geographer commanded and the other students, grateful that it wasn't them being picked on this time, stared excitedly at the poor girl. 'Tell me, Ivanova, where did you get that garb? You think it might pass for a nice dress, right? Where did you get it, I'm asking you?'

The girl, blushing, lowered her eyes while the class giggled and Leonid Josephovich continued his one-man show, 'Your mommy got it at the homeless people's shelter? What, you couldn't find a more decent outfit to wear to school?'

The rest of the classmates were chuckling.

'And you, Ovchinnikov, what are you laughing at?' The geographer, satisfied with himself, proceeded to the next pupil, 'you would certainly sell a kidney in order to get under Ivanova's skirt!'

The class would break out in disgusting laughter. It'd continue that way till the bell announced the end of the geography session.

I had hated Leonid Josephovich from the very beginning. Noticing that I was not laughing, the geographer would pick on me too, 'And you, Taiga-boy, close your ears! It's too early for you to listen to these kinds of jokes! You are still being breast-fed, aren't you?'

I noticed that the other teachers also tried to avoid Leonid Josephovich as if in fear of being humiliated themselves. Even Nina Olegovna, that young vice-principal to whom I had always felt grateful for enrolling me in the gymnasium, would blush and lower her eyes, unintentionally exposing that dark-brown mole on her left eyelid—she couldn't escape Leonid Josephovich either.

'Nina Olegovna has not shaven her legs this week, or why else is she wearing her husband's pants again?'

I simply couldn't understand how this man could be so outrageously insulting to everyone and still be working at the gymnasium. Not only his behavior but his whole presence—malodorous, jaundiced, malevolent—was debasing the Humanities Gymnasium much more than any ritual bribery. Later on, I learnt that the man had close ties with the city administration and, in spite of his looks and attitudes, he was a respected geographer, an academician, and even a director of the Regional Youth Center.

'Leonid Josephovich occasionally dines at the governor's house,' some teachers whispered to one another in the corridors. 'It was the governor himself who appointed Leonid Josephovich to teach at the gymnasium.' 'The governor has commissioned Leonid Josephovich to write the regional anthem!'

The story was that the man had been teaching for the last twenty years, yet he talked about everything except geography during his classes. His jokes were sleazy and low-minded, the most vulgar things I had ever heard but, of course, the class lapped it up (so long as the subject of attention was someone else). Yet I was not the only one who seemed repulsed.

Andrey did not laugh at that stand-up comedy either. Moreover, Andrey was never humiliated by the geographer, was never asked any questions. On the contrary, for some reason, the geographer seemed to treat Andrey in the most careful, most polite manner.

❧

Gradually speeding up with my studies I grew more and more comfortable in the new environment. I learned the meaning of the word 'humanities' (as well as how to spell 'Epicurean') and from that point on was grateful for being a part of this school, which encouraged its students to study human culture and wouldn't terrorize them with any 'sports inclinations'. Adapting to the new surroundings, I was learning things quickly and soon the others seemed to have forgotten that I was from Taiga.

Meanwhile, my mother's business was on the rise too and we finally managed to redeem our necklaces and her earrings. I spent my after-school hours helping her in our esoteric basement just as I did back in the days when we had our own store. And as my mother became more and more involved in the practices of her gypsy colleague, I got more chances to learn things about the adult life of the big city and those who tried to make it better.

My mother's little Asian stall and the psychic's room indeed made a perfect match. Those visitors who were waiting for their sessions with Isabella Davidovna would normally buy something from my mom, and our own clients would inevitably get interested in the practices of the psychic. My mother and I welcomed the guests in the waiting room, making sure their appointment was all right, while in her turn Isabella Davidovna encouraged some of her unfortunate clients (most of them were inevitably such) to look for luck among our feng-shui or Indian talismans.

After a few months of working together in the basement, that matron of whom I was so afraid at the beginning had succeeded in making me like her. It even started to seem to me that this Siberian gypsy looked exactly like my beloved Anna Akhmatova in her later years. She had never touched me, hardly spoke to me during the day, but her small, piercing eyes were powerful enough to communicate all that was needed. Isabella Davidovna would just stare at me, and I imagined her saying, 'I'm not going to eat you, boy, you can trust me. I know I'm big and frightening, but there's nothing you should be scared of when you are with me.' Perhaps, this was what each of her clients felt, too.

After a day filled with sessions (she handled some fifteen cases per day with an endless queue of people stretching from eight in the morning till eight in the evening), and when my mother had locked the doors after the last customer, Isabella Davidovna would collapse on her own daybed.

I watched her closely. I saw the black line of her mustache tremble as she exhaled great gusts of air. The woman didn't sleep, but I could see that she was absolutely exhausted. 'No matter whether she really knows white or black magic,' I thought to myself, 'she certainly works hard.'

One would imagine that a clientele such as ours was very particular and consisted of some exceedingly emotional, unhappy, and trustful ladies, but that was not the case at all. In that waiting room, from behind my stall, I saw all sorts of people seek her out: young and old, rich and poor, housewives and businessmen, professors and politicians, mafia men and their bimbos, doctors, nannies, students, coal miners—the list was endless. Most of them were returning customers, who came for weekly sessions in the same fashion as many Westerners visit their psychiatrists. Little by little I learned the stories of some of those people. Sometimes at night, while my mother was dealing with her bills and accounts, Isabella Davidovna, relaxing on her daybed, would tell me all sorts of problems that she had tried to solve that day. She was discreet enough never to disclose the names or point to the persons directly, but I would do my best to guess at who was who.

I remember, for instance, a couple who came back over and over again. They both looked crushed, desperate, frightened. The gypsy told me that they had lost their teenage daughter two years earlier and ever since she had been trying to help them to find her. The girl got mixed up with the wrong people in a club and was presumed kidnapped. The police did nothing. The father of the girl was ready to take his kitchen knife and rescue the daughter himself, if only the gypsy would tell him where to search for the child. Unfortunately, all that she could 'read' about their missing girl (Isabella Davidovna used tarot cards, runes, and palm reading) was a peculiar collection of signs and details. For instance, she kept saying that a bear was involved, that a small wooden cottage was part of the puzzle, and that aquamarine was everywhere. But how could that help to find the girl? The couple kept coming back over and over again but to no avail.

There was also an older man, with a double chin and tiny eyes set deep under his eyebrows, who came multiple times to see Isabella Davidovna. He wore crumpled expensive suits and yellowish shirts with buttons never closing over his belly: the typical appearance, in other words, of a provincial government official. The man did indeed serve in the city administration, though it was not his professional but private life that required the gypsy's assistance. The man craved a boyfriend.

People with health issues were another common category of Isabella Davidovna's customers. For instance, there was the seemingly endless stream of women with breast cancer who had been refused treatment by the local hospital. The practice in the city was that everyone who happened to have the disease in its final stages was left with no medical assistance at all. 'There's nothing we can do for you here,' those women were told by the doctors. My new friend was their only hope.

There were all sorts of people with all sorts of problems, demands, dreams. I couldn't tell if Isabella Davidovna was really helping them or not, but at the end of the day, picturing that big, exhausted body resting on the daybed and the somewhat relieved, lightened impressions on her clients' faces, I became convinced that she was doing her job with full dedication. Much better, at least, than the medical specialists and the policemen of our city.

Little by little, the fierce woman seemed to have become attached to me in the same way as I did to her, and our evening sessions, when she talked with her eyes closed while lying on the daybed and I listened to her stories of that day, became our tradition. She kept mumbling on in a monotonous voice with zero excitement or interest while I didn't dare move, afraid to interrupt the stream of her stories. But one evening, when she sat me in front of her and lay down on the bed, she asked me a direct question.

'Aliosha, you are a grown-up now. Tell me, what is the dream of *your* life?'

She was very serious and I knew she expected a serious, honest answer from me. But I only felt confused and scared. I didn't know what to say.

'Think about it a little,' she said knowingly, '*What do you want?* But sit here, don't go away. You think, and I will rest.'

I stayed motionless in my chair, thinking of my dreams as the gypsy seemed to be drowsing away on her daybed . . .

Before moving into this big city, where everything was confusion, I thought of spending my life in Taiga, that small town where I grew up. The only tertiary education institution there was a college where they taught you how to become a repairman or how to drive a tractor, that sort of thing. So back in Taiga, I thought to myself that, if I got lucky, I might be accepted into that college and learn some useful skill that would help me survive when I grew up. But now . . . now, when we had to leave my hometown, when our store had been burnt down, when it was just me and my mother against the world of cockroaches, staircase junkies, and sixteen-year-old fashion models, I didn't know what was to become of me. The world of the big city was so strange, I didn't know how to relate to it. Of what could I possibly dream?

The train of my thoughts circled round and around, but she was still there, that fierce, powerful woman was, like a huge rock, lying in front of me, waiting for my response. I had to give her an answer.

Maybe it could be something about my everlasting passion for poetry, or the fact that I was impressed by that little daughter of my mother's friend, Marina, whose books were neatly positioned on her desktop, but after some ten minutes of thinking I replied to Isabella Davidovna that my biggest dream . . .

'The only dream I can think of . . . is to have my own library. To have many books placed next to each other on my own bookshelves.'

It was the most honest answer I could produce back then. Without opening her eyes, Isabella Davidovna smiled almost unnoticeably and told me to go.

Just when I had started to get used to her presence, and the company of Isabella Davidovna had become an unexpected source of comfort to me, we had to say farewell to each other. The couple who had been looking for their daughter for two years had reported on our esoteric basement. Their child was long dead, they had discovered, and they decided that the gypsy knew it and was simply draining money out of them. The police came after my friend and she had to escape.

The couple's daughter, by the way, had indeed been kidnapped by a man involved with the mafia, who went by the nickname '*Mishka*'—'Teddy Bear'. The man had raped and killed their girl, leaving her body in the cellar of his small wooden cottage. When the body was discovered, it was wrapped in blankets of an aquamarine colour. Isabella Davidovna had read all the signs correctly, but it wasn't enough. Now she had to move to some other city, hide in some other basement, begin some other life.

My mother too was forced to find a different place for her business. Soon she managed to make her way into the Central Department Store on Kirov Street. It was a big old grey cube with three levels of hopelessly sooty, smoke-blackened windows. The store proprietor (another friend of the governor, who also owned the city stadium, the hockey team, and the biggest collection of samovars in Siberia) was leasing so-called *boutiques* as well as bare square meters in the middle of the corridors to petty merchants.

On the last floor, right in the middle of the hall, my mother rented two square meters for her Asian stall. From now on she had to stand on her feet from nine to nine every day including weekends and with only two days of rest per year (on the first of January and on the day of Resurrection at Easter)—that was the management's rule, and she had to obey it if she wanted to remain working there. Even though I could tell that it exhausted her, I think she was very glad to be finally out of the basement.

One of those nights, when my mother came back home very, very tired and I ran to greet her at the door, she passed me a plastic bag.

'This is for you,' she said, 'Isabella Davidovna stopped by the kiosk today to say goodbye.'

I took the plastic bag and looked inside: there were five brand new volumes of Jack London. I knew nothing of this author and yet I cannot express how much I was touched by this gift from our friend. Carefully I placed the books next to the three volumes of Pushkin on my desktop and for days couldn't stop admiring what appeared to be the beginning of my library . . . Just think of it! My very own library.

Chapter Six

Sixteen

'I'm afraid that I love you,' my classmate spoke quickly and quietly, but I managed to catch his words before they melted in the evening smoke.

We were standing on the sixteenth-story balcony, on the top floor of the tallest building in our city. Neither he nor I lived in that block, but we knew that each level gave access to a public deck overlooking the vast provincial drabness in which we did live. First, we would stand by the locked door downstairs, waiting for some resident with a key; we'd tell that someone that we wished to visit Masha, or Sasha, or Dasha, or some other nonexistent friend, and hopefully be let in; then we'd ride the doddery, stinking elevator to the top, walk through a dark corridor and, after pushing open a rusty, creaky door, at last reach that secret place of our own.

The three walls of the balcony were smothered in smut and graffiti, its floor was thick with grime and cigarette stubs, but we were left alone and felt safe there, far from all the turmoil down at ground level. Hundreds of minuscule grey vehicles moved up and down Lenin Prospekt; their lights—red ascending, yellow descending—were the brightest points of interest on offer and our eyes, having nothing better to focus on, kept following them. If you went with the red stream, then after some mixing and tangling the lights inevitably merged with the thick smoke streaming endlessly, mercilessly, from the chimney stacks in the factory zone; and if you followed the yellow lights, the cars would steer your gaze to the ochre city center and then all the way on to the train station. On that balcony we spent hours talking, watching our bleak and dire town, which seemed even gloomier than usual on that miserable mid-April night.

'And you, do you think you love me?' my classmate turned away from the town and looked at me with both a glimpse of hope and the certainty of rejection evident in his wild black eyes. I stood still, shivering slightly, shocked by this confession which, to me, seemed to have come out of nowhere.

He was older than me, smarter than me, braver. Although, right now, he looked very scared, perhaps at his own words or at my reaction to them. But how was I meant to react? What could I possibly do to him? Punch him? Push him from the balcony? Hug him? Kiss him? No, I was left speechless. He, in turn, remained silent.

We used to talk a great deal every day after school. Back then we'd set out walking aimlessly, criss-crossing the town from one side to the other, from west to east, from south to north, diagonally. He was my guide because I was, after all, no more than the Taiga-boy, the outsider, the alien. When we got tired or cold, we'd take a tram to observe the same street scenes unfolding outside the scratched and filthy windows.

There was nothing beautiful or charming about our experiences in the big city, but later, when I looked back on those months, I knew that it was a most delicate time: the omnipresent drowsiness of the place, the rough streets, and our old reddish tram. Yes, that trembling Soviet tram, once painted a bright red and white, but by then worn out, grey and flaking like everything else in our world, with the doors bulky and mighty enough to split one in two, with stairs so steep that old women needed assistance to board or were left downstairs looking hopelessly up at the passengers above them, and with an unavoidable controller, a *konduktorsha*—usually, an obese, morose woman—staggering through the thick crowd, carrying a heavy black bag full of coins slung around her neck and screaming imperiously from her big, rouged mouth, 'Pay the ride! Pay! Show your passes! Show! Pay!'

The *konduktorsha* addressed men as either *muzhchina* ('Man over there! Have you paid?') or *malchik* ('Get the heck out of here, boy!'), so you were either manned up or still wet behind the ears. She addressed women as either *zhenschina* ('Woman, hurry up!'), *devochka* ('You've got a school pass or what, girl?'), or *babushka* ('Granny, sit still!'). Oh, that ruthless tactless tasteless post-Soviet Russian language! Where was your *Sir*, your *Madame*, your *Senore* or *Monsieur*? Or at least, *What's good?*, or a *hi, friend, please,* tovarish? All crushed under the wheels of a brutally inhuman uprightness. A woman knew for sure she'd gotten old when the controller in her daily tram started calling her *babushka*.

Enveloped in the Siberian winter, we couldn't possibly walk for more than an hour even on a good day without stopping somewhere to get warm. The city had few shops. Their security guards were unwelcoming: they humiliated us by checking our pockets and even the sleeves of our coats as we left. The few cafés scared us off with their prices. We dreaded the school when classes were over and the bullies let loose. But the tram . . . the tram offered us a relatively safe refuge with its warm engines right under our seats. Once we climbed aboard and showed our school passes, we'd sit one behind the other—this was how the seats were arranged—and start calculating the numbers on the tickets we'd been issued: there were six digits on each, so if you summed together the first three, then the last three, and the two numbers coincided, then you'd won a 'happy ticket'. 'I got a lucky one!' one of you would exclaim. 'Eat it!' the other had to respond. If you didn't then chew and swallow that flimsy, dirty piece of paper, happiness would never come to pass. Never!

The tram ran for hours, or what seemed hours to me. Visitors from Moscow and most locals considered the city a small provincial place but to me it felt enormous: a megapolis with dozens of bus and tram lines, with hundreds of streets, hundreds of thousands of people, constant noise at night, something always happening outside the barred windows of our flat. I didn't know the place and always got lost, which was dangerous. You were taught to trust nobody, not to open the door, not to venture far from home—but of course we did.

My classmate volunteered to be my guide, showing me the sights: the bridge, the circus, the observation deck above the industrial zone (with its splendid view of coal plants and chimneys belching soot, that deck served as a vantage point for wedding photos or panoramas for the odd visitor from Moscow) and, finally, the margins of the city where all the trams and buses ended their journeys. At the final station, we had to get off and jump on a tram heading in the opposite direction. Each time we did so, we asked ourselves, why don't these trams go in circuits instead of running back and forwards? Then Zemfira, the Bob Dylan of the Russian music scene, struck upon the same thought in one of her songs, 'How strange the trams never run in circles but only from edge to edge,' and we knew she wrote it about us.

Although we spent every day together, the idea of our being something more than mere friends had never crossed my mind. It was way too adult for me—I was not yet sixteen, I looked thirteen, and felt like I was still eleven. I felt younger than everyone else in that new school where I'd met Andrey.

One day in late February, six months after I'd started attending the gymnasium and some time yet before Andrey made his confession, the boys in our class gathered to prepare for the forthcoming eighth of March. After a brief talk, we collected the money for one of our number to go to the city center to select the obligatory gifts for the girls and the female teachers. Usually sceptical about such matters, Andrey surprised everyone by volunteering and after the meeting he asked if I wanted to join him. I was thrilled! Never before had I participated in the gymnasium's extracurricular life or talked with Andrey in private.

Snow was deep everywhere on the streets, but on that day it felt as if spring was approaching. The sun was finally giving some of its warmth away and not just hanging about indifferently behind the heatproof glass as it did all winter. We took our hats off for the first time that season and strolled downtown, chatting as we went. When we reached central Kirov Street, we entered the department store, quickly selected some souvenirs on the ground-floor level, asked if they had two dozen of them, paid without giving it all much thought, and left.

'Have you ever been to the pine forest?' Andrey asked as we left the store.

'The pine forest? No, I haven't, I'm not very fond of skiing, to be honest.'

Andrey laughed. I knew that the forest, which was right across the river from the city center, was popular among skiers. Having resisted skiing ever since the mandatory marathons of my previous school, I had never cared to visit the place.

'Don't worry, I'm not going to force you to ski. We'll just have a walk,' Andrey reassured me, and we headed off to the tram station.

At the first stop after crossing the river, the tram paused, hesitating, yet not opening its doors. No one rose from their seats, but Andrey quickly approached the driver, asking him to let us out. The moment the doors were opened, I felt a breeze of freshness fill the tram: it was as if there was some cold sea, the North Ocean, right there, right behind the wall of majestic pines confronting us.

Andrey was right, no one was to be seen in the forest that day: only the perfectly parallel lines in the snow told us that someone had been skiing there some time earlier. Having no better alternative, we stuck to the ski trails, our legs sinking knee-deep in the snow every now and then, and when I looked back, I saw that the skiers' two perfectly parallel lines—lines destined never to meet—had now been rearranged into a chaotic, criss-crossing tangle of footprints.

The soft aroma of the frozen pine trees, the sand-like sparkling snow, the overwhelming quietness of the winter forest broken only by the regular distant rattle of a woodpecker and the occasional soft *fwhump* as some bundle of snow slid free from the branches of a pine—I couldn't imagine how, in the middle of this noisy industrial region, such a solitary, pristine place could survive. Andrey, seeing I was mesmerized, seemed proud to have been the one who introduced me to this refuge, and on his face, for the first time since I had begun to watch him closely, I read signs of—if not yet happiness—at least some ever-blossoming, pink-cheeked, hopeful anticipation of joy.

Returning home that evening I was excited and cheerful because I felt as if this was a day which a couple of friends had split in two and shared. As soon as I reached our flat and said hi to my mom, I went straight to my desk to write in my diary. It felt so special to get close to the class-mate whom I had observed for so long, to be in touch with a character who had lived in my pages for months already.

Then my mother walked into my room with a bucket of water and went crawling on all fours, washing the floor with a wet rag. I offered to help her. She looked at me in a very strange, bitter way, and went on with her silent cleaning . . . I couldn't write anymore. I sat mo-tionless, trying to figure out what had I done wrong. Could it be the very endless, exhausting day she'd spent standing by her stall in the department store? Could it be my own unexpected happiness that was causing her bad mood?

Finally, she approached me, pierced me with her eyes—wet cloth in her hand, hair sticking to her burning face—paused, and then ex-claimed angrily:

'Why didn't you stop by my kiosk today?'

I stared at her, confused.

'I . . . I . . . We didn't plan to go through the whole department store . . . I was just following my classmate,' I explained lamely. 'How did you know we were there?'

'I saw you.' Her lips softened a little then, and she added in a quieter tone, 'And I was so happy to see you . . . So I waved to you . . .'

At that moment, I saw the face of my mom, the strongest, most self-controlled person, change dramatically.

'And you . . . you just turned away from me.'

Kneeling back down on the floor, she broke into tears.

'You're ashamed of me. Ashamed of me and my pathetic kiosk . . .'

No bullying at my Taiga school, no difficulties at the gymnasium, no absence of my father had horrified me as much as my mother's tears that evening. Never before had I seen her cry, and now the simple sight of her filled my eyes with tears.

'Mama, *mamochka*,' I fell on my knees next to her. 'How on earth could I be ashamed of you? What are you saying? How could I possibly be ashamed of you? You are my greatest pride!'

I also wept, trying to hug her stiff, shaking shoulders. Gradually she let go of her silly thoughts and hugged me back. We remained sitting on the floor of our new home, holding each other tight, in silence and fear.

Silence and fear—those were the two implacable chaperones our family never seemed able to get rid of. As far back as I can recall, my mother and I were extremely close to each other, and yet I sensed there were always, always things that were not to be mentioned between us, but rather to be feared and avoided. It was as if there were dark rocks lurking, shallowly, below the opaque stream of our lives. These rocks, these taboos could have become stones in a wall permanently separating us—but that didn't happen.

It didn't happen, thanks, in part, to my grandmother, my *babushka*, who had always shared with me her all-encompassing, all-knowing, all-uniting powers. She was my dad's mother, of course. It was my mother's family, not his, which was largely the source of all the fear and the silence. I knew I could never raise this subject myself, never talk with my parents about it. Instead, it was my *babushka* who—out of the blue one day—began telling me the story of my mom's youth.

Born in the mountainous region south of our world, by blood (and passport) tied to a tribal Mongolian race and community, my mother left her family when she was eighteen, never to look back, or at least never to speak of, to me, her own child. Her people, like all native Siberians, were colonized by the Russians generations earlier, but it was only in the twentieth century, only under the Soviets—the socialists!—that the complete annihilation of their native culture and their language was successfully achieved. Under communist rule, these free tribal people were turned into wretched, filthy drunkards, lousy servants of transient, pale-faced guests from European Russia. One of the reasons—though not the main one—why my mother never returned to her home was that she had decided to marry a pale-faced Russian man.

My *babushka* told me how they all drove in one car to Altay to ask for my mother's hand, and how they were scorned and rejected by a dark, drunken little woman, and how bitterly my mother cried that night. And how—by the time they were ready to leave the village— they discovered their car had been completely dismantled: its wheels, lights, bumper bars, windscreen-wipers, and everything that could be detached stolen and carted away by the locals.

Even the act of inviting her family to the wedding, even the simple business of telling *them* that she was going to marry, must have been a soul-torturing exercise for my mother. Though, in fact, she was the effective head, heart, and hands of that family: the eldest of five children. Five children, each from a different father. A father that never was . . . never was a father at all—but just another man who didn't stay around long enough to leave his name but only a few rubles. A few rubles and one more child. One more child to be raised—to be fed—by my teenage mother.

Together they wandered the dirt roads of their village—it was never really one village for they were truly nomads, moving from Altay to Kazakhstan to Uzbekistan and back to Russia—my mother and her four siblings, her little children, picking lice from each other's hair, wearing plastic bags instead of shoes, walking the dirt roads, begging and collecting bottles and trying to sell berries or mushrooms or whatever they found on their way—to Russian men, always to white Russian men, the only people with money. While the children did that, their mother sold the only possession she had: her own skinny bones. To the usual customers.

Unloved, uncared for herself, my little mother—*moya mamochka*—a child herself, made to care day after day for four others, one fatal morning lets one of them, one of her younger sisters, slip out of sight as they trudged through yet another town, yet another crowd. The girl had somehow become detached, lost, my mom searching frantically for her until suddenly . . .

A screech of brakes! The ear-piercing shriek of metal on metal. Human cries, screams! What horror! A passing tram! Her little sister is lying in the dust and oil, under the bright, shining silver wheels of a Soviet tram—in her own dirty pink blood! her blood!—cut in two. In front of my mother's eyes. Eyes put there for one purpose: never to lose sight of her family.

This and many other blood-stained stories of my mother's past were never to be raised, her remaining family was never to be visited. Only her rice-shaped eyes, only her sun-tinted skin, only that Russian passport of hers which mercilessly stated 'Nationality: Altay' and ruthlessly demanded a patronymic, a father's name that she had to invent—those were the only unspoken reminders of her otherness.

My only grandmother, then, was the one on my father's, my Russian side. *Babushka* adopted my mother, cared for her warmly, and taught me, inculcated in me the lessons—the stories—of love. I always knew that my duty was not only to surround my mom with love and care, but to make sure that she read all the signs, all the evidence of it, in our daily life.

How much is written about love, romantic love, and the myriad ways of expressing it. But how do we love our parents fully? How do we make sure that they feel loved, when love itself is so often beset by silences and fears?

※

Since our first walk in the snow-vestured forest, Andrey and I became inseparable. Almost every day after school he asked me if I had any plans and we spent hours and hours walking the city and riding trams until nightfall. Andrey was happy to be my guide, even if there was scant to show. We circled the central block of streets over and over again, gradually making our circle bigger, stepping out into the endless suburban reaches. There was certainly nothing to see there either, but then, I guess, seeing things was not really the point.

One day Andrey led me to Pushkin Square (the name alone made my heart soar). The square was not big, a mere sixth the size of Soviet Square, the mammoth space next to it, yet there was a life-size statue of Alexander Pushkin in the center with pretty, beige and ochre-red four-story residential buildings all around. Those houses looked strikingly different, shorter but with much bigger windows than the typical five-story Soviet blocks. They had elegant moldings around their doors and windows, arches and porticos. I was very impressed.

'All built by the German prisoners of war,' Andrey commented.

'How strange it is . . .' I responded hesitantly. 'How strange that the only beautiful buildings we have here are built by the German prisoners . . .'

He nodded, grinning.

'In the Stalinist Empire style, on top of that,' Andrey added.

I replied that Stalinist Empire was my favourite style of architecture (today was the first example of it I had seen in my life). My friend looked at me with an odd, reproachful smile. Embarrassed, I tried to explain myself.

'These houses are different from all those identical, ugly, five-story panel blocks with minuscule flats and pitch-dark staircases we live in. It feels like they were built for rats, not people.'

Andrey told me that the buildings I was talking about were called *Khrushchevkas,* that they'd been thrown up in their thousands all across the USSR in the sixties, as temporary, prefabricated, low-cost social housing units.

'Of course, as with everything temporary in our country, it became permanent,' Andrey said with a smirk, then suddenly became serious and, after a brief silence, added: 'You realize why they built so many of these identical ugly, as you say, five-story flat blocks all around the country in the sixties, right? And why there are just a few older Stalinist palatial residences here and there?'

Honestly, I had no idea, but I looked back at Andrey's somber face and knew that he expected an answer.

'Maybe,' I replied, 'Because there were many more working class people under Khrushchev? And they had no place to live?'

'And where were those working class people under Stalin?' Andrey asked, looking straight at me.

I stayed silent . . .

'Come,' he said, 'let's sit.'

Andrey walked to a nearby bench. I followed, and we sat down. I waited for him to speak. He looked again at the Stalinist buildings in front of us, breathed in deeply, exhaled, and began the story.

'When Stalin came to power in the early 1920s, he promptly realized that Russia was losing the race to industrialize and that some drastic measures had to be taken. The British already had their subways running, the Americans drove their cars, and we still shat under the bush. Here roads had to be built, factories and power plants set up, dams constructed, cities brought to life. Stalin had practically no resources, no skilled specialists, no labour to achieve all those goals. All he had was a country full of hungry, uneducated, mostly drunk peasants—the sober and the capable ones had either escaped to Europe by then or been killed by the Bolsheviks. So what do you think Stalin did?'

Again, Andrey looked at me with the most morose expression on his face, expecting some answer, but I couldn't understand where his words were taking me.

'Why do you think that Stalin's Great Purge began in the early 1930s?' he asked.

'Because Stalin had a phobia . . .' I tried to respond with what I knew from the school program, 'a phobia that other people might take away the power he had . . . so he went on arresting all the *dangerous elements*?'

Andrey gave me the sceptical gaze he so often offered our teachers.

'Do you *really* think that all of those twenty million people who were killed under Stalin were dangerous elements? Do you think anyone even bothered to check whether they were dangerous or not? Do you think anyone even cared?'

Andrey frightened me more and more. I had never thought of any connection between Stalin's politics and architecture. Yet it did seem strange to me when Andrey explained it all: how, if the leader of the nation was scared of the opposition, he could go on arresting and even executing all those who protested. But an opposition of twenty million?! The population of Moscow and Saint Petersburg combined, and doubled?! Most of those arrested were obviously innocent civilians, all the same comrades, workers—the proletariat.

'Dear Alexey, please tell me,' Andrey went on, the irony in his voice growing more and more bitter, 'who it was that built all those energy plants, all those factories, dams, roads that we now enjoy? On whose bones does that wretched longest railroad in the world run? Who built the first nuclear plant on the planet?'

Little by little, I began to see his point.

'What Stalin did,' he continued, 'was throw millions of people into gulags—with no care for their political views or social position—he simply needed slaves, he needed free labour to fuel the industrial revolution. He organized this colossal labour system, a whole army of slaves. There were more slaves under Stalin than the Egyptian pyramids had ever seen! All those Russian and Eastern European people, arrested with no explanation and thrown into labour camps, worked in the most horrendous conditions. And how comfortable that was for the state: slaves, prisoners did not need to be paid or even fed. If one didn't work, one got shot! That was all. The entire fucking motivation!'

Andrey grew more and more emotional.

'Stalin had created a new type of economy—a slave-based industrialist one. It's a mistake to call it socialism or Leninism. There's nothing social about raising your damned industry on the bones of your own citizens . . .'

He couldn't stop now.

'Why do you think it's only with Khrushchev that they started to build all those, what you call, *ugly* five-story blocks? Because in the 1960s, for the first time in Soviet history, the government had finally decided that something had to be done *for* the people, not made *out of* the people. They built those thousands of low-cost, panel and brick social housing blocks all across the Union because the Gulag system had finally slowed down. Suddenly there were actual working-class people. Not slaves, but workers.

'But they didn't stop at that. Oh, no! The NKVD, the security agency responsible for all the repressions, is still here with us today, only under another name. But at least the genius of Stalin—his vision of turning rivers around to make the deserts bloom, of building the longest railroad in the world over permafrost, and so on—all of that is over. And if anyone . . . if anyone ever tells you to be proud of those Stalinist achievements, you should spit in their face!'

He stopped abruptly. This young man, this boy really, now seemed to be overwhelmed by the horror of his own words.

Still breathing heavily, he looked aside and kept silent for some time. Without turning back to face me, he added more quietly, 'That's why Stalin had no need to build any social housing. All these, what you call, *beautiful Stalinist buildings* were made for the few who ran the labour camps and other leaders of the state. Half the rest of the population of Siberia lived, laboured, and died in the camps.'

We sat on the bench without speaking for a while. I was ashamed of my own ignorance and scared of the things Andrey had said. He kept on looking away. I stared at the cement under my feet. Alexander Pushkin stood dumbstruck above us.

When he did finally speak again, Andrey asked me if I knew how old my hometown Taiga was or how old our big city was.

'Sixty or seventy years?' I guessed.

'Don't you see . . . ?' He was calmer now. 'Most of the cities here, with the happy exceptions of Tomsk, were built as labour camp stations at the beginning of Stalin's *industrialization*. All the settlements that we live in now were originally nothing but gulags. Who the devil do you think would go to Siberia of their own free will? Stalin himself had never crossed the Ural mountains. He arrested scientists, artists, writers, professors, doctors and millions of peasants, workers, his own comrades and sent them as forced labour to dig the coal, to pump the oil, to cut the wood, to build the damned railroads. They were never paid. They were treated like cattle. And if they dared resist, you know what would happen to them?'

Now I nodded. Now I knew.

Later, we rose from the bench and walked away from Pushkin Square, the look of which I was now ashamed to admire. The route, leading from the square, was a quiet, long street with rowan and birch trees on both sides. The trees were beautiful with their branches totally white, crystallized by the humidity and the cold.

'What's the name of this street?' I asked Andrey, trying to change the mood of our conversation, 'It looks so pretty here.'

Andrey said it was Ostrovsky Street.

'Oh, is there a maternity hospital at the end of it?' I realized that I knew the place. Had no memories of it but still knew it.

'There certainly is.' Andrey pointed to another five-story block at the far end of the street.

'Well, at least, the street I was born on was not named after some wretched tyrant like Kirov or Dzerjinsky,' I said cheerfully, 'but after a writer!'

Andrey gave me a surprised glance and then, unexpectedly burst into laughter. 'Oh dear, dear,' Andrey laughed, 'I don't know if I should tell you this or not . . .' My classmate looked at me with the smile of a caring, loving friend now.

'Tell me what?'

'All this time you've been proud to be born on a street named after a writer . . . only if you paid attention to the signs you would notice that it was not named after A. N. Ostrovsky, the playwright, but after N. A. Ostrovsky, the Communist Party leader.'

I couldn't believe it. Until that moment, I had indeed been proud of the place I was born in. Now we approached the corner of one of the buildings and took a look at the street sign. 'N. A. Ostrovsky Street' was written on the plaque.

'Although, to be fair,' Andrey continued, 'the man did write one book. It is considered one of the most influential works of communist propaganda.'

I turned away from Andrey. If he had seen my face, he'd have noticed that it was as red as the communist flag, red with shame and anger.

꙳

Virtually none of the kids in our gymnasium shared Andrey's interests in the history of our region or its architecture, and maybe they were right to ignore these dark subjects and to focus instead on the glamour that the future seemed to promise them. Xenia Chernova was preparing for and promoting the city's beauty pageant, and many girls could think only of that. Other students were obsessed with academic matters, working hard for their so-called red diplomas, those containing only 'fives', only excellent grades for all subjects.

However, there was one schoolmate with whom Andrey was in a

close relationship. Vilena, the girl with the safety pin earring, seemed to have quite a lot in common with my new friend. The two of them enjoyed ironizing the history of things, gossiping about classmates, challenging the authority of teachers, even the principal, and occasionally shocking passersby with their behavior or fashion choices.

It was not very difficult to impress the denizens of our city. Ten years had passed since the collapse of the Soviet Union, but people on the streets still looked and behaved as if anyone who dared stand out was a target for persecution. Clad mostly in grey or black, they walked through the streets at a quick, self-focused pace, doing everything in their power to conceal any sign of an inward life or emotion other than an instinctive distaste for any expression of individualism.

Vilena, in her extravagant goth clothes and outlandish makeup, seemed to actually enjoy being the target of angry looks and verbal insults. To her, this was simply a confirmation of her difference from all the people she despised. Andrey, I saw, admired her courage in standing out against the crowd, though he rarely acted out his own sense of otherness.

These two were great cinephiles and often dodged classes to visit the movie theater across the street. I had never been to the cinema before that year (there was no such facility in Taiga, and even though the dusty board on our local Pioneers' House of Culture permanently advertised some long-forgotten film, there hadn't been a single movie shown in the thirteen years I spent in the town). When my classmates discovered my shocking inexperience, the cine-initiation became inevitable.

One day during a break, when I was calmly preparing for the next class, Vilena walked up to me and commanded, 'Come on! Get your stuff! Let's go!'

Without waiting for an answer, she swept my belongings into my bag, grabbed my right hand and pulled me out of the classroom. Andrey was already waiting on the stoop of the gymnasium. He laughed cheerfully at seeing us, took my left hand and the three of us ran away from the school.

'It's already started! Hurry up!'

Holding hands, we ran across Lenin Prospekt, through the gloomy park, and then across the square to the big grey cube decked out with a huge red signboard above its entrance: 'The Theater of the Jubilee'.

'The jubilee? Which jubilee?'

'The jubilee of the Great October Revolution, of course,' responded Vilena, 'but these days it's mostly about Brangelina in there.'

Indeed, the film which was shown that day in 'The Theater of the Jubilee of the Great October Revolution' was *The Cage*, a cheap thriller with Jennifer Lopez. The movie did nothing to impress, but the theater itself did. It was built in the early seventies and seemed not to have been renovated since. It consisted of one enormous screening hall, with seating for a thousand viewers, and so the sounds of the film echoed hollowly throughout the auditorium.

Andrey and Vilena didn't seem very impressed by the film either, and after some twenty minutes they began loudly mocking everything that was happening on-screen. Other people in the audience hushed us and complained. In protest, Vilena drew from her overcoat a packet of 'Jelly Worms' and started throwing these soft candied creatures into the room at the scariest moments in the drama. People yelled and squealed as they felt the worms landing on their heads and shoulders in the dark, and the movie swiftly became much more entertaining.

Vilena had also been the one who'd brought Andrey and me to that sixteen-story block of flats one day. She seemed to know all the tricks and codes for living in the big city, and taught us how to look especially pitiful, shaking from cold or fear, when asking residents to let us in. On reaching the top floor balcony, the two friends usually lit up a cigarette.

'What a good boy,' Vilena grinned at my stubborn refusal to smoke, 'One coin less in the Patriarch's pocket.'

I gave her a questioning glance.

'Our darling Patriarch Kirill of Moscow,' she went on, tapping her ash all over the land beneath, 'His Highness Bishop of the Russian Orthodox Church, the fucking leader of Orthodox Christianity, has personally profiteered through the importation of cigarettes. The church doesn't pay taxes, you see, so the Patriarch is making a fortune from selling tobacco. Four billion rubles and still climbing. The *Tobacco Metropolitan* is his nickname.'

I stared at Vilena. Andrey continued speaking for her.

'Of course, the church is the largest supplier of tobacco in Russia. Everyone knows that,' he stubbed his cigarette on the railing, 'Before becoming the Patriarch, the man was known as Tovarish Gundyayev, another KGB prick.'

It all sounded like a bad joke to me.

'Speaking of which,' Andrey kept on, 'did you know that the mediocre KGB agent Vladimir Putin made his first million by importing heroin, which didn't exist in Soviet Russia . . . ?'

'How do you know all that?'

They both turned to me.

Vilena smiled sarcastically.

'Alex,' Andrey responded, 'Everyone knows these things.'

'Everyone?' I made a timid protest of my own, 'Do you think ordinary citizens, simple people know about all this?'

Leaning on the railing, he looked down on the grey cityscape below. Waiting for a response, I watched his face: his eyes cold, his lips were pursed tight. A white blob of spittle appeared from his mouth, gradually stretching into a long string before dropping over the edge of the balcony.

'Simple people?' Vilena broke in. 'Simple people love their tyrants.'

'Simple people . . .' she uttered once again, 'simple people flooded the streets of Moscow when Stalin died, they cried bitter tears, cried in hysterics, mourning the death of their beloved Father. Their beloved killer. They will do the same when Putin expires.'

'But that won't happen any time soon . . .' Andrey added.

The day was ending in front of us. The sun was burning in the dust.

'Have you ever asked yourself, Alexey, why I have such a weird name?' Vilena turned to me suddenly and stared into my lost, sheepish face, 'What does it mean?'

'Your name?'

'Yes, my name. What does my name mean?' She went on looking at me.

I didn't know what to think.

'Vladimir Ilyich Lenin,' she said.

I couldn't understand.

'What . . . ? What does Lenin have to do with it?'

'V. I. Lenin,' she repeated the man's initials, 'Vilen is the name for a boy. Vilena, for a girl. I was named after the biggest motherfucker in history. By my own parents . . . simple people . . .'

She dropped her still burning cigarette over the balcony and walked out the door, brushing me with her shoulder on the way. I stood still, unable to comprehend it.

'She's just angry,' Andrey said to me, 'angry. But not at you.'

We followed Vilena.

By the end of March, the snow had melted and a nasty slush filled the streets—the gloomiest time of the year had started, the time when the days are still short, the trees naked, the sky hopelessly grey, and the crystals of snow that used to light the world with their shimmering whiteness have betrayed their purpose and turned black.

The three of us spent many days together. Vilena liked walking through the 'toothless beast' that she despised so much. I learnt that her home was in an area Andrey and I had never set foot in before, and she promised to take us on a tour one day.

'The place where I live is over there,' she told me, pointing vaguely in the direction of my own block.

'You mean, in the sleeping sector?' I asked her.

'No, behind it,' she responded.

To me, the blocks seemed to mirror one another over and over again, and this mirror land looked endless. I believed there was no such thing as 'behind it'. From Vilena I learnt that there was another whole world surrounding our seemingly boundless zone of apartment buildings.

We didn't walk on Lenin Prospekt or other major streets when Vilena took us to her home. Instead, we walked across it, through the inner yards of the blocks, away from the center and away from the sleeping zone. I realized that while the tiny city center was surrounded by hundreds of social housing projects, this area in its turn was besieged by an immense concentration of wooden slums, hundreds, thousands of run-down, rotting *izbas*—this was where Vilena's home was.

'What is this place called?' I asked my friends quietly when stepping on the dirt roads, not much different from the streets of Taiga, 'Does it have a name?'

Vilena only grinned in response, but Andrey replied, 'They call it "the private sector".'

I looked at him questioningly.

'Private, because people here live in the separate, coal-warmed, handmade hovels, not in the communal blocks like ours.'

As we walked through the slums, I saw a few skinny stray dogs prowling around, children playing in the muddy snow, drunkards tottering here and there, prostitutes exposing their freezing flabby thighs to no one, gangs of mean-looking teens staring at us with spite.

Vilena was at ease with the surrounding misery, people seemed to know her and stayed away from us. In that context, her black eyeliner, her long, heavy coat, her sharp manners seemed to be very appropriate. It became obvious where her sarcasm towards the glamour of the gymnasium came from.

'Isn't Yagunovka somewhere nearby?' Andrey asked Vilena. That settlement was indeed twenty minutes away, she admitted.

'Let's go have a look.'

We walked further and further through the slums . . . There was no road under our feet, only mushy blackness. There was not a single sound, not a single feature or colour that wouldn't depress you. You didn't want to look around. You wanted it all to disappear. You were scared and you were ashamed of your own clean hands.

'Here,' Andrey said when we reached some wasteland, 'here is the place. Yagunovka.'

He took out his cigarettes, lit one and passed it to Vilena. They smoked quietly.

I looked around: in the distance, bare forests climbed the snowy hills while behind us the smoke of the city was rising. A few hovels lay scattered over the wasteland. I couldn't really see any settlement, just a vast, palling emptiness.

'This was the place of mass execution,' Andrey's voice cut through the silence.

I stared at him.

He continued.

'Through the thirties, forties, fifties, simple Russian people, the dwellers of our city and the surrounds, were brought here in groups to be executed. On a regular basis.'

'Here?' I asked, 'In this place?'

'Yes, Alexey. Here.'

I looked down at the black snow under my feet.

'Twenty minutes walk from the city.'

Up to that day I had always believed, I was sure, that all those gulags, the Red Terror, the Great Purge, Stalin, Khrushchev, KGB were part of some other, distant reality. It was not right here, under my feet, but somewhere else, far away, far in the past. At least, this was the impression I had formed from our history classes: that gulags had been only few in number, that the victims had been 'dangerous elements', that all of that had been left behind, in someone else's world.

Nowadays we were expected to be proud of our homeland, we were supposed to repeat docilely slogans from the billboards: 'We love our city!', 'We are proud of our homeland!', 'We thank the President for our happy childhood!' Until that day, I had doubted what Andrey and Vilena had been telling me. I'd thought they'd been massively exaggerating.

'Have you heard how the locals made a discovery at this place recently?' Andrey asked me. 'The people of the private sector needed some wood to repair their *izbas*. So they came to this abandoned village, Yagunovka, and started to gather up the old logs that were once used for the barracks but by now were just rotting on the ground. They wanted to build new homes with them, you understand?'

I nodded.

'Then they saw some scribbling on the surface of those logs. There were words, names, curses . . . Those were the last prayers, the pleas for help, the damning spells laid on the Party . . . Some fifty years ago, locked in the barracks here, only five or six kilometers away from the city, the condemned comrades spent their last hours scribbling notes on wood.'

Andrey paused.

Vilena kept smoking, looking away.

I listened.

'So when our contemporaries made such a lovely discovery, they called the police. Special Services came next and immediately set fire to the logs. They burned them all straightaway.'

'No evidence—no crime.'

'No man—no problem.'

'All as bequeathed to us by Great Stalin.'

$$※$$

My mother noticed that I was spending more and more time roaming the streets with my new friends. She asked me about Andrey. She wanted to know what he was like, what sort of family he came from, but I didn't know much. Andrey had never invited me home, nor had I ever heard him speak about his parents. It didn't seem strange to me at first, but with the passing of time, I did notice that Andrey went to great lengths to avoid the subject. I knew there must be some reason for his never mentioning his mom and dad. I was afraid to ask him directly so one day, when the two of us had also become close friends, I asked Vilena instead.

'He hasn't told you?' she gave me her usual smirk. 'Andrey's folks work at the FSB.'

A shiver ran through my body.

At home, I talked to my mother about it. I wanted to know if the FSB was what I thought it was. She confirmed my suspicions.

Ever since the Bolsheviks had established their secret security service, the so-called Cheka, which was responsible for punishing those who disagreed, for establishing the Gulag system, for destroying some twenty million lives—that organization had evolved and, with time, changed its name multiple times to disguise its incarnation. Andrey's parents both worked for the satanic institution that he talked about so often with so much contempt.

I remembered all the fierce speeches he had given me about the Great Purge, the mass executions, the Patriarch's profiteering and involvement with the KGB. I wrote in my diary that Andrey was a hypocrite, being so furious while coming himself from such a background.

Then, realizing that he had never said a word to me about his family, I wondered whether he simply felt ashamed of it. With time, as we grew closer and he was more open with me, it became clear that Andrey was not only ashamed but scared of his parents.

On a regular basis, his mother and father practiced on him the investigative techniques they had learnt at their KGB school. While his dad asked the questions ('Have you been involved in anything illegal?', 'Have you missed any classes?', 'Have you smoked?'), his mother held her right palm on Andrey's back and her left hand on his pulse. He never told me what exactly happened if there was any sweat on his back or the wrong number of heartbeats in his veins.

Understanding and trusting him more and more, I brought Andrey home and introduced him to my mom. She seemed happy that I had finally made a friend. We spent many evenings in my room, talking about everything, doing homework together, learning to rely on each other.

After a few months, I dared question Andrey about another matter that had been bothering me from the beginning.

'Are your parents the reason why the geographer treats you so . . . ?' I asked Andrey about our teacher Leonid Josephovich.

'Treats me how?' Andrey blushed slightly.

'I don't know . . . The geographer never picks on you, never humiliates you, never even asks to see your homework . . . Is he scared of your folks?' I suggested.

'Scared? Him? He's the governor's personal friend. He's the author of our region's bloody anthem. He can say or do whatever he pleases.'

We dropped the subject and didn't return to it for some time, until one day at the gymnasium the geographer passed by as Andrey and I were chatting in the corridor. There was a boy walking next to him, no more than ten years old. Leonid Josephovich was so absorbed in his conversation with that boy that he didn't even notice us.

'That must be a new one,' Andrey said quietly.

'What do you mean, *a new one*?'

Later that day, in the darkness, in the calmness of my room, Andrey unrolled for me the geographer's maps: the most respected teacher at our school, the governor's friend, the author of the anthem, that repulsive, sallow, senile man picked a boy to his taste each year; the geographer brought the little boys over to his flat for extracurricular activities, showering them with gifts, feeding them sweets, molesting them.

'How do you know all this?' I struggled to believe it was true.

'I saw a framed photograph of that new boy in the geographer's bedroom,' he replied.

'What were *you* doing in the geographer's bedroom?'

Andrey offered me many reasons, anxious to explain himself. He told me that his parents admired the geographer, that Leonid Josephovich had taken him a few times on Youth Center trips, that Leonid Josephovich had helped him with his studies . . . I didn't know what to think.

'It's absolutely disgusting! He is absolutely disgusting!' I said, overwhelmed by it all.

'Oh, yes, he is,' Andrey confirmed with a strained smile. 'He has food all over his place, candies everywhere, he buys little boys' clothing all the time . . .'

'What do you mean? He wears it?' I was way too naive to understand the shades of it.

'No, silly, to give it to his little boyfriends,' Andrey said, 'He usually chooses ones that come from poor families or have some troubles at home. He talks to the boys' parents, first, offering to take care of their children, to help them with their studies. He tells them, "Oh, your boy is so talented. A little help from a teacher, and he has a reserved place at the university." Normally, parents happily give their consent. And he does help, by the way. All of the boys he has lain with got excellent grades, and not only for the geography class.'

None of that nonsense would settle in my mind.

'And you . . . ? Do you . . . ?' I didn't know how to put it, how to phrase it so as not to hurt Andrey.

'Oh, I'm too old for him! Thank God,' he laughed.

'But didn't you tell me that he had taken you on some trips? Did he ever try to . . . ?' I didn't finish that question because I saw Andrey turn red, nervous. Then he summoned all his courage and unburdened his mind rapidly.

'Well, on the train, for example, he was always arranging things in such a way that I had to sleep in the same compartment with him. He'd bribe the train conductor to give us a cabin for two,' then Andrey's voice changed, he was back to his normal, sober state, 'But no, when he tried to get closer, I pushed him away.'

Back then I believed it all. I believed everything he said. I couldn't imagine that Andrey was one of the molested boys. He never looked like a victim to me. Yet, later on, I came back to the subject again and again, and gradually things became clear.

Andrey was from a two-parent, well-to-do family. A two-parent, well-to-do family of KGB agents. Andrey's parents were very protective of their single child. They were obsessed with security, scared of someone affecting their son in a bad, indecent, un-Soviet way—and that was exactly the reason why, when the most respected teacher of the Humanities Gymnasium, the author of the regional anthem, the director of the Youth Center, had shown up on their doorstep, offering his help in educating and protecting their gifted son, Andrey's parents were very pleased. Ecstatic when they learnt that the geographer occasionally dined with the governor.

From the age of nine, Andrey had accompanied Leonid Josephovich on most of his trips, followed all his courses, and paid him private visits for extracurricular activities on a regular basis.

'You are lucky you are light-haired and fair-skinned,' my friend told me, 'Leonid Josephovich prefers the swarthy ones.'

On that miserable mid-April night, however, when Andrey first dared to unveil his feelings on the sixteen-story balcony overlooking the city, I had no idea about any of that—about the geographer's bedroom, about the Youth Center trips, about the KGB parents. Back then I didn't even know my own self, let alone what part I could possibly play in this strange, increasingly puzzling new world.

'So . . . what do you think?' he had asked me on the balcony, suddenly turning away from the bleak view and facing me. 'You think you feel something in return towards me? Or you think I am mad?'

He was just like a child in that moment. I looked at him, but he was just like a child.

'No, I don't think you are mad,' I responded, 'But . . . but I never saw this coming. I thought we were just friends . . . I've never known that you . . . That we . . .'

'Oh, forget it!' he grew angry.

'Just give me one night,' I begged him, 'let me think it all over, ok?'

Andrey turned away from me, hurried to the elevator, pressed frantically on the button any number of times.

'Think *what* over?'

Inside, the walls of the tiny lift were covered with obscenities and it smelled nasty. The lift crawled its way down. I wanted to say something to Andrey, to make him feel better, but the right words would not come. He stared fixedly up at the dim lamp above us. His hands nervously squeezed the sleeves of his winter coat.

We walked silently back home. It had got much darker in the meantime. We reached the place where our ways parted.

'I'll see you tomorrow at school,' I told him as gently as I could.

He didn't say anything, merely turned abruptly, crossed Lenin Prospekt and disappeared around the corner.

Alone, at home that night, I let it all flood in: the evening, the balcony, his words. With the fire-bird throbbing in the cage of my chest, I set down in my diary, in my childish handwriting:

Today Andrey and I went for a long walk as we always do after school. As usual he told me about things I didn't know, showed me places I hadn't seen. At night we reached the sixteen-story block, we climbed up . . . Then, something happened . . . There he told me . . . he told me that he l . . . m . . . What should I do now? How should I respond? What does one do when his best and only friend opens his heart this way?

I had no answers that night. I closed my diary and went to sleep. But the next day and many days after that, in my literary attempts to pair off each one of my classmates with another, I wasn't suffering anymore, trying to imagine whom Andrey could love and who could love him in return, for his love had been found in the most unexpected place.

❦

From that April on, through the following spring months and the summer, my classmate introduced me to many other new and bewildering things.

First of all, he brought me films—those of Francois Ozon, Lars von Trier, Tom Tykwer, Pedro Almodovar, Peter Greenaway, Gregg Araki—strange names with enough Rs to make you stumble along the way, not let you pass untouched. Those stories opened up for me worlds that I had never thought existed. How could those VHSs with their strange bright covers appear in the midst of Siberia? By what force, in whose hands were they brought into our land? More importantly, where did they come from? What soil had nurtured these seeds? Who were those people, those creators? Were they as wild as their creations? What had inspired them to tell those stories? Stories that had nothing to do with either the frightening reality around me or with the distant tales of Tolstoy, Chekhov, Leskov so familiar to me. Was it real life that was depicted in those movies? Where was that reality hiding itself from me?

Watching the films Andrey brought me, I would draw in a surprised 'Ah!' every ten minutes, my eyes would open wider, my heart would pause—especially at *Dancing in the Dark, Sitcom, Fucking Åmål, Princess and the Warrior*—but in addition to the shock there was also relief. It was as if another part of my brain was being activated and I could drink from new springs of energy from then on.

Watching Almodovar or Ozon was like discovering a new land: it was Columbus approaching America, it was Gagarin entering space. I had thousands of questions for Andrey. 'Why is the camera shaking?' 'Why are the colours so strange?' 'What is the purpose of that music?' 'Why all that suffering, shown with so much passion, as if one's supposed to enjoy another person's pain?' 'What kind of family is that?' 'Is that true love?' 'Why are they all naked?' My questions were countless. My classmate was often left smiling, sometimes laughing at my innocence, sometimes simply proud to be the one to explain it all to me.

Very soon I was head over heels in love with that universe, especially with Ozon's and Almodovar's. I learnt their vocabulary, I felt every heartbeat of their characters. I knew what those artists wanted to tell me with every melody, every shade of colour. At the same time, they left so many questions unanswered, and I felt grateful for that, I didn't want to be told what to think, what to do exactly with all the excitement they had provoked in me. Me—had they ever thought of me watching those films while sitting in the low-ceilinged tiny flat of a run-down five-story social housing unit in the heart of Siberia?

One of the most puzzling questions which emerged as a result of my sudden dip into the cinematographic world was connected with *Life is Beautiful*, *The Pianist*, *Schindler's List*, and other brilliant Holocaust films.

'There seem to be so many great movies about Hitler's genocide of the Jews,' I expressed my concern to Andrey, 'but where are the films about Stalin's extermination of millions of his own citizens? Do you know at least one such film?'

That question of mine is left unanswered to this day.

After the movies came the music. It was a divine pleasure to hear—for the very first time!—the voices of Ella Fitzgerald (she sounded just like my grandmother), Nina Simone (like my mom), Billie Holiday (a sister I never had); to dance to Pet Shop Boys or to Madonna's first records—a first for me as well as for them.

Then, came the books! Even though we were fully loaded up with the classics in Tamara Alexeyevna's class, Andrey brought me many titles that were never talked about at the Humanities Gymnasium. One author who touched me deeply was Slava Mogutin.

Everything we read at school—no matter how much I loved my Tolstoy and Akhmatova—was very, very far from our world. Those great novels, those wonderful poems were, though eternal, the songs of another time, one very distant from our post-Soviet reality. To start with, none of those writers had ever walked closer than some two thousand miles to the place we lived our lives; even if many of them—from Pushkin to Brodsky—were sentenced to exile in Tobolsk or Omsk, that was as far from our place as Lisbon was from Warsaw. Geography was the simple reason why Andrey and I fell in love with Slava Mogutin. He grew up on the Chemists Prospekt—one of the most dreadful ghettoes in our city. He was the only writer we knew who was born in Siberia, had managed to escape it, and had published a few books abroad.

What Andrey introduced me to was so astonishing for a simple reason: no global web of wires had caught us yet in its nets. No Ellen DeGeneres had ever appeared all gay and proud on our televisions. Even Elton John and Freddie Mercury were still straight in Russia. There was no information of such a kind—of *that* kind—available to the simple folk of our country.

To get in touch with my friend, I still had to go out to a red phone booth at the corner of our block, phone the operator (that complete stranger!) and dictate a private message—which the operator then forwarded to my friend's pager. There simply was no access to any alternative worlds for the people of my kind unless . . . unless you had a friend like Andrey.

An even more surprising treasure that Andrey once found for me was the two thick volumes by Igor Kon, the Saint Petersburg sexologist. The *oeuvre* was romantically titled 'Moonlight at Dawn: Love that Dare Not Speak Its Name'. Published in limited edition in the first years after Perestroika, Kon's impressive work tried to explain to the Russian public the inexplicable: why love takes different forms. Each chapter, filled with surveys and case studies, ended with examples taken from the private lives of the dead and famous: Tchaikovsky, Nureyev, Rimbaud, Sappho, Proust, Wilde, Genet, Tsvetaeva and even James Dean,

T. E. Lawrence, Valentino, James Baldwin, and, to top it all, Shakespeare, Michelangelo, Leonardo da Vinci . . . Much later I realized how lucky it was that Igor Kon had managed to work on and publish his magnum opus in the 1990s: those were the short years after the collapse of Soviet tyranny and before the establishment of the new regime when the kind of love the name of which had only been whispered until then could be talked about.

The names of da Vinci and Shakespeare (not to mention Ozon, Kon, or Araki) were not familiar to young people on the streets of our Siberian town. Nobody could blame them for that. I knew where those kids came from. After all, we didn't come from very different places.

After the collapse of the Soviet Union, the propaganda billboards with messages like 'Together We Step into A Happy Socialist Future' and 'Lenin's Words Are Always Alive' were rapidly replaced with capitalist ones like 'Discover Heavenly Joy' and 'Be The Part of Generation Next'. Except that Generation Next could not afford heavenly joy.

In the 1990s and the early aughts, juvenile violence flooded the streets of cities across Russia. Those guys always looked the same: close-cropped heads, scarred white faces, shabby black sports suits, a cigarette behind the ear. Soon that appearance became to me what the swastika was to Jews: the sign of utmost horror.

They were between ten and eighteen years of age. Some of them had been to prison. Most of them had already adopted prison lifestyle and codes of behavior. All of them reminded me of skinheads. In fact, I didn't quite know the difference.

Perhaps, the skinheads had some rationale for violence, for killing. The only rules and values of those Russian boys were as follows: never act alone, hold tight to each other; the stronger survive, the weaker perish; spare the life of the young woman—she's sacred; God forgives everything, a life is worth nothing; kill the faggots—cleanse the Earth. The immense number of fellows like these all around the country, or outside Moscow city center at least, was such that they were given a special name—'*gops*', or '*gopniks*'. Millions of them acted the same way, looked the same way, fought the same way, killed the same way—and thus were impossible for the police to identify. Not that the police could care less.

'Why are they called *"gops"*?' I asked Andrey, 'why are there so many of them?' He didn't know the answers but together we did some research at the library and discovered an entry in one of the dictionaries. The term '*gop*', we learnt, was an abbreviation of '*Gosudarstvennoye Obshezshitye Proletariata*'. 'The State-Run Dormitory for the Proletariat' was first created in Saint Petersburg (a.k.a. the capital of culture) soon after the 1917 Revolution, to accommodate the peasants then emigrating in thousands from their villages to the city. These newcomers, under the chaotic government of Lenin, quickly turned into regular street rogues. Hence, the residents of Saint Petersburg went on calling all young, troublemaking rascals '*gops*', after the state-run institution where some of them spent their nights.

'But . . . if they're called "gops", while we are called "fags" . . . can we be that different from each other?' I asked Andrey.

'Of course not,' he answered. 'But it doesn't stop us from hating each other. In fact, maybe that's one reason why we do.'

Nearly a century had passed since the Revolution. The country went through a World War and the Great Purge, both resulting in millions of Russians being sent to labour camps and regular prisons. The simple folk quickly adopted prison morals, gradually bringing jail standards and language into everyday life. The collapse of the Soviet Union and the turmoil which followed only reinstigated the rise of the *gops*. After all, most of the gulags were finally shut down with millions of ex-convicts streaming onto the streets of Siberia. The capitals, Moscow and Saint Petersburg, were too far, too hard to reach while the Siberian cities and villages started to resemble limitless open-air prisons, where the only fence was the wall of taiga, and the only supervisor—the empty sky.

During a century of active development, life in the Soviet prisons and labour camps gave birth to the strictest code of behavior known simply as 'The Prison Code' with its own hierarchy, laws, and modes of punishment. Of course, originally this code was meant to function only behind bars. However, with a big percentage of the population having served sentences and with the collapse of the Gulag system, 'The Prison Code' became the norm in the everyday life of Siberia. By 2000, ex-convicts not only enjoyed living free by their own standards, but established their own political party, and had their own genre of music, romantically titled '*chanson*'.

A day, literally a single day would not pass without a gang of teenagers stopping me and Andrey right on the street, in the middle of a crowd, at a bus stop, or in a kindergarten yard (the closest semblance to a park in our neighbourhood). They would surround us, force us to a pitch-dark corner, insult and humiliate us, threaten us with a beating, sometimes with a knife, and in one instance with tearing off my ear by means of a plumber's wrench, before carrying away our money, clothes, or whatever else we might have had which was to their liking.

Each time Andrey and I were approached that way, we were interrogated in the same way as newcomers were questioned on their first day in prison.

'*Who* are you in life?' the typical inquiry would begin.

And after you'd mumbled something like, 'I'm just a regular school pupil,' another demand from prison would come.

'Prove it!'

You had to know the correct answers to give. You had to present yourself in an appropriate way. If you didn't know how to 'prove' your words, you'd be 'downed'.

In the established hierarchy of 'The Prison Code', the lowest caste consisted of 'the downed'. It was a prison term for those who were raped by cellmates on a regular basis. In Russian prisons 'the downed' were not allowed to eat with the others, they were given the most shameful tasks and held at a distance. Anyone who touched one of 'the downed' (rape and beating did not count) or even shared an object with him would be automatically relegated to the same level.

'The downed' would often be marked by tattoos (a spot or a triangle above the upper lip) or by having his front teeth knocked out. In short, there was nothing worse than being a 'downed one' in the moral mindset of Russian convicts: homosexuals, who had chosen to be identified as such voluntarily, were considered lower than animals and were meant to be erased from the surface of the Earth.

By the time Andrey and I turned sixteen, all these prison-originated codes were fully integrated into the everyday life of Siberia.

❦

Having no better place to celebrate the occasion, on the morning of Andrey's birthday I came to the sixteen-story block with my pockets filled with colourful rubber balloons. As usual, I begged my way in and proceeded upstairs, level by level, blowing up and then attaching one balloon to each balcony railing. When my task was finished and Andrey came to the building, as was agreed in advance, there stretched above him this colourful stream of balloons—sixteen of them, one for each level and for each of his years. I was waiting for him on the top floor.

This tall tower made our best hiding place. In relatively good weather we stayed on its balconies and watched the town; in freezing cold, we hid in the dark of the staircase, on the steps in between the levels. The stench of it, the dimmed light, the scratched walls, the spiraling smoke of his cigarettes, our recurring terror at the sound of climbing or descending footsteps—the backdrop to our burgeoning love.

The echoey room of the Theater of the Jubilee, with its inevitably bad but very distant film and its endless rows of empty chairs—served as the shelter to our first touch. In the dark, he covered my hand with his, he caressed it. I responded, the heat mounting under my skin. The bliss. The fire. The painful longing . . . And yet nothing more, nothing but the burning pressure of his right hand on my left.

The darkness, the timidity, the gentleness—proved a false protection. Gossip about the unusually warm friendship between the two boys from the Humanities Gymnasium spread across the streets of our city in the course of a month.

By the doors of our school, they waited morning and evening.

I begged Andrey not to fight, not to react, to agree silently to anything, to submit.

'If you start fighting back, they will kill you.'

'They put no value on life, yours or their own.'

'Bear it all. Keep quiet.'

'Give them all you've got. It is your resistance that they want.'

'Let them feel the glory of the victory before you are under their feet.'

'Run as fast as you can when they are not looking.'

That was our adopted code of behavior.

But not only ours.

Andrey told me about a particular bench on Spring Street—second on your right as you're coming from the direction of the theater—where if you sat and waited long enough, you could make friends with those similar to you.

He said that in our local newspaper's classifieds, one could always find an ad or two that mentioned 'watching Cadinot together'. This was code for a gay date, Cadinot being the French erotica filmmaker.

No, we were not the only ones. And yet we were on our own.

We learnt to visually scan the street at any given moment in search of possible danger or for a possible refuge: a shop, a pharmacy, an open staircase door, where we could run and hide in case of an attack, perhaps buzz the door of a stranger, pretending that that was our home, pretending that we did have someone who could help. Though in fact, we could only count on ourselves.

Ask for help?

Ask whom?

Try to explain to the police the grounds on which you were abused?

Try to explain it to your parents? To your own KGB agents?

Try to find the shelter in the teachers' room?

One day when, after classes, we learnt that once again the school was surrounded by *gops* waiting for us to come out, we had no other option but to talk to the principal in search of protection.

'Oh, please, don't exaggerate!' was all we heard in response. 'It can't be as bad as you describe! Also, you might feel better if you act and dress more discreetly. You know how people feel when someone stands out?'

'And do you know how it feels?' I wanted to reply in response, 'do you know how it feels, when every time you start your day, every time you step out of your home, go to school or to work, you look around and realize that people detest you—do you know that feeling?'

Do you know how it feels, when you don't *do* anything, you don't attack anyone, you don't insult anyone, you don't even say a word, yet these simple people already wish you dead? Young and old, rich and poor, those who have never seen your face before and those who see you daily—these simple people of your own sex and colour reject you for the way you are, for the way you look, for the way you walk. Do you know how that feels? Have you ever felt this way in your entire life . . . ?

As Andrey went on fighting with the principal, demanding that she call the police or do something, I kept on staring at her face, asking my silent questions.

Yes, most of the school knew all about me and Andrey. People were talking, asking questions, and we stubbornly refused to lie. When they asked us, 'Is that true . . . ?' we would respond, 'Yes, it is.'

We had Arthur Rimbaud in our heads. We had Oscar Wilde on our minds. We wanted to keep our dignity by staying honest. We didn't see anything shameful in our love.

Tamara Alexeyevna, our literature teacher, was the only staff member who protected the pair of us. Perhaps it was because she knew better than anyone else of Mayakovsky living with the Briks, of Kuzmin's novels, of Cocteau, of Auden, of Cavafy, of Michelangelo and da Vinci. And of those 126 love sonnets written by Shakespeare to a young man.

But she was the only one. The rest of the gymnasium staff, including the geographer by that stage, humiliated us.

One day, when Andrey sent a message on my pager to let me know that he was sick at home, I attended on my own the obligatory class with a title I could never quite grasp—'The Basics of Vital Activity Security'. Only boys had to attend that lesson, while girls, I suppose, were given some instructions on domestic science or childbirth. Our teacher, an austere military man in his sixties, always in uniform, mostly talked to us about the importance of serving in the army. The obligatory two years military service—from which some returned handicapped while others came back in coffins even in peacetime—

awaited all male pupils after they had graduated from school. Male university students were drafted after they'd completed their degrees.

After that 'Vital Activity' class, when the military man had finished with the theoretical part, the pupils started asking him questions. The very first question, the concern of everyone, was about what made you ineligible for serving in the army.

'Well, you may only be freed from military service if you have some serious disease like tuberculosis, epilepsy, schizophrenia, or *gomoseksualism*,' the teacher kindly explained, while my classmates laughed, pointing at me. 'Yes, yes, there's nothing funny about it. Pederasty is the very worst shame that can fall on a family. It is very difficult to cure. Therefore, such individuals must be isolated so as not to infect the others. So, faggots . . . excuse me, pederasts, do not go into the army.'

Even if a teacher wanted to use less obscene terminology, he simply couldn't because Russian vocabulary lacks words to describe gay persons without insulting them. Every now and then, our native tongue would absorb a seemingly neutral term from English—'gay', 'homosexual', 'LGBT'—only to see these words turned into abuse by the population overnight: 'gei', 'gomoseki', 'shit-covered lgbt-shniki'.

The teacher added, however, that in order to avoid army service based on homosexuality, one had to deliver proofs of that particular state of being to the authorities. 'Prove it!' the Russian army code demanded in exactly the same fashion as 'The Prison Code' did. What those proofs were supposed to be remained a mystery.

By the end of that 'Vital Activity' class, I felt destroyed, I felt that not only were the people around pushing me down, but so too were those who were above, who were supposed to be in charge, who were meant to help, to guide, to protect you—your teachers, your supervisors, your police officers. To say nothing of my classmates, who gathered around and taunted me that day as I tried to escape.

'You'd better come up with some proofs, you've heard it?'

'If not, you'll be fucked to death once you're in the army!'

'You're faggot, aren't you? Or what do you even call yourself?'

How to respond to this? What, indeed, are you supposed to call yourself when your own language is against you?

I remember putting my headphones on and playing music loudly, very loudly, to block out their voices. Back in those days, my favourite band was t.A.T.u. That was a music duo, without which—I'm sure of this fact now—I wouldn't have managed to stay sane in those years.

In spite of that aggressive, oppressive society, those years in Russia were still surprisingly liberal in the sense that the media was mostly independent, the ideological vector was still set towards liberalization, and it seemed that even if today was no good, then tomorrow would be much better.

It was also the time when t.A.T.u. released their music album. These were two girls from Moscow, no older than sixteen, singing about their love for each other and their fight for the sake of it. In the famous music video of their first single, the two girls in school uniforms are shown kissing in the rain behind barbed wire with an outraged crowd pointing and screaming at them from the other side of the fence. At the end of the video the girls discover an opening in the wall behind them and, holding hands, they walk off, leaving the angry crowd on the other side of the fence.

These teenage songs helped me drag myself through the oppressive school, through the violent streets, past the junkies on our eerie staircase until I finally reached home and locked myself in my safe misery.

In their second video, t.A.T.u. hijack a truck and drive off through the snow-filled land. *200 km/h in the Wrong Lane* was the title of the album—just as it was the spirit of my own days.

For the *gops*, Andrey and I were the easiest, most exciting targets. They found every possible reason to knock us down, to empty our pockets, to piss on our clothes. The title 'monster' thrown at me from a deformed pustulous mouth (with some teeth missing and others substituted with fake steel) close-up in my face and reeking of last night's dried fish and this morning's cheap beer—became the most common compliment attached to my identity. It took me a long time to learn how to raise my eyes and look back at those aggressors in an effort to understand what was driving them, where all that malice was coming from, what made those simple people, people of my own race, sex, colour, language, and nationality so inexplicably aggressive.

Who were those *gops*? Where did they pick up these beastly mindsets and methods? Where did they go to school? *Did* they go to school? Where were their families? Who were their parents? There cannot be any excuse for violence, especially for routine violence. Yet I did try to understand what force was driving those hundreds of hate-filled young men.

Could it be a feeling of guilt, acquired from their years in prison or in the army, mixed with bitter envy? If once, driven by your own animalistic impulse, you have violated another man, what thoughts and feelings would swamp you when you came across someone who reminded you of your years behind bars? And when you saw someone who seemed to live in freedom, who seemed to be more hopeful, to have some chance of a brighter future? How hard it must be *not* to long to smash those chances, those hopes, that freedom against a cement wall.

Trying to understand them, I came across a scary statistic: in the decade following the collapse of the USSR, the death rate among Russian citizens increased nearly tenfold. There was no clear explanation for why people were dying. The death toll was similar to the numbers during the Second World War, only there was no such war in the nineties. It was said that the overall life expectancy at age fifteen in Russia was at the same level as that in Ethiopia, Gambia, and Somalia, only there wasn't as much wealth in those countries as there was in Moscow alone. Where was all that wealth? Who had ever seen it?

The researchers kept asking, why did Russians keep dying? And the only answer they could find was that they died because they didn't see the point in living. Because they saw no value in life, their own lives or anyone else's. Because the Soviet Union kept teaching its citizens, decade after decade, that their individual lives were worthless. Because people witnessed the great confusion of the post-Soviet leaders, who changed course over and over again: it was obvious that even those in charge of this troubled country had no clue what to do with it. Those who could—the mafia leaders, the oligarchs, the governmental officials—raped the miserable land, squeezed all the oil and gas out of it and ran abroad to put their dirty money in clean Swiss banks.

People, simple people, were left with nothing: no money, no certainty, but most importantly, no hope. My mother, looking at the life around her, kept saying to me year after year, 'Nothing good will ever happen here. Nothing good.'

How scary is that . . . Just think of it!

Nothing . . . Ever . . . Here . . .

The *gops*, those young, cruel, angry Russian men, were not just looking for money in our jackets. They scanned the city, too, their eyes searching for some form, some evidence of life, some hope under the skin of those who seemed a little bit more hopeful than them.

That was the basis, the meaning of those scary statistics.

All that made us climb over and over again up into our sheltered place, on that sixteenth-story balcony, from where Andrey and I could hardly see our fellow denizens, crawling like zombies over the city— and they definitely couldn't see us. We enjoyed being above it all. We were determined to stay alive, to stay hopeful.

But were there any statistics, was there any research ever done on how many people were 'downed' in those years in Russia? Was anyone counting how many homosexuals were violently killed? Did anyone ever bother to count *those* deaths?

No answer . . .

Silence.

Nobody talks.

Nobody stands up.

Neighbours do not report. Police do not investigate. Media do not cover.

Nobody counts how many people are humiliated, beaten, stabbed, destroyed for being queer across the country. Russian people destroyed by other Russian people on a daily basis all across the nation.

And nobody counts.

Even the victims' families do not know or do not admit the true reasons for the violence. Because even the families humiliate, beat, reject, destroy their sons and daughters for the very same reason.

And their neighbours . . .

And their friends . . .

Years pass by, things change, hopefully, for the better.

Families and friends of the victims of mass persecutions on a religious or racial basis speak out, seek justice, raise monuments in memory of those fallen.

But will the families and friends of persecuted homosexuals ever speak out?

A Black mother will not say that her child was not Black: what will the mother of a gay woman or a gay man say?

Jewish people stand up for Jewish people. Black people stand up for Black people. Gay men and women keep hiding in countries like mine because, unlike minorities who share the same race or the same religion, when one gay person stands up for another, only then everyone suspects that he or she must be gay, too.

'Don't provoke,' they whisper. 'Don't show off . . . If you want to stay alive.'

So, tell me now . . . Is this how it always goes? Is this the logic of life? Does evil always walk hand in hand with good? Do the two run parallel all the way, like the ski tracks in the pine forest? Do they ever cross or become one at some point? Or have I got it all wrong?

If the 1998 crisis together with the so-called organized criminal groups had not terrorized my quiet hometown and if my mother's shop had not been burned down, would we have stayed in Taiga and never moved to the big city?

And if the geographer had his maps straightened out and his compasses well-fixed, might all those boys of his have never found themselves confused, not taken the difficult paths, but instead all be married happily with children?

If the streets of that city had not been so terrifying and if the human beings down there had been more humane, would we never have had the need to hide on that balcony, and never seen the world from above?

And Andrey, would he have never been standing there, on that cold, black mid-April night, facing the bleak town, too scared to look at me, while trembling, while asking, 'And you? Do you think I am mad? Do you think *you* might love me?'

Chapter Seven

Better Places

From then on it was the three of us against the world. The streets, their grimy cars and nasty stench; the crowd, its hateful glances and sharp elbows; even nature itself, its unbearable winters and stifling summers—I felt like all of that was against me, didn't want me there, was pushing me away. The only way I had learnt to resist it all was to hate it back.

Love did not deserve to be conferred on such a place: one where people killed one another over a half-empty bottle of vodka; a country where those in charge were glad to toss such a bottle into a crowd and then laughingly observe the murderous rage which ensued; a land where nature, the same nature that was meant to be above us, thought to be helping us, guiding us, feeding us, was instead the cruelest, most oppressive force. With its frostbites and snowstorms, with its yearly floods and summer heat, with its forests and swarming mosquitoes, its barren ground on which one had to toil like a slave in order to harvest a single potato, its temperatures that dropped to minus forty in December only to climb up to plus forty in July—nature itself seemed to be hating me, hating us, hating everything that simply wished to stay alive.

I remember standing with my mother at a bus stop one typical winter morning. The buses didn't have any reliable schedule, one never knew when a bus would come or if it ever would. It was minus thirty-five and my mother, giggling in a slightly hysterical way, kept jumping up and down on the spot.

'Jump, Alioshenka, jump!'

On such a day in Siberia, unless you moved your feet, unless you rubbed your cheeks, played with your fingers inside your mittens, you would lose your feet, cheeks, fingers to frostbite within an hour. We had already been waiting for the bus for some thirty minutes at that station, and before that we had had to make our way there.

My mother tried to smile, but I knew she was just playing the hero, as usual. The lens of her glasses had turned to ice, her cheeks were not pink anymore but almost white. Laughing no matter what, ignoring danger, staying absurdly positive—that was *her* way of fighting back.

Then the bus—a small, squat, Chinese vehicle, one of those sold to our region secondhand—finally appeared out of the smoky air. We needed to wave to make it stop and pick us up. But to wave, we had to know what the bus's number was (if you stopped the wrong one, you were cursed by the driver). But in order to know the number, we had to be able to read it first.

'What is it, Alexey? What's the number?'

The bus's windscreen was frozen, ice covering the piece of cardboard with the number on it. At the last moment we could read it— and it was the one we had been waiting for! We raised our hands, we jumped, we waved . . . but the bus passed by without even slowing down. We only caught a glimpse of its driver shrugging his shoulders— it was too late, he wouldn't stop at the last moment because the road was glassy, and the brakes wouldn't help.

I moaned, feeling that I had no more strength to resist the cold.

'Oh, don't worry, Alioshenka, there will be another one,' she would merely say, 'Jump! Keep jumping! Jump!'

Waiting for some magic vehicle to appear out of the smog and to pick me up on the way to a better place seemed to be all I hoped for in those months. I remember going through a Moscow magazine one evening. It was the December issue and the magazine was filled with holiday-related features. One full spread was dedicated to photo reportage of how people from different places around the world celebrated New Year: a ball was descending on Times Square; people were gathering on the

Champs-Elysées; in Tokyo youngsters wore glasses in the shape of the year 2002; fireworks exploded over Sydney while Moscow's Red Square was filled with red lights... And then, in the very center of that colourful, joyful collage, there was a small picture with the name of my own town in the corner. I couldn't believe my eyes! The name of the place we called home was scarcely even known to people in Moscow. But there it was! Surrounded by images from Paris, New York, Sydney...

Someone had surely wanted to have a laugh, plumping my city down in the very center of that glossy magazine's New Year spread. The photo featured a tattooed, half-naked, bald drunkard squatting in the snowdrift in his underwear, trying to light a sparkler but with no success. Behind him were a run-down hut and a group of yellow-faced toothless Siberians giggling at their mate. I kept staring at that picture for ten, fifteen, twenty minutes . . . Everything around me seemed to slow down and it was then suddenly as if I was rising somehow, rising above the room, above the house, above the city and observing my own life from the skies.

And so there it was. My life in the eyes of the rest of the world: an alcohol-soaked Siberian, ridiculous, ugly, hopeless, in the midst of the snowdrifts, trying to make something more or less decent out of his life, and to no avail.

My classmates would just laugh at the image and turn to the next page, but oh, not me. Not us. Andrey and I recognized our own life in that photo—or what might become of it if we stayed on. I cut that picture out of the spread and attached it to the wall above my desk.

With time, I gradually began to realize what Andrey had meant to me, how deeply he had affected my life. Yes, he had opened up a whole new world for me. But what he'd also contributed to was the destruction of the actual, the real physical world that had surrounded me all those years. I felt as if he had lifted some veil which I had used to cover over so many things: no, I was never blind to the troubles that my family went through, but before Andrey, I'd accepted all these and other difficulties as the simple facts of life, as normality, as bad luck.

Since Andrey had talked to me about the history of our country and our cities and the way it'd been shaped by the KGB, Lenin, Stalin, Putin, I began to realize that there were some repetitive tendencies, some common patterns, a scary logic in the personal tragedies of my family and the general course of events in Russia. I started drawing connections between my mother's burnt store, all those squatting Slavs on the streets, and the bloated faces of officials on TV.

Andrey had passed on to me not only his bitter disappointment with the reality we happened to be born into but also the knowledge, the strong belief, the absolute conviction that reality was not the same everywhere. That there were better places, and the possibility of a better life. He had passed on to me that hope, and I clung to it in the way a drowning person clings to a lifebuoy. I kept reading the authors Andrey had introduced me to, I kept watching his VHSs, I spent hours every day learning English, because there was nothing I could do but believe that one day I would become the part of that other, better, kinder, or at least marginally more humane world.

I didn't have any actual, reasonable grounds for that hope, for believing that other places existed where I could live safely. With one exception. There had been a time—one brief moment out of time—when the two of us had had a chance to see the world outside Siberia with our own eyes.

On turning eighteen, Andrey and I became eligible to apply for an exit visa. In addition to holding a national passport, a Russian citizen wanting to travel abroad must apply for a special document from the state—an exit visa or 'foreign visits passport'—in order to be able to apply, in turn, for a special document from a foreign state—an entry visa—in order to leave Russia.

Back then Andrey's parents made no objection to the idea of his taking a short trip abroad. Nor, separately, did my mother. After all, he and I had just successfully finished school. We had been accepted into the local university, into the Faculty of Russian philology and journalism, and done so without the need for bribes or other financial transactions. Everyone was relieved. Had we failed to gain university entry, we would have been compelled to serve in the Russian army. Nobody wanted that. The so-called 'blue ticket', a precious, flimsy piece of paper stating that a young man was temporarily exempt from the military draft, was one of the documents required for an exit visa—luckily, now in our possession.

There remained one problem.

Andrey's parents knew nothing about me or about my relationship to their only son. They were intolerant of everything imported from the West—and being gay ranked high on that list. He was too scared to introduce me to them even as his friend. Telling them that we wanted to go abroad on a trip together was out of the question.

Andrey's solution was to ask our friend Vilena to pretend to be his girlfriend. A complete scenario was created: Andrey and Vilena appeared multiple times together in front of his parents, she played her role as a loving girlfriend, and Andrey gradually convinced his mom and dad that he was old enough to go on vacation without the company of Leonid Josephovich.

One summer morning, the two of them, Andrey and Vilena, were taken to the train station by his parents. The couple waved farewell to the big city and at the next station, my very own station in Taiga, Vilena got off the train. I was waiting for the couple there, right under the plaque commemorating Lenin's passing through the town. I quickly kissed Vilena goodbye before she took the bus back to the city, and I boarded the Trans-Siberian in her place. Finally, Andrey and I were reunited. How excited we were. How happy. Finally! Finally, we were on our way out!

⁂

For the outward-bound traveler, the first obstacle on the path to the promised land is the *provodnitza*. The spirit-sister of *konduktorsha*, the tram ticket controller, the *provodnitza* is the caretaker of a train carriage, typically a blunt, sturdy, ageless woman who, with one raised finger, stops train robberies and, with one glance, makes you do whatever she pleases. This frightening character takes care of her carriage— and every carriage has a *provodnitza*—like the most protective lioness, terrorizing the passengers more fiercely than Ivan the Terrible did his subjects. The train windows, the only air conditioning on the train, are under no circumstances to be touched, opened or closed. No matter if it is summer or winter, boiling heat or freezing cold, it is only she, the Trans-Siberian priestess, who can make such vital decisions as letting a narrow stream of air into or out of the compartment. Normally she keeps the windows tightly locked (unless they are broken and then you have to stuff your blankets, pillows, and clothes into the gap to prevent the gales from storming in).

The next awaiting nightmare consists of your fellow travelers, who constantly remind you just how far you still are from where you want to be. Given their presence, you're sometimes actually grateful to have the *provodnitza* around.

People who take the Trans-Siberian are usually of two types: old ladies with their salamis and pickles, and ex- or future convicts with their vodka and dried fish (since Tsarist times, the Trans-Siberian has been the vehicle which sentenced men have had to take on their way to or out of prison). One is naturally better off sticking to the first type of traveler, for after a day of heavy drinking the jailbirds often, according to some deeply rooted tradition, start knife-fighting. Only the *provodnitza* is able to calm them.

Then, of course, you have all sorts of mundane details which go along with simple Russian living: stinky socks and sweaty armpits (most of the carriages consist of single shared zones without doors or curtains); abrupt and unexpected stops (when one can fall from the upper berth and break one's ribs on the steel table below); and, for variety, days when the train doesn't stop at all, and one has to fast. No showers, no places to store food, no places to buy or to cook food, no electricity supply. A playful imagination can easily reproduce the combination of smells, sounds, and other atmospheric features that are inevitably created during a seven-day train ride in such conditions.

If you want to escape the nightmare, there are only two places of refuge: first, the tight space between the carriages, where the thick cigarette smoke never fails to unite the ex-convicts with the future ones;

and second, the toilet—Turkish-style, supplied with only a hole in the floor through which one can admire the rail-track passing underneath.

Neither Andrey nor I expected much from our train trip to Moscow. We were in fact luckier than many of our fellow passengers, having to endure only a three-day journey from our home city to the capital, not the full seven-day ride. Besides, we had a good time listening on our headphones to Zemfira and t.A.T.u., reading books, and talking quietly. On the other hand, we had nothing to eat except the dried fruits and biscuits which my mother had forced me to carry on board.

Andrey didn't expect much from Moscow either. But oh, I did. Not only from Moscow but from the entire European part of Russia! For some reason, I had a strong belief that as soon as the train crossed the Ural mountains—that natural border which separates East from West, Asia from Europe, *us* from *them*—everything would miraculously change. Up to that day I had cherished the dream, no, I had not doubted, not even for one moment, that the landscapes, the worlds of Pushkin, Leskov, Turgenev, still existed, if not in Siberia, then certainly over there, behind the mountains, in the European part of my country.

Those envisioned white churches crowned with golden tulip-heads, those fields of rye and poppy flowers, those picturesque wooden villages, those old men fishing peacefully by the pearl-like lakes—were all gone, had somehow vanished without leaving a trace of their ever having existed. Staring out from the train window hour after hour, day after day, I grew sadder and sadder, angrier and angrier. Nothing, absolutely nothing changed in those four thousand kilometers as we made our way across the continent. The entire country, from Finland to Japan, seemed to be one vast wretched field of tilted fences, broken *izbas*, abandoned factories, and polluted waters.

'Where, but where is it all?' I kept asking Andrey, looking at him with eyes wide open.

'Together with the Tsar's family, darling, rotting in the ground.'

Just as I was about to ask him how he could be so cruel, he added, 'Actually, I'm not even sure if it was any better in the time of the Tsars. Have you read Radishchev?'

On the third day we reached Moscow. By then I was trying to coach myself not to expect anything good to come from it (the charm of the boyars' capital, the nineteenth-century mansions, the palaces turned into hotels and other naive expectations had melted away on the journey), but what I did see horrified me more than I could bear.

'Where is the pre-Revolutionary architecture?' I asked Andrey, knowing that our capital was a thousand years old.

'Most of it was bulldozed by Mayor Luzhkov. He's a billionaire by now and lives very comfortably in London. He and his wife are running a foundation in support of young British architects.'

'Why do all the people look so miserable, so unhappy and angry here?' I asked.

'Because they've been forced to move outside the city and it takes them up to four hours to get to work in the morning. Because the rent eats up three quarters of their incomes. Because the air is nastier than in our hometown . . .'

'But where are all the museums, the historical and cultural centers? Is anyone protecting the architectural heritage here?'

'Well, you've got the Kremlin and the Tretyakov . . . Where did you think you were going, Alexey? To fucking Venice?'

Moscow was a cruel, soulless, faceless monster. Its people—twenty million of them—seemed to be even less tolerant of one another than were the people in our province. Its streets were even less welcoming. Its architecture—with its horrid mixture of newly constructed, tasteless glass cubes and the same old Stalinist blocks—was even more dispiriting. But the one thing that was present in plenty in Moscow though not in Siberia was money. One could feel it streaming down the prospekts: supersized advertising boards, super-priced cars, fantastic European luxury brands. This metropolitan monster had been sucking the juices out of Siberia for two centuries. All the coal, all the wood and oil had been dragged by the same Trans-Siberian railroad to one place, Moscow, only to be sold on in the blink of an eye to Western buyers. Of course, the profit never travelled back. In the best scenario, it all stayed in the capital, in the hands of some twenty persons closest to the tsar. Ordinary Muscovites seemed as poor as Siberians but also angrier, much more bitter. Meanwhile those few related to his majesty bathed in *joie de vivre* somewhere in the South of France.

On our first day in the capital, shortly after we got off the train and dropped our bags at a hostel, we chanced upon a miserable looking tourist in the middle of Tverskoy Boulevard. The man wore only his undershirt, and he kept approaching passersby in an attempt to find someone who spoke English. I wasn't fluent but could understand him. Exhausted and frightened, he told us that he had lost his tour group and had no idea how to find his way back to his hotel. He said he was in his undershirt because a gang of teenagers had just robbed him, taking away his backpack, wallet, and his jacket. We did our best to explain to the foreigner how to reach his hotel via the subway, but then realized that we ourselves were not certain how to deal with Moscow metro. We decided to accompany him, to try to find his station together.

Oh, that much-lauded Moscow subway! Even I, probably the most naive Siberian alive, could find absolutely no charm in it. By then I knew very well what message it was meant to convey: when the Bolsheviks 'neutralized' entire classes of the *intelligentsia* and aristocracy, when they had destroyed their homes, stripped and burnt the churches and the palaces, erased any visible sign of an independent culture, and sent millions to the labour camps of Siberia—they then set about building 'The Palace of the Proletariat'. Needing to bring the peasantry from outside Moscow to the city's multiplying factories, the Soviets excavated a hundred meters below ground to establish the deepest, the largest subway system in existence. They fixed patriotic scenes all over the ceilings, placed gnarled statues of milkmaids and coal miners against the walls, attached humongous chandeliers in the middle of it all, and called it 'The Palace' in exactly the same way as they called those pitiful institutes designed to raise loyal Pioneers 'Palaces of Culture' and every crumbling school a 'Palace of Knowledge'.

From the moment I entered it, that Palace of the Proletariat felt more like a mass grave to me, even though a highly decorative one. With its incessant, mad hordes of workers moving involuntarily down a million steps to the train doors, it inevitably reminded one of a conveyor belt, delivering helpless cattle to an abattoir. Decorate it as much as you wished with your plasters and your Lenins, its essence remained unchanged: anyone who admired the Moscow subway admired hundreds of lives being destroyed, thousands of souls corrupted, millions of aspirations routinely smashed.

Andrey and I succeeded in bringing that devastated foreigner back to his hotel. It seemed to me that he was ready to burst into tears the moment he entered the familiar lobby and saw some of his traveling companions. We left him there, while we ourselves then had to make our long way back to the hostel.

I remember so vividly that Kitay-Gorod subway station, where we found ourselves after saving the foreigner. It was getting late and Andrey was trying to read the map when I saw a couple of policemen approaching us. The moment I saw them my jaws started to tremble: seeing the police was a bad, a very bad omen.

The worst and the most banal thing they could do to us was ask for our military ticket, that piece of blue paper declaring that one had already served in the army or was exempt from serving. In a country where the vast majority of boys dodged the draft, policemen were making fortunes by demanding bribes from guys like us. If one refused to pay or simply didn't have ready cash on him, he'd be drafted directly from the street into the army.

Though I knew our papers were fine, there was still nothing good about the Russian policemen approaching. When Andrey showed them our passports and our university papers, they seemed disappointed.

'What, no luck today?' Andrey, who was never good at keeping his mouth shut, taunted.

The policemen looked at him . . . In the blink of an eye, they'd wrapped his arms behind his back, put cuffs on his wrists and begun dragging him off someplace.

'What are you doing? Let him go!' But of course they took no notice. They were taking him away without explanation, their sensitive souls hurt by his comment. I was being left behind outside that Moscow subway station in the late hours.

'Don't worry, Alex,' Andrey yelled back to me, 'they can't keep me for long. They've got no reason. They'll let me go. Stay here! Wait for me! Don't move!'

I was left behind, outside that stupid Kitay-Gorod station. It was rapidly getting dark. I didn't know what to do. I stood there, in the middle of some empty space with no benches to sit on, no walls to lean on, only a few encircling trees and the last workers hurrying home. I must have looked like the typical lost provincial teenager—pale, feeble, diffident. I was so nervous, so scared of what might happen to us.

Twenty, thirty, sixty minutes passed. The streets emptied. The silhouettes of the trees, as if holding hands, formed an ever-tightening circle around me. Then I saw a man standing within their shadow. He took a few steps forwards into the light . . . He looked spiteful, sallow, dirty. He tried giving me a smile of sorts. I turned away. My knees shaking, I was about to run, but I had no clue where to search for Andrey afterwards. My friend had instructed me to wait for him right there.

Another couple of minutes passed. I glanced back at the man. With his right hand in his pocket he was stroking his crotch. An abhorrent expression played over his face.

Terrified, I looked away, in the direction from which Andrey was supposed to reappear. He was nowhere to be seen. And then, I felt someone's breath on my neck. I shuddered. The man leaned over me. His whisper in my ear . . .

'I pray God your asshole is tight enough.'

Horrified, frightened, dizzy, I moved away and began walking rapidly back to the subway entrance. Descending to the trains I heard those steps—the man was following me.

The escalator seemed to crawl. The stairs, as if leading down into in inferno, had no end. Not a soul around by that hour. My heart beating faster and faster, I ran downstairs.

The man ran, too.

I reached the platform—'Attention, doors closing!'—I leapt inside a moment before the doors shut.

Out of breath, I looked back through the glass: the man hit the door with his fist, but it was too late. He pressed the glass with his palms and, as the train began to move, he stuck his tongue out, rolled his eyes upwards and made the most inhuman face I had ever seen.

I threw myself onto a seat.

The carriage was empty but for one drunkard lying unconscious on the floor.

I kept hearing my own pulse vibrating in my ears. I was scared for Andrey, scared for myself. I didn't know where he was or how I could help him, but I knew that he had the key to our hostel room . . . Then, I remembered that Andrey was still clutching our passports in his fist when the policemen dragged him away: both passports, his and mine.

Even a couple of stations on the Moscow subway last an eternity. By the time I got off the train, it must have been far after midnight. The subway was empty, but when climbing up from below ground I approached the exit, there were two more figures standing still, blocking the way out.

'No, it simply cannot be true.'

Another couple of policemen were fishing for guys riding up on the escalator. As I used to do in Siberia when noticing a gang of street rogues, I pretended that I saw no one, walked fast, with my eyes fixed on the exit.

'Hey, wait a second!' I heard behind me. 'Hey you!'

Someone grabbed my arm. I looked back. One of the uniformed men was holding me.

'Your documents,' he ordered.

I did try to explain. I tried to tell them what had happened to me, I tried to make it clear that my friend had just been taken away and all our documents remained with him. But the policemen couldn't care less—and there I was, in the middle of the night, my very first night in Moscow, with my hands behind my back, being dragged off somewhere together with a junkie they had picked on the way.

'Where are you taking me? Where? Please, let me go!'

I was trembling in their hands, but they kept on dragging me, dragging us away. I kept begging, the semiconscious man sneered.

Then, all of a sudden, I remembered what those policemen truly wanted from me.

'Wait! I've got it. I've got it!'

They stopped immediately. One of them released my right hand. I took off my left shoe and shook it upside down. A five hundred ruble bill fell out from under the sole.

'Here,' I gave them the money.

Without hesitation, without a single word, as if this sort of scenario was the most natural thing, the policemen released me, took the money and left.

I went on standing there with my shoe in my hand. My face on fire, my eyes wet. No power or reserves left within me, I was about to collapse right there, on the marble floor of that Palace of the Proletariat.

'If some bastards attack you,' I heard my mother's voice in my head, 'give them everything you own, just give it to them!'

With that thought I burst out into laughter. I laughed, my voice echoing in the empty hall. I had never thought that by bastards my mother also meant the police.

I reached our hostel, finally. It was a shabby Soviet establishment—a *gostinitza*—where on each floor a sleepy old woman sat day and night, making sure that no prostitutes made their way in. I begged that woman. I begged her to give me an extra key to our room, I kept saying that my friend had got into trouble, that he was going to be back soon, that he had both our documents and our key. After a while, the woman sighed, passed me a key silently and turned back to her soap opera.

When Andrey came back late that night, he seemed fine. But I cried and cursed that infernal city for a long time. He tried to calm me.

'Relax, it's all right. It's all in the past,' he kept saying to me. 'Tomorrow, tomorrow, tomorrow we'll leave it all in the past.'

Indeed, it was already that next day, the day when we would see Europe.

❧

Neither before nor since have I heard talk of that manner of traveling.

It was by far the cheapest and perhaps the most intense European trip one could ever have imagined making. If you are a Siberian with not much money and you want to see Europe, here is how you do it.

You start by taking the Trans-Siberian. Then, when you are exhausted after a few shaky days with no shower and virtually no food, you reach Moscow—the scary monster of developing capitalism. After you get through your Moscow adventures, involving local policemen and other scum, you get on a bus, yes, a *bus*, packed with Russians, desperate to witness the new Old World, though never for one minute isolated from their salamis and pickles, their fried sunflower seeds, their vodka and all the other necessary accompaniments of Homo Sovieticus. Even then, for the first thirty hours of your dreamt-of trip, you don't see much, because the bus is making its way through the endless Russian and Belarusian fields. Then, on the second day of your nonstop bus ride, you reach Poland.

'Please, don't try to talk to the local people, they don't like Russians,' the bus driver, who is also your tour guide, warns you. 'Last time they threw rotten veggies in through our windows.'

As it turns out, there's not much time for talking with the locals anyway. The first of only two occasions you are let off the bus, you have a mere twenty minutes to grab some food and run back to your seat, while the second requires three hours of queuing in order to pass through the obligatory visa control. Everyone is glad of this lengthy hiatus, however, because it provides the chance to run to the duty-free shop and buy loads of cheap cigarettes and, yes, more alcohol and salamis.

Finally, after some fifty (five zero) hours on the bus (you sleep in it, eat in it, and use its minuscule toilet while the wheels keep rolling) everyone gets very excited because you are approaching Germany. Most of the people stand up in the aisle to take photos.

'Yes, we are in Germany!' the driver announces triumphantly.

Inside the bus, you hear a blizzard of camera shutters and the excitement in people's voices, but outside the window you see the same highway and the same fields as you saw in Poland and Belarus. But now you *know* you are in the West—that changes everything. However sceptical you are, you too get quite excited, because it's only now a matter of time—another five hours or so—before you'll be entering Berlin, the first European capital you have ever seen in your life.

When the bus pulls over in the city and the doors open, you feel like a released prisoner. You are dizzy not only because of being on the road for five days but also because you feel the taste of freedom—from now on, you can do with your life whatever you want! Also, like an ex-convict, you smell badly, you feel your stomach sticking to your vertebrae, and you have the look of someone . . . well, someone who has just happened to have taken a bumpy ride from Siberia.

'You have four hours! I'll pick you up from the same spot,' the bus driver yells and pulls out.

In this European city everything amazes you, everything over-whelms you: clean streets ('They wash them with shampoo!'), green lawns ('You can even sit on them!'), people picnicking ('We left our salami in the bus!'), colourful shops, automatically sliding doors, flow-er pots by the windows, even parking bollards deserve your attention and the inevitable click of your camera. Bright advertisements, polite shop assistants, many different languages—not a single thing or a per-son you encounter leaves you cold-hearted. McDonald's makes a par-ticularly strong impression.

At that time, the closest McDonald's to our Siberian town was about two thousand miles away. The only time I saw a burger before that trip was when our classmate, a girl whom no one seemed to have noticed before, came to the gymnasium one morning with a Happy Meal. Her dad had just landed after a night flight from Moscow, bringing for his daughter that delicious, rubbery, day-old Big Mac. When the girl cat-walked through the corridor, holding that bright red and yellow bag close to her heart, she was immediately catapulted to the status of the most popular person in the school.

As soon as Andrey and I had reached Moscow, we too went to Mc-Donald's of course, even though that restaurant was considered to be one of the chicest places in the country and we felt quite intimidat-ed. Famously, on the day in 1990 when McDonald's first opened in Moscow, thirty thousand people queued by its entrance for days and days. That aura of exclusivity still clings to Russian McDonald's premises. The German McDonald's, by contrast, was a big disappointment: somehow it lacked the atmosphere of utter luxury that its Moscow branch flaunted.

As you chew your burger, you glance at your watch. Oh, what horror! The time is up! Suddenly you realize that your four hours in German paradise have expired and you have to run back to the bus!

With a light head and a broken heart, you step back inside your Russian wagon. Even though the bus has been a part of Western Berlin for hours now, it still smells of Moscow food and rotten alcohol. You hate it, but cannot do much except be mean to your fellow travelers— you are mean to them because you don't want to be *like* them, even if you know that you are.

Hour upon hour passes, the bus keeps running through European countries—Germany, the Netherlands, Belgium. Everything you see out of your window seems miraculous, thrilling, overwhelmingly beautiful. You don't talk much, don't read and don't sleep, you just keep watching, watching, watching while others in the bus are arguing with the driver for going too slow.

'We won't ever reach Paris this way! Can't you go faster like you did in Russia? Don't you see there are no policemen on the road! No one will ever know!'

Yet you don't mind going slow. What entertains you most is watching the cars overtaking the bus. Your seat is higher than those people in the passing cars—Western people! European people! Foreign people!—and you can study them closely: the Westerners in the speeding vehicles are chatting, laughing, getting restless, growing bored, listening to music. No matter what they do and how they do it, to you they all look endlessly lucky and, somehow, free.

At one point you notice a convertible car, something you've only seen in movies before. A good-looking driver is at the wheel and his girlfriend in a striped silk blouse sits in the passenger seat beside him, while on the back seat a young man in sunglasses lies with his elbows behind his head and his legs crossed on the car door. Suddenly, he smiles, perhaps because he sees you staring at him from the bus or maybe simply in response to something his friends are saying: that moment, that particular second, you are ready to give up everything you have in your life—your friends, your family, your own soul—everything just to be no one else but that smiling guy in sunglasses on the backseat of that car. The convertible speeds up and soon disappears. You feel something green and poisonous filling your chest.

When the bus reaches Paris you realize that your desires are much greater than what four or five hours in the city can deliver—Champs-Elysées, Tour Eiffel, forty-five minutes in the Louvre . . .

Yes, the Louvre! I remember how Andrey and I walked down the road in central Paris, away from the museum towards Place de la Concorde, in between two lines of hot, trembling cars stuck in traffic: the drivers facing us, us blinded by the molten sun. We walked holding hands, for the first time in our lives—and it felt like a small victory.

Another hour, and then—all of a sudden!—it's time to turn back, time to head East, to ride home to your beloved Moscow. The salami bus is waiting. Your European trip is over, and you can only melt back into your seat, counting how many hours you have actually spent in this bright new world . . . Ten? Fifteen? Too few excruciatingly happy hours while you were walking those streets, breathing that air, feeling safe, feeling human, feeling free . . . The rest of the week you'd spent inhaling the aromas of your own compatriots.

As the wheels turn faster and faster, you sit and recall the brightest impressions which, in spite of the shortness of your visit, cling stubbornly to your mind . . . Perhaps oddly, it was the lawn, the green sunlit lawn that we saw in each European city that impressed us the most. Those lawns in the central parks where groups of friends and families were picnicking, having parties, or just peacefully lying around, reading books, or napping—it was those lawns that stayed with us. To be free . . . free and careless to the extent that you can allow yourself to relax in a public space—just like that!—walking barefoot on the grass, clean, clean grass, or simply lying prostrate there, right there, in the heart of the city with no fear at all, trusting yourself to those around you . . . And those around you doing the very same thing—eating, or opening a bottle, or just walking dully along.

The sight of that lawn which we managed to catch in Berlin, then again in Paris, in passing through some other smaller places, the sight of that lawn made us both so full of admiration, awe, and envy. There's nothing easier than relaxing on a public lawn. There's nothing, nothing harder.

On the way back to Moscow the bus stopped in Amsterdam. Once again the driver gave us some ridiculous ninety minutes to enjoy the city before the full forty-eight hour nonstop ride back to the Russian capital. The simple reason for that, of course, was that no passenger from our bus could afford a single night in any European hotel or a dinner in a European restaurant—hence the speedy bus tour with its salami and vodka onboard.

By then Andrey and I had lost our euphoria and were simply very angry, feeling that our trip was way too short, too impressive, too heartbreaking.

'That bus of ours is like a zoo,' Andrey said bitterly on our brief break, spent walking the cobbled quays of a Dutch canal. 'You sit in that bus like a wild, dangerous animal, locked in your cage, and all you do is watch real life happening outside.'

After a few minutes of silence, he added, 'I don't want to go back! No!'

'Of course not,' I responded. 'Neither do I. Neither do I . . .'

Walking in the streets of Amsterdam, counting the minutes before our departure, my friend grew more and more agitated. Finally, he decided to get himself a joint to release the stress or for whatever other reason.

'C'mon, Alex, it's Amsterdam! We cannot leave this place without smoking!'

But I was simply never into it. In spite of being Russian, no, in spite of being Siberian, I had always felt repelled by strong alcohol, drugs, and even cigarettes. Andrey was much more experienced and adventurous than me. He would say that drinks and drugs were the only ways to stay sane. Perhaps he was right. I couldn't help it.

'No, I won't smoke,' I told him that day in Amsterdam.

He stopped in the middle of one of those pretty roads that run by the canals with those neat townhouses on each side. He looked around slowly and then focused on me.

'Listen, Alex,' I saw that he was very, very serious all of a sudden, 'you know that it's now or never, right?'

'You can do whatever you want,' I replied stubbornly, 'smoke whatever you wish, but I won't do it. I'll just sit next to you and laugh at you.'

'No, you don't understand,' Andrey continued. 'I'm not talking about the joint. I mean . . . Listen, it's now or never . . .' He stared at me with the hopeful eyes of a madman. 'Either we go back into that wretched stinking bus that will inevitably take us back to Russia or . . . or we just leave it all behind and stay on here. What if we just stay on here . . . ?'

I gave a nervous laugh. But I looked at him more closely: he wasn't joking. This young, smart, intelligent boy was as scared as hell at the thought of going back where we came from, scared of his KGB parents, scared of our city, but most of all scared that his life was going to be this way—silenced, oppressed, ridiculed—forever.

He was scared to go back, but he wasn't scared to stay in this country where he had spent only a few minutes.

'Listen to me,' he said. 'We simply don't need to get back on that fucking bus! All our lives we've been doing something we didn't want to! So why don't we finally do what we consider right? Why don't we finally start living, start doing what we want? Start from scratch?'

He went on and on in that way.

'We're here now! We are finally here! Don't you feel like a human being?! Not like an insect that everyone spits on, but like a human being?! Don't you feel that this is where we must be? This is where we belong, you and me! We love it here. We are not needed back in our Russia. Those people will be happy to get rid of us—us ugly perverts. We are just going to rot back there, you know that! If you don't get stabbed in your staircase, then you will hang yourself one day. It's as simple as that!'

What he was saying had been spinning about in my own mind for a long time. Those were all my thoughts, too. And he knew that like nobody else.

'Listen, Alex. Today we are young and we can resist that world over there, but what's next? What's going to happen to us when we are thirty? Forty? Sixty? How do you imagine the future in Russia will be for a fucking gay poetry lover like yourself? What do you think is going to happen to us? *What*?'

Andrey was beyond control, his own or mine, at that moment.

'We either get killed in one of those street fights, or we simply kill ourselves. That's what's gonna happen to us. You know that very well.'

I kept listening. My heart was throbbing. I couldn't summon enough strength to reply. I knew he was right about it all.

'It's enough!' he yelled so loud that some passing cyclists turned and gazed at us. Then he smiled and took my hand in his—a gesture that he would never dare making back in our world. 'It's enough, Alex. We are staying here and not going back.'

He said it calmly. I kept silent, my face downcast.

But then, if only for a minute or two, I did join with him in his excitement. An image crossed my mind of our bus, indeed our zoo, leaving for Moscow without us. I looked around and imagined us staying on in lovely Amsterdam. I could see that happening. I could imagine that better life which lay within our grasp. We would find shelter somehow. Surely there were some people here, some organizations which would help us . . . We could ask for asylum. We could be given a chance. We could work. We could . . .

Then I glanced at my watch. We had twenty minutes until the bus departed . . . How scared we would be as soon as the bus left without us! I thought of night falling on Amsterdam, how cold it would be to sleep on the street. On that green, green lawn. I thought of getting hungry. I thought of my mother alone in Siberia.

'Andrey, listen . . . What are we going to do here?' I said quietly, sheepishly. 'We don't have any money, we have no place to stay, nowhere to go. We don't know a single person anywhere outside Russia.'

He dropped my hand. He looked at me with spite.

'Oh, don't give me this bullshit! We'll manage somehow. Anyway, it's not that important what happens after. What's important is that we're not going back!'

'Have you considered that legally we are not allowed to stay in Europe for more than ten days? Our visa only lets us stay till the next week. As soon as it's over, they will deport us.'

'We won't show our passports! We'll throw them away!'

'But how are we going to get a job without any documents? They won't even let us clean their toilets without a work permit.'

'Oh, fuck it!' he yelled, 'Fuck all that!'

He stepped aside from me, turned away—faced the water.

I heard him sniff a couple of times. I saw his right hand tightening, gradually forming a fist.

'Andrey,' I said gently.

I tried to touch his right shoulder, but he pulled roughly away. Then, suddenly, he turned back to me. He looked at me as if it was in me, in me that he saw everything he hated about life.

'You! Go away!' he yelled, pushing me, 'Get lost, fucking crybaby! You're just a scared little mommy's boy! You can't do anything with your fucked-up life! What do you have to lose? *What*?

'Go back to your bloody Siberia if you want to and let all those bastards rape you, kill you, throw your skinny body under a bridge! This is what you want, right? Right? This is what you want?'

He kept shaking me, jabbing his fingers into my chest, pushing me away, then shaking me again. I was powerless. I stepped aside. I turned away from him.

❧

At sunrise, back in Siberia, over the broken surface of my yard, an old yellow Volga was slowly wobbling away. The taxi grew more and more blurry until it became merely a distant yellow stain, and then that patch of colour reached the corner of the building, and vanished. I was left behind, standing there with my right hand holding open the downstairs door as if waiting for someone to come through it. I stayed motionless, breathless for a while: I knew that this was one of those moments when your life changes once and forever, and there is nothing to be done; I also knew that for many years to come I would keep seeing that blur of yellow here and there but that it would never signal his return.

This was how Andrey left. Only one month had passed since our European trip. Nearly three years—since his declaration on the balcony, the first day of our love.

During those years we spent together, my mother frequently welcomed him, letting us spend long evenings at our place. Andrey's parents, realizing that their son was growing more and more independent, became suspicious.

One night they welcomed him home with a collage of small white papers which covered the entire full-length mirror facing their front door: those were our love messages, the little 'telegrams' that for three years we'd been exchanging through an anonymous operator of our paging company. In the best traditions of the KGB, Andrey's parents first obtained our private correspondence, and later that night made him face an interrogation. When his father finally retired to his bedroom and his mother was brushing her teeth in the bathroom, Andrey unlocked the front door, ran downstairs, crossed the street, walked to the center of the city bridge, and jumped off it.

Siberian rivers are bottomless, borderless, merciless. Yet Andrey didn't die. People told me later that he was seen that day wandering the city streets, soaking wet, in a state of shock.

When he finally returned to his senses, Andrey went to Leonid Josephovich, the geographer, and made the man give him enough money for a one-way flight to Moscow. Andrey then came to my place, told me what had happened, and stayed with me overnight. Knowing his parents would raise an entire army to find him, he couldn't stay longer: next morning at five o'clock, he got into the yellow Volga and left for the airport. That was all. That was the end of the story.

I fell on my bed, buried my face in the pillow. I tried to stay silent, not wanting anyone to know about my teenage tragedy. Yet I wept and wept and wept.

After some time, I heard my door opening. I felt my mother sitting by my side. Her hand on my hair. Her shaking voice.

'Alioshenka, please, don't be like this, don't be . . . Tell me what's happened to you, tell me.'

What could I tell her? How?

'Please, please . . . Don't be this way . . . You're everything to me . . . Tell me, I will help . . .'

I heard my mother's voice breaking, but I kept silent. It still wasn't clear to me how much she knew, how much she understood about me and Andrey.

'Tell me, Alioshenka, is it because of . . . Andrey?' she said.

I froze for a second, then sort of nodded, with my head still buried in the pillows.

'But why? Nothing is wrong . . . Why are you crying?'

Then she became silent. Lifted her hand from my body. Her voice grew harder.

'Is it because you are . . . because both of you are . . .' Harder. Harder! 'Because both of you are boys?'

In that moment I became certain that this was the day when I would lose all the love I had in my life once and forever.

'If that's the only reason to cry, then don't, my dear one,' she placed her hand back on me. 'There's nothing wrong about you two being together. There's nothing wrong.'

My mother! My most precious, my most treasured mother. From where, how, from what wondrous sources could she possibly draw this deepest love, this limitless kindness, this overpowering all-acceptance? Given her living without a moment of security, given her wretched upbringing in a run-down village, her four younger siblings, each from a different man unknown to the family, her communist schooling, her country torn apart by the KGB and the mafia, her white-faced, white-haired, snow-white country where even the mere words 'segregation', 'colonization', 'democratization' are taboo . . . given all of that . . . from what possible source could this Altay orphan, this Soviet, jobless engineer, this single, singular Russian woman, my mother, have gained this most understanding, most beautiful soul?

I didn't say anything to her by way of reply, I didn't let her know the details of my drama, I didn't even tell her that there was no Andrey in my life any longer. Instead, I rose from the pillow and held her close.

When I woke it was noon, and it all seemed like a bad dream—the yellow car, the messages from our pagers, the bridge, his parents . . . They had panicked, of course, as soon as they learnt their son had run away. They had their colleagues positioned in the airport and at the train station, hoping to catch Andrey as he tried to escape, but they were too late. They didn't know he had already flown to Moscow.

They hastened to our school and the university, they talked to our teachers and our classmates. They certainly talked to the geographer, and he must have told them what he knew. Finally, they reached me.

His father came banging on my door, threatening to bring the police, to break in, but I refused to let him in. Andrey's mother kept calling me day and night, day and night. Day and night. Each time I picked up the phone, she began cursing me and couldn't stop.

'You, dirty little pervert! You have destroyed everything! You have destroyed, have spoiled our son! Are you still hiding him under your bed, tell me, are you?'

She was screaming hysterically. I would just hang up on her over and over and over again, but she kept on calling. Then, at some moment, I couldn't hold it in anymore. When the phone rang again, I gathered all my strength, I brought all the force I could muster into my voice, I picked up the phone and yelled back at Andrey's mother.

'Now listen to me, madam. Listen to what I have to say! Listen to me, I said!'

She finally quietened down.

'Your son has gone. He's in Moscow. Stop yelling! Listen to me,' I said. 'If you want to blame anyone, anyone for what has happened to Andrey, look in the mirror. Blame yourself!'

I hung up. The woman never called me again.

For a few days, Andrey's father kept coming to our house. He would come and stand motionless for twenty, thirty, forty minutes under my barred bedroom window. Maybe he was trying to spot Andrey, but he was mistaken. Andrey was no longer a part of my life.

A couple of years later, Vilena (with whom I wasn't as close after our friend had left) had chanced upon Andrey in Moscow. When she got back to Siberia, I called her to ask if Andrey had any thoughts of ever coming back home. She told me that he had already been back.

Andrey's father, after months of trying, had finally managed to track him down in the capital. He'd asked Andrey to forgive them, himself and his mother. He said that they had realized all the mistakes they had made and they wanted their only son to come back home.

The boy was touched. He was just a boy after all.

So, one day Andrey did fly back to Siberia. On his first night at home, his parents must have cried, saying how much they had missed him. And that wasn't a lie. But next morning Andrey woke to a buzzing at the door. He looked through the peephole: there stood a number of army representatives come to draft their new recruit.

In the same way as Andrey's parents had, in the past, entrusted their boy to the care of the geographer in order to secure their son's future, this time they'd decided to report him to the army: the military would surely make a real man of him.

Andrey was no longer a student by then, so it was fully legitimate to draft him, and he'd been dodging it for months already. His loving parents had grasped the chance.

Refusing to open the front door, Andrey managed to escape from a window. Thus, after only one night at home, he had run away again, taken a bus to Novosibirsk, and flown from there back to Moscow the very same day.

When I talked to Vilena about it all, I asked how Andrey had looked when she saw him that last time in Moscow. Was he all right? Was he eating well? She said he looked very skinny. She said he was troubled. She said he was on heroin.

Andrey had left Siberia, left his family, left me. But he had also left so much *to* me. He had passed on to me a part of his personality and his experience. He had changed me in many ways, and at the same time he had helped me to understand myself better.

Later on, I kept asking myself over and over one simple question: would my life have gone in the same direction had Andrey never told me that he loved me? On that sixteenth-story balcony, one bleak April night.

Of course, there was something in me that attracted him. Some unusual tenderness of character, extreme sensitivity that most men lacked, some compliance, some kind of gender ambiguity. This had been a part of me ever since I could remember. None of that had been 'given' to me, it was fully mine from the beginning. Andrey had only opened up a possible way in which my soul might function in the modern world. Because of him, unfortunately, I was also made aware of the way this modern world treats that kind of person—my kind.

In the midst of an ordinary sunny day, on my way to school, in my own hometown, the town I was born in, born just like them—them, my compatriots, my contemporaries—one or more of them would approach me and whisper in my ear:

'If I see you here again, I'll smash your face into the wall.'

Other days guys would catch me, push me around, grab at my genitals, laughing wildly, checking to see if I was a boy or a girl.

On the day of my graduation I received an anonymous message on my pager. 'If you come to the event,' they threatened, 'you'll be downed.' But I decided that I should attend no matter what. 'I won't be intimidated,' I thought to myself.

On one occasion, when Andrey and I were on a tram, sitting side by side, I noticed some cold, strange feeling on my back. I touched the spot—the hair and skin on the back of my neck were slimy. I looked behind. There were two adult men, sitting behind us, spitting onto our heads all through the ride . . . Horror, absolute horror. Most routine, most usual horror! And the worst part was that I clearly understood why those people loathed me so much, why they found me so wrong.

It was the same thing about me that made my primary school classmates, those little boys, bully me and call me an alien . . . The same thing that pushed these street guys to call me a hermaphrodite . . . The same thing that made my grandmother's village neighbours mistake me for a girl . . . The same thing that made my father distance himself from me and eventually leave our tiny family . . . The very same thing which Andrey loved in me: what he called 'being like an angel'.

What was that thing exactly? I knew it. I felt it. Yet it had always stayed a heartfelt mystery to me.

I always craved to understand myself. And I think I did, to some extent. I longed to understand the people around me. And I think I did that, too. But what I could never truly quite grasp was why we call ourselves humans, if to be 'humane' meant being compassionate and sympathetic with one another.

Maybe because of the way our story—Andrey's and my story— eventually ended, maybe because of the way other people had treated me—him, us—something became twisted in me when my only love vanished. Without Andrey, I didn't feel as though I had stopped being who I was, but I didn't feel like I wanted to be that miserable gay young man either.

Gradually, after a few months of being alone, I decided to keep it like that. To stay alone. Little by little I came to the conviction that the only way for a human being who was born different to keep a decent life in the circumstances I lived in was to maintain celibacy. All other options—whether it be a lavender marriage to a woman or a closeted relationship with a man—were in my eyes inevitably based on a compromise and a lie. To maintain dignity, to keep self-respect, I decided to have no close relations at all. If I couldn't have the right place for myself in the world, I wouldn't take any place in it whatsoever.

Chapter Eight

A Siberian Dream

My pillows, my blanket, my linen, and even the curtains, which separated my bedroom from the barred reality outside, were all covered with white stars on a blue background, and red stripes on white—in pale imitation of the American flag. I'd picked out the fabric myself at the drapery shop and my mother had put it all together on her Soviet sewing machine, the same one she'd used to make clothes for me and my father when I was a child and he was a young man.

The colourful collage on my wall, which had begun with the magazine picture of how Siberians celebrated New Year, grew bigger and bigger, and by the time I was about to enter university almost the entire wall above my desk was covered in magazine and newspaper cuttings. They were all there to remind me of what I wanted to accomplish in life, and the thing I wanted above all was to go West.

I had also scotch-taped a map of the world and, using pins of three different colours, marked the places of interest. Red pins denoted the cities I most longed to live in—New York, London, Venice. Yellow pins indicated the birthplaces of famous immigrants—Valentino, Joseph Conrad, Mikhail Baryshnikov, among others. Blue pins marked the seas I dreamt of swimming in.

One of my bedroom walls was almost entirely taken up by a large mirror. In front of it, I practiced daily the physical routine I had invented for myself, still stubbornly determined to become a dancer one day, in spite of what my father had to say about it. Or maybe because of that. On both sides of the mirror I'd glued sheets of white paper, one above the other, so that they formed a continuous scroll from the ceiling to the floor. In large black letters, I'd written a quotation, no, not from one of my classics but from an Adidas commercial:

> *Impossible is just a word thrown around by small men who find it easier to live in the world they've been given than to explore the power they have to change it.*

When visiting us one day my father entered my room and seemed startled by this sudden explosion of the blunt maximalism of youth. He studied my map and my clippings, he read the quotation, and then commented, still looking around, 'Well, who knows, maybe one day you'll become the new Lenin, after all.'

He left then, but I loitered there, bothered by his reaction. To become the new Lenin—especially, 'after all'—was the last thing I wanted to happen to me. I was conscious of the silliness of my own grand ambitions, but to dream big, to try hard, to reject what was already hostile to me seemed to be the only way to pull myself out of the misery we all called Siberia.

When you are young, everything seems to happen so quickly. All the events in your life seem to be of such dramatic importance, and each of them tends not to know how to keep a distance from the others. One day you are a child, the next you are insulted if a *konduktorsha* calls you '*malchik*'. Then, in the blink of an eye, some people are gone, and you cannot believe that everything you've shared with them has actually happened. Andrey and I were still doing our homework together in May. Our bus trip across Europe took place in July. By the end of August, he had disappeared from my life. On the first day of September, the classroom seat next to me was empty.

I was fortunate enough to be one of the six people from the gymnasium who were selected by the admissions committee to go to university without entrance exams and without bribes. In those days, education was still free but the exams were draconian and the entry standard extremely high. I wasn't especially close to the other students selected. They all seemed to care about nothing but their red diplomas.

On our first university day, there was an orientation meeting held in one enormous lecture hall that resembled an amphitheater. Our dean, a morose, sallow man, greeted us with imperious contempt.

'Journalists? Don't dare call yourself journalists! You must work like slaves before you deserve to be called journalists!'

The dean never did tell us how we journalism students should refer to ourselves. All through our university years, he ritually referred to us simply by our family names, 'Morozov, go grab me some chalk!' Though at other times a lot more crudely.

Despite the promise of Perestroika, by the early 2000s Russian universities remained Soviet to their marrow. Education was free, the textbooks were old, the professors underpaid, tired, and openly contemptuous. They taught by what they called the Socratic method, giving them the license to dispense for hours on end the most discouraging, sometimes simply obscene, remarks upon their students: the stick method, with no carrot in sight. The academic program was set in stone for all (including obligatory sports and economics courses). The university building itself was a constructivist monolithic Palace of Knowledge, within which some eighteen thousand students massed daily.

Being enrolled at university was the single biggest dream Russian parents cherished for their child, and the children themselves could not foresee a future without these five standard years at a higher institute. There was no choice between applying or not applying. If you managed to pass your high school final exams with average or higher grades, you absolutely had to try to pass the university exams. That was the rule. It did not derive from a universal respect for knowledge, but from fear of the future and the ideological complications of the Soviet past. This was especially the case for boys, for whom tertiary education was the surest way to avoid the army.

In communist times, once they had graduated from university, students were given direction as to where they were to go next. An employment list with the proposed job options would be hung outside the dean's office. Students with the highest academic merit were given the first choice, because one would have to choose not only between various factories and companies but—as happened with my parents—between different cities, regions, and republics in the vast Soviet territory. My family had been lucky to be sent to Taiga because less successful students could end up in, let's say, Kamchatka, which could fairly be dubbed the Siberia of Siberia.

However by the nineties, this whole employment system had broken down. As soon as the Union collapsed, all the particles of it were derailed. Factories closed one after another, workers went on federal strikes, there were no job options left for fresh graduates—not even in Kamchatka. The list by the dean's office disappeared once and for all, while the massive universities themselves stood still. It seemed that academics could survive without being paid for much longer than coal miners.

They must have been in their fifties, but they looked much older. Their clothes were never too bright, too clean, or too ironed. Their haggard faces bore an expression of permanent intolerance toward us, ignorant youngsters, children of the new country. With their foreheads lined with unresolved questions and their eyes exposing an almost childlike innocence and fear (as if they were constantly asking themselves, 'How did this happen to us?'), our morose professors treated us as if we were the source of all their problems, as if they blamed us for the collapse of their cherished Union. We feared them but only for the first few months. Gradually we learned more of who they really were and went on to despise them mercilessly as only youth can.

We realized that, in spite of their knowledge, their education, their experience, they were, in the new century's vocabulary, nothing but losers. They had lost their battles, they'd been lied to and cheated, they were not needed, they were forgotten, left behind like some superannuated parts of a broken machine. If they ever had been practicing journalists, then their lies were long exposed, their successes devalued. And now, now they were not even paid for their work, and they endured it, did not protest, did not raise their voices. What kind of journalists were they? What sort of journalism could they teach us? We sensed quite quickly their broken spirits. We scanned them with our eyes and our brains, while they read out their lectures in a low, rapid, uninterested manner, and we thought we knew everything about them.

They were born, raised, educated, and worked under the Soviets. It was them—those who went to practice as journalists in the provincial versions of *Pravda*, *Izvestia*, *Komsomolskaya Pravda*—who were to blame for all the lies, for all the dirt, for all the vulgar cruelty that the Soviet media had planted in the hearts and minds of millions of people. Now the monster had collapsed, the scary truth was exposed, and the gulled masses of their readers had every reason to spit in those journalists' faces, but even that they'd forgotten to do.

The head of the department was Vladimir Vladimirovich Banalin, the dean who never permitted us to be called 'journalists' or even 'students'. We understood quite early on that he and his father were both named after Lenin, while his surname was emblematic of the repression of original thought. As if reading our minds, he was always vengeful towards his students, every now and then pausing in his monotonous lectures to criticize one of us. While lecturing, he had old Soviet textbooks and his own dusty notes open in front of him. He typically sat with his elbows leaning on the desk and his fingers locked, forming a sharp triangle with his upper body. We never once saw him smile.

His topics were 'The Theory of Journalism' and 'Genres of the Soviet Press'. After listening to his enthralling lectures, we were required to write and to publish materials strictly following the neat set of guidelines presented in textbooks from the Soviet times. After each of the first four semesters, in spite of the specialization we had chosen, we were supposed to submit our printed pearls for his approval. Vladimir Vladimirovich Banalin would refuse to accept, let's say, a review because it did not fulfill the genre's requirements, or a news report because it was fifty letters too long or too short by his standards, or an analytical article because it lacked adjectives. The content didn't matter. What mattered was that our publications satisfied the rules carved in stone for each genre. Many of us couldn't bring ourselves to follow those dusty textbooks and their definitions. It was said, for example, that a film or a book review must contain between four and five thousand words, while we were already buying and loving the glossy Western-style modern magazines that had short notes on music, movies, and books.

'These are the reviews!' we would protest, pointing at our magazines.

'No,' the dean would parry, 'these are!' pointing at the newspapers of his youth.

Not just Western magazines, but the entire West was the actual problem for Vladimir Vladimirovich and his team.

'Those Americans, they cannot wipe their own arses!' he used to say. 'The end of the world for them will come when they run out of toilet paper. The stupidest people!'

'Oh yeah, the Russians certainly know what to do in such an emergency,' I was desperate to respond, 'that's the only reason *Pravda* is still in print!'

But I never dared say it, even though it was the sad reality: toilet paper was only introduced to Russia in the year 1969. And it was met with zero interest by the public. Toilet paper only became popular after a special newsreel. Up until 1970, a thoroughly crumpled edition of *Pravda*, to which every comrade held a subscription by default, did the job just fine.

The second most important person in our department was Irina Makarovna Banalin, the spouse of Vladimir Vladimirovich. She was pallid, dried out, fragile, with blue circles under her eyes and very thin hair. We knew that before university, while her husband worked at one of the *serious* publications, she was a librarian. That experience had bequeathed her a voice with no volume, and we dragged ourselves through her mandatory classes in complete boredom and disrespect. She delivered the history of Soviet journalism, talking mostly about Brezhnev, Stalin, Khrushchev, and about how the press had functioned under each of them.

Irina Makarovna would typically skip over or fast-forward through the dark parts of those stories, focusing on the high morals and deep values of the institutions like *Literaturnaya Gazeta*, the biggest literary newspaper in the USSR, famous not only for its five-thousand-word book reviews but also for publishing loads of dirt on many free-thinking writers. Via its zillion monthly copies, the Soviet newspapers destroyed hundreds of literary careers, muted thousands of independent voices, ruined innumerable lives—but we were taught none of that in Irina Makarovna's history of Soviet journalism.

I remember being in one of the university's classrooms (a long narrow hall with a chalkboard in front of us and a dusty window behind), listening to yet another of the teacher's tirades, and feeling that all this accumulated pain, this disappointment, this despair was so thick in the air that one could scoop it up with a spoon. It wasn't just the teacher. It wasn't simply the subject. It was the whole atmosphere in that university: the halls and the corridors were shabby and dark, the expressions on the students' faces were sullen, hopeless, almost senile; the classes lasted from eight-thirty in the morning to four, sometimes five, in the evening: night fell so early and the sun rose so late that we had scarcely had a chance to walk in the light.

One day, trying to concentrate on the Banalin's lecture, I felt the winter sun falling on my back through the grimy window behind. I couldn't take it any longer. Suddenly I stood up, pulled my coat on and left the room in the middle of the class without asking permission. I walked all the way through the labyrinthine corridors of the university and, finally reaching their end, heaved open the heavy doors.

Outside, the day was clear and full of light. The sun's rays, reflected off the snow, were glistening in billions of tiny rainbows. I muffled myself up in my coat, pulled up my hood, and walked away in the direction of the riverbank. Of course, the river was frozen, but its vast current was by then transformed into a silent flow of crystal white snow—the world felt fresh and hopeful, whatever our teachers had to say about it.

❧

Being enrolled at the journalism department required that I complete internships not only in the printed media but also at the local TV channel, adding serious television reports to my portfolio of equally serious newspaper publications. The university simply didn't care how and when we found time to fulfill all its requirements. As a result, we attended classes during the day, wrote notes for the newspapers on our knees under our desks, did our reading at nights, and worked at the TV station during weekends and in between semesters. Of course, the TV channel we were assigned to work for was fully controlled by the state. It simply couldn't be otherwise.

As TV interns, we were expected to do the same job as any other reporter. For each aired report, we would be paid the equivalent of one lunch at the student canteen. Naturally, we would only get paid if the news program was also approved by the TV channel's director. That person reported to the governor himself, who, in his turn, reported to the president.

Watching the packs of reporters running around the studio and then around the city, digging up the subjects, hunting for interviewees, fighting like dogs with each other over the opportunity to be aired and to make that ten dollars—all that scurrying 'busyness' made it seem to me like we were living inside a lunatic asylum. What depressed me most, however, wasn't the low morality or the high ambition which ran amok in that TV channel's corridors but the ubiquity of the censorship involved.

In the short time I spent there, I saw a reporter being fired simply for picking the wrong subject. That journalist, a young woman recently graduated from my faculty, had prepared a piece about the miserable state of residential buildings in the city. She had noticed, like myself and many other people, that those crumbling Soviet housing projects were only repainted (though never repaired) a few days before some Moscow official visited the city. And only those parts of the buildings were repainted that faced the street along which the official's motorcade would travel. My own block had that same sad fate of possessing two faces: one, relatively neat, to make the officials happy, the other—the one which greeted residents of the building—absolutely run down.

This was the subject the reporter had chosen. She was fired the same day she tried to have the story approved for release.

The 'Governor's Swimming Pool', the 'Governor's Fitness Center', the 'Governor's Meat Market', the 'Governor's Department Store' ... As I criss-crossed the city, searching for suitable subjects for my news pieces, I was amazed at the number of organizations, companies, sports centers, cultural institutions, and even petty shops, beer stands, and kiosks, that were falling out of private ownership yet again and reverting to the state. Each new acquisition by the local government was proudly announced on billboards: the 'Governor's Kindergarten', the 'Governor's Tennis Court', the 'Governor's Spirit Factory'. It was all the more absurd for being fully standardized, legalized, and presented *comme il faut*.

At first, I merely laughed at all that ridiculous nonsense: what does the slogan 'Governor's Gift to the City' mean, when written on a tram or on a medical center, if all of these facilities are built and maintained by the people's taxes? But when I realized that even the TV van in which I rode, the seat I was sitting on in a classroom, and the lunch I'd eaten at the students canteen, were also the 'Governor's'—it didn't seem funny anymore. Moreover, I was expected to thank him for it all.

One day when I was alone at home someone pressed the buzzer at our apartment door.

'Who's there? Who?' I asked loudly, still imitating an adult manly voice to discourage people from breaking in as I'd been taught to do years ago.

'Me . . . It's only me, sonny . . .' came a voice there was no way of mistaking.

Immovable and bright as a beam of sunshine in a dark room full of dust, my *babushka* stood there in front of me.

'And here I am . . .' she said timidly, her eyes gleaming, her little smile spreading over her rosy face, her white kerchief over her hair.

'But . . . how . . . how did you get here, *Babushka*?'

'How? How . . . On *elektrichka*, of course . . . If no one is coming to visit me, am I supposed to wait forever?' She giggled, emptying her sacks of pickled vegetables and jams.

After handing me her homemade treasures, she stepped shyly through our modest two rooms, then lowered herself carefully onto our sofa (my mother's sleeping place) and remained sitting there, unmoving, for many long, long minutes.

'I'd be afraid to touch anything, dear,' she said matter-of-factly, with no sign of reproach. 'Here it's your mother who's the hostess.' She paused, then whispered to herself in the same timid voice, 'And how to live like this? You two poor things . . . In such a tower with so many flats, like two birdies in a birdhouse.'

It pained me to see how alien, how out of place my own dear *babushka* seemed in our new home. Only when my mom returned from work at night and we sat down to have dinner did the conversation gradually start up again.

Bashfully, grandmother began asking me questions about my new life—the university, my friends, the work I was doing at the newspaper and at the television station. How proud she seemed when I told her that I had made a couple of reports for the evening news! The program she watched daily was about to begin and so I turned on the TV. She put her thick glasses on and placed the chair right in front of the set.

I recalled then how seriously she had always taken everything that appeared on the screen, how cheerfully she greeted the newsmen, how passionately she argued with the soap opera characters. How real that televised reality was for her! And as the pictures leapt onto the screen and those heavily censored, dramatically falsified reports were being presented, I watched my own grandmother . . . She became very excited now, waiting for her grandson's name to appear on the screen.

Typically, the first news reports were about yet some more of the governor's successes in bringing order and happiness into the world.

'Oh, how lucky we are to have such a great man in power!' my grandmother exclaimed in the most sincere, heartfelt tone. 'Ever since I can remember he was there for us! Always for us!'

The next couple of news pieces were of the opposite kind, covering the situation outside the region, including one piece about a train crash in nearby China. Those items were presented in a very dark manner, and I listened as my grandmother responded.

'Poor people. Poor people . . . When I just look at what's happening abroad . . .'

The next report was more radical: some villagers from a distant Siberian region shared an incredible story. According to them, the Americans had recently come to their village in order to collect blood samples from the local population. When the interview was over, the journalist kindly clarified that the foreigners were most likely in the process of inventing a new weapon of mass destruction, directed specifically at Russians.

'Dear Lord! Oh, dear!' my grandmother was so impressed. 'Why do all those foreigners hate us so much? Why do they all wish us harm?'

The program ground on to its final reports—feel-good stories about local life. This was where the students' work would usually be shown, but on that day there was nothing of mine. Instead they showed a large village family: the man had lost his job in the city and had decided to move with his wife to a farm and to start living off the land. The woman had borne him five children and was pregnant again. Before the camera, the couple shared their gratitude to the state for letting them have such a nice life and only complained about not having a church in the vicinity. My grandmother felt very sympathetic.

'Oh, you see, Alioshenka, even today when you work hard, everything's all right! You see, one has to have a family . . . traditional values . . .'

It was only on that day, only during that half-hour which I spent watching my grandmother as she watched the news, that I fully realized what a dramatic effect television had on her: there was not a single particle of her that doubted what she saw on the screen. She accepted everything the screen told her as the absolute truth. This was how she had always been. This was how the Russian people of her age and even younger, that majority of people who grew up without the screen, treated it: as some divine force, as the source of wisdom, as the source of ultimate knowledge. And this was exactly how Putin had gained and retained power. Without TV, he would be nothing at all. Perhaps the surest way, the easiest way to reduce our tyrants to nothing—I thought to myself that day—would be to turn all those screens off once and forever.

I saw no reason for trying to prove to my grandmother that the TV had been lying to her. That I myself had been lying to her from the screen. But watching her that day, I grew so bitter, so ashamed of myself, so angry toward the state which owned and ran this devilish business, that I decided to quit my TV internship as soon as I could and to give up on all sorts of screens for good.

Nothing was said or done during her short visit in relation to my father, her son. But later on, in a couple of weeks or so, when he appeared one Saturday, and then again, and again, without my mother seeming to mind—only then did I realize what the true reason for my grandmother's sudden visit had been. She only wanted to try her best to fix our family—to make it more like a nest, less like a birdhouse.

❧

In spring every Russian university presented a series of concerts which gave an opportunity for students, regardless of their field of studies, to demonstrate their talents. With minimal financing and maximal enthusiasm, each faculty put on a show. A jury picked the best acts and sent them to the National Festival of Student Arts.

From the time when, as a child, I'd recited poetry on the stage of the Pioneers' House of Culture, I'd always loved the performing arts. At university, I volunteered to be a part of the faculty show and was swiftly chosen as director of the entire thing. During the weeks preceding the festival, every day, after some seven courses of Antique literature, Soviet history, economics, and the rest, I hurried off to rehearsal.

The idea was simple: we would choose the casts, the most talented students, and try to create something altogether extraordinary. Of course, that was merely our vision of it—*extraordinary*. In reality, any professional artist, dancer, or musician who happened to wander into our rehearsing space would have seen nothing but some amateurish extravaganza. But to us, it was a project of huge importance.

It felt great to design and paint the sets, to sew the costumes, to create the choreography, to select the music, to stage the whole thing by ourselves. The trick was to combine our different talents into one unified show, to create a complete musical from scratch. I had been sleeping under the American flag for long enough to have no hesitation in deciding on the theme: we would spend that Siberian spring of 2004 in the Manhattan of the seventies.

> *We want to be playing tag on the green,*
> *wearing just shirtsleeves, tidy and clean.*
> *If the weather is rainy rather than dry,*
> *while doing the homework we want not to cry.*
>
> *We shall finish the textbook with exemplary zeal.*
> *That of which we shall dream will always be real.*
> *We shall love everybody, and they will love us,*
> *It's as good as it gets, like a plus and a minus . . .*

I read Joseph Brodsky's 'Song of Innocence' into a microphone from backstage, before the curtain went up, while a couple of dancers in cream-coloured tunics were slowly spinning to Alessandro Marcello's Adagio on the apron of the stage. During Brodsky's last verses, radio waves began breaking into the music, a different melody emerged and the dancers drew the curtains apart. Super-sized collages, inspired by Lichtenstein and Warhol, served as the background. More and more dancers flooded onto the stage, impersonating the characters from *Party Monster* and *Studio 54*, films that I loved. To the first sounds of Pet Shop Boys' *Paninaro*, they all began dancing. Brodsky had landed in New York.

When the show was over, our troupe rejoiced, jumping about in excitement, kissing and crying behind the closed curtain. The audience seemed to have enjoyed our bright, exuberant American musical, and we knew we could trust our audience. The people who came to see student performances like these weren't known for restraining their emotions, often acting wildly in the same way as audiences, perhaps, used to all around the world in the long gone past. They felt free to yell and to whistle, to give standing ovations in the course of an act and to throw stuff on stage, to leave the room if they didn't like what they saw and even to bring the curtain down if they found the show intolerable. There was no applauding out of mere politeness, not a whit of bourgeois hypocrisy in reaction to our amateurish Siberian extravaganza.

Only somehow along the way we'd lost sight of one thing: it was actually the aughts in Siberia we were living in, not the seventies in Manhattan. The jury, the good old jury, failed to share our excitement. The elite members of our society—those charged with selecting the acts to represent the region at the National Students' Art Festival—were neither students nor artists. They were university managers, government representatives, the people responsible for the 'Governor's Parade', the 'Governor's Ball', the 'Governor's Circus'. It wasn't long before I found myself summoned for a conversation.

'What *was* all that? No, tell us, what was all that insanity?' they asked me as soon as I entered the room. 'No, explain it to us! We haven't got a clue as to what that was all about.'

One after another, the jury members expressed their outrage at my beloved Pet Shop Boys, 'Party Monster', and Joseph Brodsky.

'And what is that Studio 45 anyway? Ok, let's say you picked the theme of the seventies,' the most progressive of the jury members said, 'but what was all that music? All that weird dancing? What you've put on here is nonsense. Vulgar nonsense!'

Only the evening before I had seen that very same jury give a standing ovation to a group of semi-naked female economics students performing a belly dance. That, they hadn't found vulgar. Listening to the jury now, I was shaking with anger and frustration, because it was all my idea, these were my choices, that had been my voice reading my favourite poem.

'And to round it all off . . .' a younger woman, the director of the Governor's Theater, concluded, 'who was that fairy, reading those so-called "poems" at the opening? Couldn't you find a more masculine voice, one pleasant to the ear?'

Listening to this 'critique', this barely disguised, pitiless attack, I found the same outrage rising inside me as when Andrey's mother had kept shouting her insults down the phone at me. I couldn't keep silent any longer. I raised my eyes, took a deep breath, and responded, as calmly and clearly as I could.

'It is not the students' problem if the jury is incapable of understanding youth culture. Perhaps it is the jury itself that needs to be updated. In fact, if the jury gets itself all hot and excited about a band of eighteen-year-olds shaking their bellies, then I have no interest in the opinion of such a jury.'

I rose from my chair.

'Listen, young man,' a voice at my back rang out, 'in Soviet times . . . in Soviet times, you would be in a labour camp for such a speech!'

I didn't respond. I preferred my imaginary Manhattan to their Soviet realism.

By that year I had learned a thing or two about living among Russians. With the help of Andrey and the passage of time itself, I'd come to understand how much, how easily I let things affect me, how many of those brutal words and actions I accepted as normal. I had developed a deep-rooted habit of never responding. I was like a quiet pond into which people threw stones without the circles ever appearing to spread on the surface—while underneath, deep down, the tormented waters churned in reaction to each assault.

Until I was eighteen, I'd made no effort to shield myself from what the world was throwing at me. When people spat in my face, screamed 'Monster!' at me, I'd merely stay quiet, I'd wait for it all to pass, and then run back home to stand in front of the mirror for a long time asking myself the same question:

'What is it that is so unbearably, intolerably wrong about me?'

But now, by slowly drawing connections, by studying Andrey's books and films, by taking that seven-day bus ride to Europe with him, I'd begun thinking the unthinkable: that maybe, just maybe, there was nothing wrong with me.

'Maybe instead,' I even dared say back to the mirror, 'maybe instead there is something wrong with the world around?'

I was surprised to find that even at university there were plenty of students and teachers who acted toward me in the same harsh ways as those street guys did. The meanest and the most aggressive colleagues were from either the law or the sports faculties. One might wonder what the two had in common, but the explanation was simple.

Those who chose to study law were mostly from families associated with the government and the criminal world. It was a well-known fact that to be enrolled in the Law Department, a student only needed to load his academic book with cash and pass it to the professor. The teacher would take the cash and award a grade, depending on the amount presented. As a result, the crowd in the Faculty of Law was itself lawless.

In post-Soviet Russia the sports and the criminal *avtoriteti* were closely linked. Few parents would send their boys to the Sports School for one simple reason: it was from there, from the youth sports centers and the university sports departments, that the criminal and the government authorities selected the strongest athletes, the best boxers, the fastest runners as their bodyguards, their problem solvers, their killers.

For the representatives of those two faculties, I was a particularly attractive target. The Sports School was based on the ground floor, a level below the philological one, and so I couldn't make it to Dostoyevsky without passing through his underworlds. The sports teams usually hung out at the university entrance. More than often, they'd block the doors when they saw me coming, they'd surround and bully me for as long as they pleased.

No, I couldn't fight back. Fighting back against a full team of professional boxers wasn't wise. Nevertheless, I also felt that by that time I had had enough. Once, passing through the crowd, hearing the routine insults rising around me from all directions, I stopped in the middle of the hall.

'Faggot!' a common compliment was yelled from the crowd.

I paused. I turned around to the one screaming.

For the first time, I looked calmly into the eyes of the aggressor.

'Do you think that I still don't know that?' I responded. 'Do you think you're offering me some kind of enlightenment? Do you think that no one has ever told me this before? If you want to keep on having fun like you do every time I pass by, maybe you'd better think up something new to say.'

What I did that day wasn't much, no. It felt like some sort of self-humiliation, too. But what else could I possibly do? Who was I to ask for help? Where to look for justice? Among the future lawyers?

The longer I lived in Russia, the more obvious it became to me that the prison laws were the only ones that functioned well in my country. Prison morals and a prison worldview were widespread not only among the ex-convicts but also among the students and the art festival jury members, the high school teachers and the university professors.

There was one professor in our department, however, who stood out. He had only joined the staff in my third year. Loquacious, cultivated, and charismatic, Vlad Konstantinov handpicked a small group of students and reigned over them. He only wanted to teach those few who—to him—seemed more progressive, more 'modern'. I was very glad to be in that group because for the first time at university I felt that I had met a person who could actually teach me something relevant.

He wore jackets and jeans, ties and polished shoes, which seemed extravagant in comparison with the dire uniform of other professors. He gave his classes while standing, without notes or textbooks, talking clearly and openly. We knew that he came from Moscow where he'd worked for the central TV channel, and we respected him for that (no other teacher of ours had had anything to do with modern day journalism). While educating his students, Vlad Konstantinov allowed himself to be audaciously rude about his own colleagues, mocking our dean and his wife, making jokes about them, criticizing them for their lack of openness to the new world. They were the same toothless dinosaurs in his eyes as they were in ours.

When the time came to choose an advisor for my final thesis, I couldn't think of anyone else but Vlad Konstantinov. I made an application and he accepted me willingly. Russian university required you to start working on a thesis when you were still in your second year, to submit what you had achieved to date at the end of every second semester, and to complete the project by the end of the fifth year.

When I met Vlad Konstantinov in his office to discuss the thesis I'd been working on, he asked me whether I wanted to change my topic. The one I'd chosen without his advice was rather unorthodox (it focused on the entertainment media), so I thought that my professor wanted me to select something safer. I was absolutely wrong.

'How would you like to focus on something like . . . let's say . . . gender stereotypes in mass media?'

I gasped. I was stunned by the boldness of his suggestion: subjects like women's rights, queer studies, ethnicity and race, even human rights were unheard of in Russian universities.

'Aren't you interested in this particular field?' Vlad Konstantinov asked me, looking pointedly into my eyes.

I nodded, feeling that my face was glowing red.

'That's what I thought,' he said, with a knowing smile, 'I know a thing or two about people. I can see what kind of man you are, Alexey . . . After all,' my professor paused, smiled again, and winked at me, 'we are not so different.'

Embarrassed by this thinly disguised revelation, I tried to change the subject. We continued talking about gender stereotypes and how I could possibly apply that theme to post-Soviet media, but after a while, the conversation took a turn in the direction of personal experience.

'I understand you very well, Alexey,' my advisor said, 'but you see, no matter what you think and want from life, you must be careful here . . .'

His index finger pointed down to his desk. I nodded.

'A man in *our* position must make certain smart choices in life in order to stay safe, in order to be successful, in order to accomplish something.'

I kept nodding silently.

'Eventually, you must find and marry a discreet, undemanding woman.'

I stopped nodding. I looked at him with dazed eyes.

'Yes, yes. I've been married for almost twenty years. We even have a child.'

At those words, he giggled. It was a flat, unpleasant, even complacent laugh, or so it seemed to me.

'Yes, a son of your age. It doesn't stop me from enjoying life. They are not that smart after all.'

I was confused.

'Who? Who are not that smart?' I asked him quietly, as if we were sharing some dark secrets.

'Women.'

I left my advisor's office with very mixed feelings.

Nevertheless, I did follow his suggestion that I change the subject of my thesis. When I told my classmates about it, they were puzzled, not even knowing what 'gender' meant. My other professors rolled their eyes and turned their backs on me when I announced the new focus of my studies. Yet it was indeed a subject in which I found great interest. I only wondered how on earth I would ever manage to graduate with such a thesis when I'd have to present and defend it before a committee of toothless dinosaurs.

❦

I had subscribed to a mailing distance learning program in English way back as an eleven-year-old in Taiga, and persisted with it ever since. The year I joined the university, foreign language courses were removed from the academic program due to 'the subject's redundancy', as our dean put it. My mother provided a solution: she introduced me to a private tutor, an old friend of hers from the time when she herself was a student.

My English tutor was a modest, elegant man who seemed to have spent his entire life fighting the world around him with delicate manners and vast knowledge as his chief weapons. He had been teaching French for years and, even though English was not his specialization, he agreed to help me.

'Those two are practically the same language,' he argued, 'in comparison with Russian.'

Three evenings a week, I made my way through the cement labyrinths, formed by the inner yards of the panel blocks, infested with crime and urine, into the depths of Lenin Prospekt. After reaching my tutor's building, I quickly climbed four murky floors before pressing, not without relief, the buzzer of his apartment. His pretty, timid wife would open the door, smile at me, and hurriedly draw me in. There, in the limits of their cramped space, things suddenly felt safe and fair.

As we studied by the small desk in their bedroom, I could hear how my tutor's wife kept hushing their two-year-old behind the closed door to the kitchen. Sometimes, during the lesson the woman would softly knock and my teacher would say, 'Come on in, dear!' She would then enter with a flowery tray with tea and biscuits on it.

I recall their thin porcelain cups and homemade jam. Beside the teacups, there were some tiny pretty bowls. I remember looking at them without knowing what their purpose was. What was I supposed to do with them? Then I saw the thin hands of my tutor spooning the jam from the jar and placing it in the little bowl first instead of eating it straight off. To me, it seemed dangerously aristocratic and I thought that if he dared do such thing outside their minuscule world, he might be executed to the joy of the cheering mob.

Later, much later, I discovered that this man had, after a long search, managed to find a job somewhere in North Africa and moved his family there. Good manners and vast knowledge had lost their battle with Siberia.

While reading Nabokov, Chekhov, Tolstoy, Leskov, Lermontov, Akhmatova, Pushkin, and many others, I had a strange perception of encountering not only a different culture but a different language, one very far from that of modern day post-Soviet Russia. My own language was the language of the *gops* and the criminals, my speech was woven from words that originated in the gulags and *kolkhozes*. My English tutor seemed to exist somewhere in between those two different Russias, yet he was quite far from both, too.

Where were all those souls who populated pre-Revolutionary Russia? Were they the same Russians as I was? Was their tradition, their culture, completely destroyed by time, by the people, by their own country?

It was always a divine pleasure for me to read those classical authors, praised all across the world and associated with my land, but it was also a devilish torture for me because I could clearly see that nothing of that world existed on my streets, almost nothing of it remained in our lives. And those little particles that had survived seemed to be running through our fingers like sand—escaping into the deserts of Africa.

Once I saw a rare video interview with Vladimir Nabokov. I was shocked to hear him speak because the way he was using the Russian language, the way his intonation grew and descended, the vocabulary he had—all of that had very little to do with the Russian language I'd been using all my life. Later on, I heard Akhmatova's recorded voice and I was impressed in the same way. For they were speaking the same language, and that language—even though I could understand it—was not mine.

One critical book which I read at that time was Nikolay Nikulin's *Memories of the War*. Nikulin had spent most of his life working for the Hermitage State Museum. However, his one and only book, not published until the 2000s, wasn't about artists but about monsters. As a young man, Nikulin was drafted to fight the Nazis and wrote his memoir as a way to recover from the experience.

Twenty-five million Soviet soldiers died during the Second World War. The German casualties were estimated at about five million. The US lost four hundred thousand soldiers. So who won that war? How could we Russians yearly celebrate that great victory with all the fireworks and the military parades, knowing those numbers? Twenty-five million! Five times more than what the 'defeated' had lost.

Nikulin claimed that tragedy on such a scale was caused by the cruelty not of the Nazis, but of our own government. It was the beastliness of our own people that horrified him. Nikulin blamed Stalin, he blamed the Bolsheviks. After all, he pointed out, the number of people who perished in Nazi concentration camps was many times fewer than those who lost their lives and souls in the gulags. Yet Russia had never held its own Nuremberg process. Why not?

Why did we never punish our tyrants?

Was it because we were tyrants ourselves?

The scariest part of *Memories of the War* lay in its conclusion, where

Nikulin tried to see into the future of his homeland, making this observation on all the Soviet people who'd been raised, shaped, and produced by the Bolsheviks:

> *It is the selection that Russian people went through—that is the*
> *time bomb which will be detonated only in the XXI or XXII*
> *centuries—that will be when the mass of bastards, selected and*
> *educated by the Bolsheviks, will give birth to a new generation.*

Did *that* explain the beastly behavior of the people living around me in Siberia? Was that the reason for the mafia's and Putin's triumphs? Was that why millions of Russians—some eighty percent!—supported the new tyrant with so much zest? And was that also the reason why it was so hard for me to call that land home—*my home*?

Was I already surrounded by this new generation? By the grandchildren of the Bolsheviks?

And was I one of them?

By 2005 it had become evident that Putin had changed the vector of our country yet again and instead of moving toward democratization, he kept pushing it back to the ideals of the Soviets. And why should one be surprised? What could one possibly expect from the grandson of the personal cook of Stalin?

As Putin accumulated power, tragedies piled up all over the country. It was as if one couldn't move upwards without thousands of innocent people dying beneath one's feet. The Chechen War was promptly followed by the bombing of residential blocks across Russia, and when the bombings had their effect on the minds and the lives of the people (the government blamed the Chechen terrorists), almost instantly the Second Chechen War was begun. Then, in October 2003—when I was in my second year at university—more than eight hundred people were taken hostage in one theater in Moscow, with many of them killed. And when I entered my third year, in autumn 2004, 777 children together with some three hundred adults were taken and held hostage for three days in Beslan school in North Ossetia—331 of them died. How fearful Russians became! How high Putin rose! With every horrid episode broadcast on TV for hours, sometimes for days, the number of Putin's supporters grew larger and larger. The man solidified his status as the national hero, the savior, the Christ. The church fully supported him, with Patriarch Kirill of Moscow, that Tobacco Metropolitan, always present at the President's side.

In each of those tragic events, each and every one of them, independent journalists discovered evidence of the Russian government's complicity—the KGB's complicity to be precise. It is true that when you open a book or an article written by one of those activists—books like *Blowing up Russia* by Alexander Litvinenko or *Putin's Russia* by Anna Politkovskaya—the information presented there is so outrageous that it seems like yet another conspiracy theory. However, when you also notice how many of those journalists, writers, lawyers, even ex-KGB agents found the same patterns of evidence in different cases, you begin to realize how much more than a theory it is. That no matter how unbelievable it all seems, it is in fact the terrifying reality.

The likelihood that what those journalists discovered was true became even more credible when they themselves—Anna Politkovskaya, Alexander Litvinenko, Anastasia Baburova, Yury Shchekochikhin, and many others—were murdered soon after their reports became public. When you see journalists gunned down in the course of their investigation, or straight afterwards, you realize just how important, how damning, the things they were stopped from revealing must have been.

Under Putin Russia found itself listed as the third deadliest country in the world for journalists, after Algeria and Iraq. Reading that, I finally understood what Nina Olegovna, the vice-principal of the Humanities Gymnasium, had meant when she'd asked me, 'Aren't you scared of becoming a journalist *in this country?*'

❧

At the end of my third university year, I was at home one day when my mother came back from work. She brought groceries and I ran to help her with the bags.

'Guess what, Aliosha?' she said to me. 'I met your English tutor at the market.'

'Did he complain about me?' I joked with her.

'No, no. He told me that you've been a very good pupil.'

Then my mother left the groceries, paused, looked at me sternly, and added, 'He also told me something you might be interested in . . .

'He said that five students from your university this year are going to be given a chance to spend one semester abroad. Except for the flights, all charges are covered. He told me that this doesn't happen often and not many people know about it. Only those who pass a specially organized English test will be given this chance. He said you should try.'

'Where abroad?'

'Somewhere in America . . . Not far from New York.'

In those few moments while my mother was talking, I felt the world around me gradually dissolving, matter losing its gravity, and some new reality rising around me. Out of the ground, tall silver buildings were growing, lights and stars were being lit above me, and some new, friendlier people were already smiling at me.

'What do you think, Aliosha? I know that there are eighteen thousand students at your university and only five spots, but would you like to try to pass that test? What if you could be one of those lucky five?' my mom said with a hopeful yet nervous, even dolorous expression in her eyes.

In the next few months my index cards multiplied with such speed that soon every drawer in my room was filled. I forgot about everything except preparing for the English test. I didn't mention any of this to anyone. I was too afraid of destroying that misty, marvelous dream by my own words and rash actions.

Inside, I felt an explosion of hope.

'Even if I pass the test . . . Even if they give me the green light . . .' exhausted from all the studying, momentarily losing all hopes, I told my mother one evening, 'Even then, how on earth will we get the money for the flight ticket? And what will I eat when I'm there? *If* I'm ever there . . .'

'Don't worry about it. Just study. I'll get the money for the flight,' was all she said.

Then one night, a few hours after she'd returned from her kiosk, I saw my mother getting dressed—dressed very differently from what she wore in those years. She had her red lipstick back on her lips, her old Tom Claim suit on again, a sweet perfume.

'Where are you going so late, Mother?'

Silence.

She returned in the middle of the night. I waited impatiently in the corridor. She returned not quite her usual self—lighter in image, darker in soul.

'Look what I've got,'—a flop of cash on the kitchen table.

Money can only come from a man. Always from a man.

That's what she had learned from her mother. That's what I learned from mine.

'Now you can pass the test and get on that plane,' she said, and then disappeared into the bathroom.

The water ran for a long, long time—I fell asleep to the sound of it. In the morning, she acted as if nothing had happened, it even seemed that she was relieved, even a bit proud. And I knew, I sensed it, that if I or someone else commented that it was the wrong thing to do, wrong thing to happen—that she was bought, abused, harassed, treated unfairly—she would only shrug her shoulders, and respond:

'That's not the worst thing that can happen to you.'

'What would be the worst thing then, Mother?'

Silence.

'The worst . . . is when no one wants you alive.'

Finally, the day of my English test came. I did my best, of course, but was still very uncertain about the result. I remember the text I had to translate. It was something from zoology, and one word kept appearing over and over again: 'squirrel', 'squirrel', 'squirrel'—I hadn't the faintest clue what 'squirrel' meant and was quite upset afterwards.

Time passed, and one day I got a call from the student office. I hadn't gotten the highest grade but I was in the top five. They told me I could start collecting papers for an American entry visa.

'What papers?'

'An application, a military ticket, a police clearance, a medical certificate, a birth certificate, copies of your academic books, your parents' work booklets, their passports, their bank statements, proofs of everything they own—a car, a flat, whatever—all of this has to be presented on paper, translated into English, the translations notarized by a lawyer . . ,' the university secretary was talking so fast. 'But first of all, and most importantly, you have to provide a written statement of approval from the dean of your faculty.'

'A statement of approval?'

'Yes, a statement of approval. Your dean, Vladimir Vladimirovich Banalin, has to agree that it's a good idea for you to spend a semester in the United States.'

Everything collapsed at that moment.

The mist cleared.

It was the end of the whole affair.

Knowing the tone of the conversation in advance, I walked gloomily to the dean's office the next day.

'Those Americans panic when they run out of toilet paper! Stupidest people!' once again the dean remembered the stupidest of jokes and laughed at it himself. 'Did you hear that, darling?' he addressed his wife, who sat beside him. 'Did you hear that? Those Americans, at the first sniff of a crisis, they'll buy all the toilet paper in the world!'

They kept on giggling as I sat pale, miserable, hopeless. Not a single student in his department had ever been allowed to go to study abroad, the dean told me.

'And you have no reasons for going there either!'

The conversation was over.

After discussing the situation with my mother, it was decided that I had to see my very progressive academic advisor, Vlad Konstantinov.

Mother bought a bottle of cognac and told me to slip it to him—privately.

The man invited me over after class, after dark, invited me to an apartment—not his home but a nearly empty, unfurnished, bare-walled place on Fifty Years of the October Revolution Street, between Red Army Street and Lenin Prospekt.

'Have you come to talk about gender stereotypes?' Vlad Konstantinov greeted me cheerfully. 'Though, perhaps, these days you are far more interested in American studies?'

He already knew about what had happened. He poured me a drink, the strong spirit instantly filling my eyes with moisture. I complained bitterly that the Banalins wouldn't let me take my first and perhaps my only chance to go to America, to change my life for the better.

'Well,' Vlad Konstantinov murmured, filling his glass. 'And why exactly do you think it will be for the better?'

I was bewildered. We obviously shared something in common, my academic advisor and I. Or did we?

'I went there,' he said. Then he lowered his eyelids, 'Hm, this is a good one,' he said, after tasting the cognac. 'I went to the West, you know. I spent some time in Europe . . . But if you expect people there to be particularly cultivated, different from Russians, I'm afraid you are mistaken, Alexey.' He placed his drink on the floor by the sofa.

'Once, for instance, I was at the supermarket in Paris,' he went on. 'You know, buying groceries. There was a Black woman at the cash-desk. I paid for my purchases but then they just lay there on the desk between us. She made no move. "Pack them!" I ordered her. The poor thing then started agitatedly packing my groceries, as would be normal in any civilized countries. But people there are not, you see. They are not that civilized.'

I kept on listening silently to my professor. He kept on sipping his drink and talking freely. He seemed confident that he had found a young apprentice, someone who trusted him. Now he wanted to make sure that I would follow in his footsteps, make the same smart choices as he had.

I tried, tried very hard to explain to him how I felt about living in

Siberia, how alienated I had been all my life and how much I wanted to see the world. He listened to me quietly for some time. His glass was empty.

'Alexey, I'm afraid your problem is much, much bigger than a simple geographical one,' he said finally in a softer tone, placing his palm on my shoulder. 'You see, I study people, I know them better than they know themselves. Look at you,' he slapped my back a couple of times, 'Just look at the way you are, the way you talk, the way you deal with the world, the way you are with others! One day I was driving across the bridge, and I saw you walking alone there. You walked with a display of such boldness, such haughtiness and self-regard that I couldn't imagine anyone beside you . . .'

He paused there. I shrugged his hand off my back. My eyes now blurring with tears, I glanced at him silently—though in fact all I wanted at that moment was to shout back at him. I wanted him to know how wrong, how mistaken his judgement of me was. How if he couldn't imagine me in any other way than as a willfully, congenitally perpetual loner, then this was simply the result of his feeble imagination. Of his not knowing a time when Andrey was the core and heart of my life, when we were inseparable, when we walked the streets and bridges of our city for hours—forever afraid to walk too close to each other. Or when, hand in hand, we walked the streets and quays of Paris and of Amsterdam during our brief moments of freedom there. How—even now—months and months after that dirty yellow prison van of a Volga had torn him out of my life forever, I still, in moments of loss and madness, saw him, saw Andrey in the street, ran after him, shouting, calling his name, only to have the startled, frightened deer I was hunting turn his stranger's face on me, before running off himself. I could have told him . . .

But what was the use? Why rehearse all that history and pain to someone who—even without the benefit of a bottle of cognac provided by his own student—was unable to imagine it. Unable to see that the very thing he believed me incapable of was the thing I desired most. Having once known it, only to then lose it in the cruelest way imaginable. Unable to see, to comprehend his own—*their* own—set of rules and mores, judgements and expectations to be the very reason for my walking—my living—alone. Unable . . .

Was he really unable to see all that in me? Were we, Vlad Konstantinov and I, his pupil, his protégé, so different from each other? Or were we only separated by age and time now? Was I simply the kind of boy he used to be, and he, the future version of myself? The version I would become once I acquired his logic of life, once I married a woman, had children, and started teaching younger boys the language of silenced love.

I said nothing to him. Yet he heard me, it seemed, for he turned away and for a while stared abstractly off to one side. In his checkered light brown jacket and blue jeans, with his softening gaze and lost smile, he himself looked out of place, lonely, miserable. But then, then he resumed his former familiar expression, turned back to me and continued his lesson.

'Scientifically speaking, Alexey, you lack an associative group. You do not belong to any major or minor community, whereas it is the association with others that makes us happy in life. What I'm afraid of is that it won't be any better for you there than it is here.'

I lowered my eyes, all hope at that moment slipping away through my fingers. What if he's right, I wondered. No associative group, no community, no others . . . Forever alien. Of course he was right. Here, or over there—what did it matter? I felt no more strength left in me.

I gave up everything then, my own body included. My advisor moved closer. I didn't resist his touch this time. Why should I? What was there so precious to protect? His breath was the worst-smelling air ever to have touched my hair. His lips were soft, too soft—and too wide, capable, it felt, of swallowing me whole.

At night, after it was all over, I fell into tormented sleep: I dreamt I was climbing on the roof of my grandmother's house, scrabbling hands and feet up its steep slope, fighting off the enormous scorpion that crawled after me. I kept throwing down bunches of flowers, armfuls and armfuls of flowers so that the beast would lose its grip and slide off the roof, leaving me alone on top, almost intact.

How hard, how heavy our dreams can be. How frightening to see a glittering dream reduced to a nightmare. How hard to resist, to fight back—to protect one's sanity.

Yet eventually, I did just that. I shrugged off what my advisor had said and done that night. I regained the confidence to believe that I did in fact deserve happiness and freedom and that I would find it—if not immediately, or on my continent, then with time on somebody else's.

I told myself that he was mistaken to think that there was no place, no community to which I could possibly belong. I thought that he was projecting too much of himself onto me. And probably he was. Because the very next morning he phoned the dean's office and in five minutes solved everything, setting me free, making me the happiest man in Siberia.

With the exam over, the necessary permits granted, my paperwork complete and the fares for my flights processed—everything now seemed set for the best in the best of all worlds. Except that on my bed, reflected in the grand mirror of my dreams, my mother was left alone, disconsolate, wrapped in bedsheets bright with the colours of the American flag.

⁂

'Not gonna get us!' the girls from t.A.T.u., my favourite band, were screaming on the radio. 'They not gonna get us!' the song from their album *200 km/h in the Wrong Lane* was playing in the car as my father and I drove back to Taiga, to say goodbye to my grandmother—before I took the plane to New York.

'Damned lesbians!' my father grumbled at t.A.T.u., hammering the off-button with his iron thumb. 'Damned perv . . .', he cursed, but before he could finish, the vehicle in front of us dropped its speed suddenly and my father wrenched the steering wheel to overtake it— throwing our car into the wrong lane at insane speed.

'You must drive in such a manner that the others are all scared of you,' they taught you at the driving school. 'The speed limit may be 120 km/h,' they said. 'But if everyone else is going at 200 km/h, then you must go as fast or faster.'

And what, I always wondered, if one doesn't abide by such mad rules? Would that make one saner? Or just madder than the rest?

'Damned perverts all around,' my father finished his sentence when we were back on the right side of the narrow road, covered as it was with silver ice and clad with snow on its edges. 'Now even on the radio, you've got those faggots screaming.'

I sat quietly—as always—because I knew that I was in his hands, in his car, in his country. At 200 km/h in the wrong lane. But not for long now . . . Not for long, Father.

A yellow blur appeared on the road in the far distance ahead of us. Amidst all the white and grey, that bright yellow taxi, that trembling old Volga evoked something vital: an image, a signal of burning memory that pierced me through.

'Where was *he* now?' I asked myself silently.

The taxi grew bigger and bigger. We were overtaking it rapidly.

Here I was, about to leave it all behind and go West—as the two of us had always dreamt. But where was he? Where was Andrey now?

As my father increased speed, cursing once again as he overtook the yellow Volga, I stared across into its windows as we passed—and saw him, my boy, my Andrey sitting in the back seat.

My heart jerked.

'Father!'

The icy road bent sharply then straightened.

'You still get all excited when overtaking,' he lit a cigarette. 'But it's no . . .'

No . . . Of course, no . . . It couldn't possibly be Andrey in the taxi. It was just the blurred reflection of my own pale self.

There was no Andrey now. And yet there, in that momentary image, he was—me.

'It's time to go. Time to set sail!' My father burst into the flat, as I was trying to part ways with my grandmother as gently as I could. He had dropped me at her place in Taiga fifteen minutes earlier—just time enough for the final goodbye, in his opinion.

'Already . . . ? Oh, well . . . Can't you stay just a minute longer?' my *babushka* begged her son and me. 'Please, here . . . here . . . take some pickles with you for the road . . . Wait a bit, I'll put some aspic in a jar. Take some jam . . .' she mumbled on.

'Mom! We don't need your stuff!' my father yelled at her. 'These days we can buy it all in a shop, don't you get it?!'

I couldn't believe my grandmother's son's cruelty.

'Well . . . Alioshenka,' *Babushka* followed us into the corridor of her minuscule flat. 'Well, Aliosha . . . Tell me, do they at least have cows over there?'

'Cows?' I laughed.

My father spat on the cement floor as he descended the staircase, 'I'll be waiting in the car.'

'Do they have cows where, *Babushka*?'

'There, where you're going . . .'

'In America?'

'In America . . . Fresh milk is important. I'll pray for you, my dear one . . . Only you promise to write to me, will you?'

'Write?' I laughed again, thick pressure building deep behind my eyes.

'Well, yes . . . If you have a couple of empty pages left in the end of your notebooks . . .'

'Then I should tear them off and write you a letter?' I continued for her.

She nodded. Her smile was the smile of a timid schoolgirl. Seven years, not older.

The cold iron door of her flat creaked like a tin can. I backed my way out, eyes still locked on her face. Slowly I began descending the staircase, the same sooty, scary staircase of my pitch-dark winter mornings. I reached the ground-floor landing, the one where youths gathered at night, youths whom no one kicked out since there was no place else for them to go.

I looked back up at my grandmother through the crooked bars and railings of the staircase: framed in the narrow opening of her heavy door, the perfect oval of her face was whitening out to a degree even brighter than the whitewashed wall behind her.

'I'll pray for you, Aliosha,' she made the shape of a cross with her trembling fingers. 'I'll pray for you, and you write . . .'

'For you, *Babushka* . . . I will . . . For you . . .'

Acknowledgements

This book, together with its second volume about Alexey's peregrinations in America, was written in solitude, in a deep-frozen state—my natural habitat—in a Venetian attic in 2014. However, my imperfect English would have never been brought to a publishable form without the help and advice of my brilliant mentors, the wonderful Australian writer John Clanchy and his awe-inspiring and very effective superintendent Brigid Ballard, or without kind encouragement from my beautiful, scintillatingly smart and talented friends Eithne Nightingale, Artis Henderson, Catherine Allen, Melanie Cantor, Kyrena Karmiloff, Jenny Chamarette, Lyn Dickens, Julia Mathison—all of whom I met (with the exception of Catherine) at La Muse Writers and Artists Retreat in Southern France, where I used to dust furniture and pick cherries.

Without my beloved partner and my parents, I simply wouldn't be *here*.

Translation of Joseph Brodsky's verses is by Shimon Edelman, and of Anna Akhmatova's by Andrey Kneller.

Biographical Note

Born and raised in a small town in Central Siberia at the time when the Soviet Union was falling apart, Artem Mozgovoy began his career as a cadet journalist in a local newspaper when he was sixteen; at twenty-six he was an editor-in-chief. In 2011, as Russia began legalizing its persecution of gay people, he left his homeland. Having lived in six different countries, including the US, and worked as a movie extra, a yoga instructor, and a magician's assistant, Artem today holds a Luxembourgish passport, speaks five languages and, with his Romanian partner, lives in Belgium.